HAND OF
FATE

**Center Point
Large Print**

Also by Lis Wiehl with April Henry
and available from Center Point Large Print:

Face of Betrayal

**This Large Print Book carries the
Seal of Approval of N.A.V.H.**

HAND OF
FATE

A Triple Threat Novel

LIS WIEHL
with APRIL HENRY

CENTER POINT PUBLISHING
THORNDIKE, MAINE

ISBN: 978-1-60285-743-8

Library of Congress Cataloging-in-Publication Data

Wiehl, Lis W.
  Hand of fate / Lis Wiehl and April Henry. — Center Point large print ed.
    p. cm.
  ISBN 978-1-60285-743-8 (lib. bdg. : alk. paper)
  1. Radio talk show hosts—Fiction. 2. Murder—Investigation—Fiction.
  3. Women lawyers—Fiction. 4. Female friendship—Fiction. 5. Large type books.
  I. Henry, April. II. Title.
PS3623.I382H36 2010b
813'.6—dc22
2009053734

For all the *Face of Betrayal* readers who made Allison, Nicole, and Cassidy's first appearance such a success—especially Bill C. in Corvallis, Oregon, who wrote, "I'm 88 years of age, and anticipating *Hand of Fate* is an incentive to live for." Now that's both inspirational and humbling. And for my daughter Dani.

*It is usually more important
how a man meets his fate than what it is.*

—KARL WILHELM VON HUMBOLDT

CHAPTER 1
KNWS Radio
Tuesday, February 7

Jim Fate bounced on the toes of his black Salvatore Ferragamo loafers. He liked to work on his feet. Listeners could hear it in your voice if you were sitting down, could detect the lack of energy. He leaned forward, his lips nearly touching the silver mesh of the mike.

"Can massive federal spending and a huge new layer of government bureaucracy really make the United States a better, safer place? Or is it a matter of simply enforcing the food safety laws the states already have on the books? For more than a century, our food safety system has been built on the policy that food companies—not government— have the primary responsibility for the safety and integrity of the foods they produce."

"So what are you suggesting, Jim?" Victoria Hanawa, his cohost, asked. "Are you saying we just let more Americans die when they buy food a company couldn't bother to keep clean?"

She sat on a high stool on the other side of the U-shaped table, her back to the glass wall that separated the radio studio from the screener's booth. To Jim's right was the control room, sometimes called the news tank, where the board operator worked his bank of equipment and where one or more local reporters joined him at the top and the bottom of the hour.

"What I'm saying, Hanawa, is that activists are seizing the latest salmonella scare to further their own goals of increasing the power of the federal government. They don't really care about these people. They only care about their own agenda, which is to create a nanny state full of burdensome, unworkable, and costly regulation. And of course the federal government, being the federal government, believes that the only solution to any problem is adding another layer—or ten—of federal government."

While he spoke, Jim eyed the two screens in front of him. One displayed the show schedule. It was also hooked up to the Internet so he could look up points on the fly. The other screen showed the listeners holding for their chance to talk. On it, Chris had listed the name, town, and point of view of each caller. Three people were still on the list, meaning they would hold over the upcoming break. Now a fourth caller and a fifth joined the queue.

"What about the Tenth Amendment? There are state laws already in place to address these issues! We don't need to add a whole new layer of government bureaucracy that could end up doubling or even tripling food prices! I mean, that would be stuck on stupid."

"But the food industry in this country is putting profits before safety," Victoria protested.

"With all due respect, Hanawa, if we let the federal government handle it, they will insist that everyone who buys anything at a grocery store sign a release form and be issued their very own government-approved barf bag. Just another example of disenfranchisement."

Victoria's mouth started to form an answer, but it was time for the top-of-the-hour break. Chris pointed at the clock and then made a motion with his hands like he was snapping a stick.

Jim said, "And you've been listening to *The Hand of Fate*. We're going to take a quick break for a news, traffic, and weather update. But before we go, I want to read you the e-mail from the Nut of the Day: 'Jim, you are a fat, ugly liar who resembles the hind end of a poodle. Signed, Mickey Mouse.'"

He laughed, shielding himself from the sting. In this business, you knew that words *could* hurt you. Even if you were only forty-one and in good shape, with the kind of traditional broody Irish looks that made most women look twice.

"Fat? Maybe. Ugly? Well, I can't help that. I can't even help the hind-end-of-a-poodle business, although I think that's going a bit far. But a liar? No, my friend, that's one thing I am not. While I'll give this a pass today, you'll need to get a little more creative than that if you want to win the NOD award. And America's Truth Detector will be right back in a moment to hear from you."

9

He pushed back the mike on its black telescoping arm.

As the first notes of the newscast jingle sounded in his ears, Jim pulled the padded black headphones down around his neck. He and Victoria now had six minutes to themselves before the third and final hour of the broadcast.

"I'm going to get some tea," she said, without meeting his eyes. Jim nodded. In the last week, there had been a strained civility between them when they were off mike. On air, though, they still had chemistry. Even if now it was the kind of chemistry you got from mixing together the wrong chemicals in your junior scientist kit.

On air, everything was different. Jim was more indignant and mocking than he ever was in real life. Victoria made vaguely dirty jokes that she wouldn't tolerate hearing off mike. And on air, they still mostly got along, bantering and feeding each other lines.

Victoria grabbed her mug and stood up. Even though she was half Japanese, she was five foot ten, with legs that went on forever. Handing him a padded envelope from a publisher, she said, "This was in my box this morning, but it's really yours."

When she pushed open the heavy door to the screening room, the weather strip on the bottom made a sucking sound. For a minute, Jim could hear Chris in the screener's booth talking to Willow, the intern, and Aaron, the program director. Then the door closed with a snick—there were magnets on the door and frame—and Jim was left in the silent bubble of the studio. In addition to the magnets and the weather stripping, the walls and ceiling were covered with blue, textured soundproofing material that resembled the loop side of Velcro.

Jim grabbed the first piece of mail from his inbox and slit it with a letter opener. He scanned the note inside. "Dad's seventy-fifth birthday . . . love to have a signed photo," yada yada.

"Happy Birthday, Larry!" he scrawled on a black-and-white headshot he pulled from dozens kept in a file folder. "Your friend, Jim Fate." Paper-clipping the envelope and letter to the photo, he put them off to the side for Willow to handle. Three more photo requests, each of which took about twenty seconds to deal with. Jim had signed his name so many times in the last ten years that it was routine, but he still got a secret thrill each time he did it.

There were still about three minutes left, so he decided to open the package from the publisher. He liked books about true crime, politics, or culture—with authors he could book on the show.

Jim pulled the red string tab on the envelope. It got stuck halfway through, and he had to give it an extra hard tug. There was an odd hissing sound as a paperback—*Talk Radio*—fell onto his lap. A book of a play turned into a movie—both based on the true-life killing of talk show host Alan Berg, gunned down in his own driveway.

What the—?

Jim never finished the thought. The red string had been connected to a small canister of gas hidden in the envelope. Now it sprayed directly into his face.

He gasped. With just that first breath, Jim knew something was terribly wrong. He couldn't see the gas, couldn't smell it, but he could feel its damp fog coat the inside of his nose and throat.

He swept the package away. It landed behind him, in the far corner of the studio. Whatever it was, it was in the air. So he shouldn't breathe. Jim clamped his lips together and scrambled to his feet, yanking off the headphones.

It was just like what had happened in Seattle three weeks earlier. Fifty-eight people had died from sarin gas in what seemed to be a botched terrorist attack.

His chest already starting to ache, Jim looked out through the thick, glass wall into the control room on his right. Greg, the board operator, was half-turned away, gobbling a PayDay bar. He was watching his banks of equipment, ready to press the buttons for commercials and national feeds. In the call screener's booth directly in front of Jim, Aaron was still talking to Chris and Willow, waving his hands for emphasis. Jim was unnoticed, sealed away in his bubble.

He forced himself to concentrate. He had to get some air, some fresh air. If he staggered out, would the air there be enough to dilute what he had already breathed in? Would it be enough to clear the sarin from his lungs, from his body?

Would it be enough to save him?

But if he opened the door, what would happen to the people out there? Chris, Willow, Aaron, and the rest? He thought of the firefighters who had died in Seattle. Would invisible tendrils of poison snake out to the dozens of people who worked at the station, the hundreds who worked in the building? Greg in the control room, with its own soundproofing, might be safe if he kept his door closed. For a while, anyway. Until it got into the air ducts. Some of the people who died in Seattle had been nowhere near the original release of the gas. If Jim tried to escape, everyone out there might die too.

Die too. The words echoed in his head. Jim realized that he *was* dying, that he had been dying from the moment he first sucked in his breath in surprise. It had been, he thought, somewhere between fifteen and twenty seconds since the gas sprayed into his face.

Every morning, Jim swam two miles at the MAC club. He could hold his breath for two minutes. How long had that magician done it on *Oprah*? Seventeen minutes, wasn't that it? Jim couldn't hold his breath for that long, but he was sure he could hold it longer than two minutes. Maybe a lot longer. The first responders could surely get him some oxygen. The line might be thin enough to snake under the closed door.

Jim pressed the Talk button and spoke in a slurred, breathy voice. "Sarin gas! Call 911 and go! Don't open door!"

They all swung around to look at him in surprise. Without getting any closer, he pointed to the package in the corner.

Chris sprang into action with the catlike reflexes of someone who worked in live radio—someone used to dealing with crazies and obscenity spouters before their words got out on the airwaves and brought down a big fine from the FCC. He punched numbers into the phone and began shouting their address to the 911 operator. He'd pressed the Talk button, so Jim heard every word.

"It's sarin gas. Yes, sarin! In the KNWS studio! Hurry! It's killing him! It's killing Jim Fate!"

Behind Chris, Willow took one look at Jim, her eyes wide, and turned and ran out of the studio.

In the news tank, Greg backed away from the window. But in the screener's booth, Aaron moved toward the door with an outstretched hand. Jim staggered forward and held the door closed with his foot. His gaze met Aaron's through the small rectangle of glass set in the door at eye level.

"Are you sure? Jim, come out of there!"

14

Jim knew Aaron was yelling, but the door filtered it into a low murmur, stripped of all urgency.

He couldn't afford the breath it would take to speak, couldn't afford to open his mouth in case he accidentally sucked in air again. His body was already demanding that he stop this nonsense and breathe. All he could do was shake his head, his lips clamped together.

Chris pressed the Talk button again. "They're sending a hazmat team. They should be here any second. They said they're bringing oxygen."

Jim made a sweeping motion with his hands, wordlessly ordering his coworkers to leave. His chest was aching. Greg grabbed a board and a couple of microphones and left the news tank at a run. Aaron took one last look at Jim, shook his head, and then left. A second later, the fire alarm began to sound, a low pulse muffled to near nothingness by the soundproof door.

Chris stayed where he was, staring at Jim through the glass. The two of them had been together for years. Every morning, Chris and Jim—and more recently Victoria—got in early and put the show together, scouring the newspaper, the Internet, and TV clips for stories that would light up the lines.

"I'm praying for you, man," Chris said, then released the Talk button. He gave Jim one more anguished look, then hurried out.

Jim wished he could follow. But he couldn't run

away from what the poison had already done to him. His vision blurred. Time was slowing down. He was so tired. Why did he have to hold his breath, again? Oh yes, sarin.

When he looked back up, he saw that Victoria was still in the screener's room. She moved close to the glass, her dark eyes seeking out Jim's. Angrily, he shook his head and motioned for her to go.

Victoria pressed the Talk button. "I don't smell anything out here. The booth is practically air-tight, anyway."

Jim wanted to tell her that "practically" wasn't the same as really and truly. It was the kind of argument they might have on air during a slow time, bantering to keep things moving along. But he didn't have the breath for it.

A part of Jim's brain remained coldly rational even as his body sent more and more messages that something was badly wrong. He hadn't breathed since that first fateful gulp of air when he opened the package. A vacuum was building up in his head and chest, a sucking hollowness, his body screaming at him, demanding that he give in.

But Jim Fate hadn't made it this far by giving in when things were tough. It had only been a minute, a minute-ten maybe, since he'd pulled the red string. But then he did give in to another hunger—the hunger for connection. He was all alone and he might be dying, and he couldn't

16

stand that thought. He moved to the glass and put his hand up against it, fingers spread, a lonely starfish. And then Victoria mirrored it with her own hand, the anger between them forgotten, their matching hands pressed against the glass.

There was a band around Jim's chest, and it was tightening. An iron band. It was crushing him, crushing his lungs. His vision was dimming, but he kept his eyes open, his gaze never leaving Victoria.

With her free hand, Victoria groped blindly for the Talk button. "Jim, you've got to hold on," she yelled.

Jim's heart contracted when he heard how hoarse she sounded. She had to leave!

He lifted his hand from the glass and made a shooing gesture, again wordlessly ordering her to leave. Instead she pushed the Talk button again and said, "I hear sirens. They're almost here!"

But his body was ready to break with his will. He had to breathe. Had to. But maybe he could filter it, minimize it.

Without taking his eyes from Victoria, Jim pulled up the edge of his shirt with his free hand and pressed his nose and mouth against the fine Egyptian cotton cloth. He meant to take a shallow breath, but when he started, the hunger for air was too great. He sucked it in greedily, the cloth touching his tongue as he inhaled.

He sensed the shoots of poison winding them-

17

selves deeper within him, reaching out to wrap around all his organs. His head felt like it was going to explode.

No longer thinking clearly, Jim let his shirttail fall away. It didn't matter, did it? It was too late. Too late. He tried to take another breath, but his lungs refused to move.

He staggered backward. Grabbed at his chair and missed. Fell over.

Horrified, Victoria started screaming. A shiver ran through Jim's body, his arms and legs twitching. And then Jim Fate was still. His eyes, still open, stared up at the soft, fuzzy blue ceiling.

Two minutes later the first hazmat responders, suited up in white, burst through the studio door.

CHAPTER 2
Mark O. Hatfield United States Courthouse

Federal prosecutor Allison Pierce eyed the 150 prospective jurors as they filed into the sixteenth-floor courtroom in the Mark O. Hatfield United States Courthouse. A high-profile case like this necessitated a huge jury pool.

The seats soon filled, forcing dozens to stand, some only a few inches from the prosecution table. Allison could smell unwashed bodies and unbrushed teeth. She swallowed hard, forcing down the nausea that now plagued her at unexpected moments.

"Are you all right?" FBI special agent Nicole Hedges whispered. Nicole was sitting next to Allison at the prosecutor's table. Her huge, dark eyes never missed anything.

"These days, I'm either nauseated or ravenous," Allison whispered back. "Sometimes at the same time."

"Maybe the Triple Threat Club can find someplace to meet that serves ice cream and pickles."

The club was an inside joke, just three friends with connections to law enforcement—Allison, Nicole, and TV crime reporter Cassidy Shaw— who were devoted to justice, friendship, and chocolate. Not necessarily in that order.

The courtroom deputy called for everyone to rise and then swore them in en masse. Allison eyed the would-be jurors. They carried backpacks, purses, coats, umbrellas, bottled water, books, magazines, and—this being Portland, Oregon— the occasional bike helmet. They ranged from a hunched-over old man with hearing aids on the stems of his glasses to a young man who immediately opened a sketchbook and startled doodling. Some wore suits, while others looked like they were ready to hit the gym, but in general they appeared alert and reasonably happy.

There would have been more room for the potential jurors to sit, but the benches were already packed with reporters who had arrived before the jury was ushered in. In the middle of the pack was a fortyish woman who had a seat directly behind the defense table. She wore turquoise eye shadow, black eyeliner, and a sweater with a plunging neckline: the mother of the defendant.

After those lucky enough to have seats were settled in again, Judge Fitzpatrick introduced himself and told the jury that the defendant had to be considered innocent until proven guilty beyond a reasonable doubt, and that she did not need to do or say anything to prove her innocence. It was solely up to the prosecution, he intoned solemnly, to prove their case. Though Allison had heard the words at every trial, and the judge must have said them hundreds of times in his nearly twenty years on the bench, she still found herself listening. Somehow Judge Fitzpatrick always imbued the words with meaning.

When he was finished, he asked Allison to introduce herself. She stood, offering up a silent prayer, as she always did, that justice would be served. She faced the crowded room and tried to make eye contact with everyone. It was her job to build a relationship with the jurors from this moment forward, so that when the time came for them to deliberate, they would trust what she had told them.

"I am Allison Pierce. I represent the United States of America." On some of the potential jurors' faces, Allison saw surprise as they realized that the young woman with the pinned-back dark hair and plain blue suit was actually the federal prosecutor. People always seemed to expect a federal prosecutor to be a silver-haired man.

She gestured toward Nicole. "I'm assisted by FBI special agent Nicole Hedges as the case agent."

Nicole was thirty-three, the same age as Allison, but with her unlined, dark skin and expression that gave away nothing, she could have been anywhere from twenty-five to forty. She was dressed in her customary dark pantsuit and flats.

The judge then pointed out the defendant, Bethany Maddox, who wore a demure pink and white dress that Allison was sure someone else had picked out for her. The courtroom stirred as people craned their necks or got to their feet to get a glimpse. Bethany smiled, looking as if she had forgotten that she was on trial. Her defense attorney, Nate Condorelli, stood and introduced himself, but it was clear that the would-be jurors weren't nearly as interested in Nate as they were in his client.

Today was the first step in bringing to justice the pair the media had dubbed the Bratz Bandits, courtesy of their full lips, small noses, and trashy attire. What was it with the media and nicknames for bank robbers? The Waddling Bandit, the Grandmother Robber, the Toboggan Bandit, the Runny Nose Robber, the Grocery Cart Bandit— the list went on and on.

For a few weeks after their crime, a grainy surveillance video of the pair had been in heavy rotation not just in Portland but nationwide. The contrast between two nineteen-year-old girls—one blonde and one brunette, both wearing sunglasses, short skirts, and high heels—and the big, black guns they waved around had seemed more comic than anything else. On the surveillance tape, they had giggled their way through the bank robbery.

The week before, Allison had heard Bethany's parents on *The Hand of Fate*, the radio talk show. The mother had told listeners that the two young women were not bandits, but "little girls that made a bad choice."

Bethany's mother had seemed surprised when Jim Fate laughed.

The father, who was divorced from the mother, had sounded much more in touch with reality, and Allison had made a mental note to consider putting him on the stand.

"God gives us free will, and it's up to us what we do with it," he had told Jim Fate. "Any adult has to make decisions and live with them—good, bad, or indifferent."

The two girls had done it for the money, of course, but it seemed they welcomed the accompanying fame even more. On their Facebook pages they now listed more than a thousand "friends" each. Allison had even heard a rumor that Bethany—the blonde half of the pair and the one on trial today—would soon release a hip-hop CD.

The challenge for Allison was getting a jury to see that what might seem like a victimless crime—and which had only netted three thousand dollars—deserved lengthy jail time.

The courtroom deputy read out fifty names, and the congestion eased a little bit as the first potential jurors took seats in the black swivel chairs in the jury box and in the much-less-comfortable benches that had been reserved for the overflow.

Now the judge turned to the screening questions. "Has anyone heard anything about this case?" he asked. No one expected jurors to have lived in a vacuum, but he would dismiss those who said their minds were made up. It would be an easy out, if anyone was looking for one.

But many weren't. Twenty-four-hour news cycles and the proliferation of cable channels and Internet sites meant that more and more people might be interested in grabbing at the chance for their fifteen minutes of fame. Even the most tangential relationship to a famous or infamous case could be parlayed into celebrity. Or at least a stint on a third-rate reality show. Britney's nanny or Lindsay's bodyguard might be joined by the Bratz Bandits juror—all of them spilling "behind-the-scenes" stories.

The jurors listened to each other's answers,

looking attentive or bored or spacey. Allison took note of the ones who seemed most disconnected. She didn't want any juror who wasn't invested. Like a poker player, she was looking for signs or tells in the behavior of a prospective juror. Did he never look up? Did she seem evasive or overeager? Allison also made note of the things they carried or wore: Dr Pepper, *Cooking Light* magazine, a tote bag from a health food store, *Wired* magazine, brown shoes worn to white at the toes, a black jacket flecked with dandruff. Together with the written questionnaire the prospective jurors had filled out earlier, and how they answered questions now, the information would help Allison decide who she wanted—and who she didn't want—on the jury.

There was an art to picking a jury. Some lawyers had rigid rules: no postal workers, no social workers, no engineers, and/or no young black men (although the last rule had to be unspoken, and denied if ever suspected). Allison tried to look at each person as a whole, weighing each prospective juror's age, sex, race, occupation, and body language.

For this jury, she thought she might want middle-aged women who worked hard for a living and who would have little sympathy for young girls who had literally laughed all the way to the bank. Nearly as good would be younger people who were making something of their lives, focusing on good grades or climbing the career ladder. What Allison wanted to avoid were older men who might think of the girls as "daughter figures."

Barrrp . . . barrrp . . . barrrp. Everyone jumped and then looked up at the ceiling, where red lights were flashing. Judge Fitzpatrick announced calmly, "It looks like we're having a fire drill, ladies and gentlemen. Since they lock down the elevators as a precaution, we'll all need to take the stairs, which are directly to your left as you exit the courtroom." His voice was already beginning to be lost as people got to their feet, complaining and gathering their things. "Once the drill is over, we'll reconvene here and pick up where we left off."

Allison and Nicole exchanged a puzzled look.

"Kind of odd," Nicole said as she collected her files. "I hadn't heard we were going to have a drill today."

Allison's stomach lurched as she thought of what had happened in Seattle last month. She clutched the sleeve of Nicole's jacket. "Maybe it's not a drill."

As Allison and Nicole turned toward the exit, they saw that one of the prospective jurors, a hunched old lady with a cane, was having trouble getting to her feet. They helped her up, and then Allison took her arm. "Let me help you down the stairs."

"No, I'll take care of her, Allison," Nicole said. "You go on ahead. Remember, you're evacuating for two now."

Allison had been so busy concentrating on the jury selection that she had actually managed to forget for a few hours that she was pregnant. Eleven weeks along now. She didn't quite show when she was dressed, but her skirt was only fastened with the help of a rubber band looped over the button, threaded through the buttonhole and back over the button.

"Thanks." She decided not to argue. At least Nicole knew her child was nowhere near here. What if this wasn't just a drill?

Allison hurried through the black padded double doors and toward the stairs.

CHAPTER 3
Channel 4 TV

Juggling a handful of colorful dry-erase markers, Channel 4's assignment editor, Eric Reyna, stood in front of the whiteboard at the station's morning story meeting. Around the table, staff passed copies of the three pages of potential story ideas that Eric had compiled. Everyone sat on a rolling office chair—everyone except the new intern, Jenna Banks. She was balanced on a bright-blue exercise ball that she claimed helped strengthen her "core."

Crime reporter Cassidy Shaw was already tired of the ball, and how Jenna bounced on it, and how her blonde cascade of hair rippled when she did, and how her tiny skirts rode up her slender thighs. But there was no point in complaining. She would just look old and bitter. It was a measure of the cruel reality of the news business that at thirty-three she might legitimately be considered old and bitter.

Eric ran his free hand through his thinning, gray hair as the reporters scanned the list. As the assignment editor, Eric was like the air traffic controller of the newsroom. He monitored scanners, managed news crews, and generated stories. And he ran the morning and afternoon story meetings that decided what aired at noon and what aired at night. He was a good ten years older than anyone in the room, but since he was never on camera, Eric didn't need to worry about his potbelly or lack of charisma.

And while no one knew his face or asked for his autograph, Eric made it clear to Cassidy and the rest of the on-air staff that he saw himself as the true brains behind the pretty faces that spent time in front of the camera.

Led by Eric, the team quickly decided which stories to follow up on. A Portland couple accused of allowing underage drinking at their New Year's Eve party was due back in court. Some environmental activists had chained themselves to the fence at the headquarters of a company they claimed used cancer-causing chemicals to line their aluminum cans. And the station's political reporter, Jeff Caldwell, was chasing down a report of misconduct at city hall.

Once the day was planned out, Eric said, "Okay, people, during sweeps we'll be running some special programming."

February—as well as May, July, and November—was a sweeps month, when the Nielsen company measured the audience watching each television program. That information set the price advertisers paid for commercial time. The more people who watched the news, the more Channel 4 could charge for advertising for the next four months. During sweeps month, every news story had to be bigger, stronger, and just a little bit crazy.

Cassidy made her voice low and sonorous. "It killed Lucille Ball, Albert Einstein, and George C. Scott. And it's caused by something you probably have in your medicine cabinet. Is your life in danger? Tune in at six to find out more."

Everyone laughed. Everyone except Eric, who continued on as if she hadn't spoken. "Cassidy will have that special piece about domestic violence that will air right before Valentine's Day. I'm anticipating a lot of viewer reaction."

Everyone looked at Cassidy. She straightened up and smiled. Then Jenna had to spoil it all by

28

patting her hand and saying, "You're so brave," in the exact same tone as she would use to compliment someone competing in the Special Olympics.

Eric continued, "In addition to Cassidy's piece, we'll be running a couple of investigative exposés. One will involve having someone pose as a streetwalker. We'll set up a hotel room and surprise the johns for a little on-camera conversation."

Cassidy pressed her lips together. No wonder Eric had singled out her piece. He was just trying to butter her up so she would be willing to go from serious to sleazy. It was bad enough that the station hadn't made her coanchor, something they had hinted doing only a few weeks ago. Now they wanted her to put on some hot pants and a pair of vinyl boots and lean into creepy guys' cars while they filmed her. Even if she would look pretty darn sexy, it was still demeaning. Well, she wasn't that desperate. She would just tell them no. And then they would beg and plead, and maybe she would work some kind of deal. Get some extra vacation days, at a minimum.

"That's so sleazy," Cassidy said. "Do I really have to do it?"

Eric smirked as if he had been waiting for her. "No one's asking you to, Cassidy. Jenna has already agreed to go undercover and do the reporting for that story. We want you to work on a different investigative piece. We're going to send you to a spa in the Pearl District. We have reports that they're using bad Botox."

All Cassidy could manage was to sputter "Jenna!" Her disdain for the story evaporated. Jenna! Jenna! But she was the intern! She was only twenty-two years old! Okay, she was smart enough, but you had to pay your dues before you got airtime. Before you got a story served to you on a platter.

From the other end of the table, Jenna gave Cassidy an exaggerated smile that showed every one of her shiny, white teeth. She coyly dipped her head toward one shrugging shoulder, miming an apology.

Right. Like Cassidy was dumb enough to think that Jenna hadn't known this was coming.

Halfway down the table, Cassidy heard Brad Buffet's soft snicker. Brad was the anchor, the once and future king. Cassidy had tried to depose him, or at least share power, and he had made it clear he would never forgive her betrayal.

Where was the fairness? A few weeks earlier, Cassidy had handed Channel 4 a story about a dead girl and a senator that pushed the ratings into the stratosphere overnight. Stations from all over the country had courted her. By now she could have been telling viewers the top story in San Francisco or Boston. Instead, she had stayed put in Portland, for the promise of coanchoring with Brad.

Sure, she got to fill the role a few times, but the promise turned out to be empty. The station manager instead told her, "We're bringing in a new gal to partner with Brad. Former Miss Connecticut. She tests very well."

"But you promised me, Jerry!" Cassidy had protested.

"We didn't promise. We said we would try it out." Jerry had sighed. "And we did give you a run in the anchor's chair, but the overnights didn't come back like we'd hoped. We gave it a shot, Cassidy, but I have to think of the good of the station. As a crime reporter, everyone loves you. But you just don't have the same impact in the anchor's chair."

And now, to add insult to injury, Jenna was getting the story that would showcase her gorgeous body. And Cassidy was stuck with the segment that would make viewers think of her as old.

When the meeting was over, Cassidy fled to the ladies' room. After making sure she was alone, she looked at herself in the mirror. Despite the fact that she had finally started getting more sleep, in the unflattering fluorescent light her skin looked somehow sallow. Did her hair—which she spent several hundred dollars getting cut and colored every six weeks—appear more like straw? She drew her fingers down on either side of her lips. Could she be getting puppet lines? Next, she

31

turned to the side and put her hand on her stomach. It was flat when she sucked it in—but not so much when she didn't.

It was at that moment that Jenna walked in, moving so fast that by the time Cassidy jerked her hand away from her belly, she could tell that Jenna had already seen it.

"Hey," Cassidy said, giving her a false smile. She quickly moved to the door with her hand outstretched.

"Do you think I'm wrong to be taking the assignment?" Jenna asked. "Do you really think that it's degrading?"

Something inside Cassidy snapped. "It's bad enough that you're doing it, but don't pretend that it wasn't what you wanted all along!"

Jenna's eyes widened. "I didn't know anything about it until Eric asked me. I'm sorry if you think I'm not being some old-school feminist, but I personally think you can still be hot *and* be a journalist."

"Of course you do," Cassidy said. She had clearly underestimated Jenna, who had managed to call her ancient and ugly without actually using the words. Without saying any more, Cassidy pulled open the restroom door.

As she walked back down the hall, Eric looked up from the police scanner. The small, black box was used to monitor police, ambulance, fire, and public utilities transmissions.

"Hey, Cassidy, didn't you tell me once that you know Jim Fate?"

"Yeah. Casually." She managed a shrug. "Why?"

"Because the scanner is saying there's been some kind of explosion over at KNWS. It's not very clear. But it sounds like someone took him out."

Cassidy went absolutely still. *Jim? Dead?*

Then Brad spoke from behind her, making her jump. "I'm surprised nobody did something to that guy a long time ago. How many people has he ticked off over the years?"

Neither Eric nor Cassidy answered him. Instead Eric said, "Cassidy, I'm assigning this story to you, given your personal connection. I want you and Andy over at KNWS right now."

She managed to get the words out past her suddenly dry throat. "Sure. But tell Andy we'll take separate cars and I'll meet him there."

Eric's eyes narrowed. "I want you on this right away. I'm going to put it on a breaking news crawl. So don't dawdle, Cassidy. I want a finished package for the noon news. Maybe even sooner. "

"And you'll get it. Don't worry."

Cassidy turned away. Her fingers were already in her purse, feeling for the key to Jim's condo.

CHAPTER 4
Mark O. Hatfield United States Courthouse

Allison had been one of the first down the stair-well. The man in front of her pushed open the heavy door, and the sound of dozens of sirens rolled over them, so loud that she winced and put her hands up to her ears. She blinked in the pale sunshine and looked out at a world entirely different from the orderly one of the courthouse. She stopped short, but then a hand pushed her shoulder from behind. She stepped to one side, so that she wasn't blocking the exit, and pressed her back against the cold granite wall.

People were running in all directions. They cut across the street without regard to traffic. Cars sounded their horns and pulled into bike lanes and even into the oncoming lane in a futile effort to find a clear path.

Chaos.

"Move! Move, people, move! Move away from the downtown core!" A policeman standing on the corner shouted into a megaphone, but his words were nearly drowned out by the sirens. "Go across one of the bridges. Get out of down-town!"

Looking past him, Allison could see what she guessed must be the source of the problem. Half a block away was a knot of fire trucks, police cars, ambulances, cops, and firefighters—but what really froze her blood were the men in white hazmat suits milling around, waving wands in the air as they checked small handheld machines. She thought of the thumbnail sketches of the victims of the recent terrorist attack that the *Oregonian* had been running. Would her picture and two paragraphs about her life be in next week's paper?

A section of sidewalk in front of an office building had been cordoned off by orange cones and yellow tape strung around spindly street trees. And in the middle, a tall Asian-looking woman stood in what seemed to be a blue kiddie pool, screaming as more men in white chemical suits and blue rubber boots sprayed her off with a high-pressure hose. Her eyes were closed, and her arms were wrapped around her head. And as Allison watched, she toppled over.

Allison didn't know where to go—just away from the sirens, away from whatever had happened to that poor woman. Get away before it got her too. A woman in a turquoise blouse darted in front of a dark sedan, and the next second she was on top of the hood, her body pressed against the windshield. Allison gasped in horror, but the woman pushed herself off the car and started running again, limping, before Allison could help her.

An older man in a heavy overcoat doubled over

right in front of her, his breath wheezing. He clutched his fur collar. "It's in the air!" he yelled. "It's in the air! Terrorists! Sarin!"

Allison's breath caught in her chest. Sarin! What could that do to her developing baby?

All around her, dozens of people were trying to clear their throats, gagging, swaying, coughing, even falling to the ground. Allison stood frozen for a second. Should she try to help someone— maybe drag the middle-aged woman who sat panting in the middle of the sidewalk? But to where? Was any place safe? Would stopping to help just strike her down too? *Dear God,* she prayed, *help me know what to do.*

Her heart was beating so fast. The air smelled sour. Her mouth tasted like metal. She took one more look at the poor woman in the wading pool. She was still now, and the men in white suits were cutting off her clothes, dropping each scrap into a red plastic bag marked with hazard symbols.

Allison realized she had to save herself. Save herself and the baby inside her. If she didn't get out of here right now, they might both be dead.

All around her more and more people staggered, coughed, fell to the ground. One woman was crawling, still trying to get away. Others had given up. And in the middle of the crowd stood a Hispanic toddler, screaming. Allison hesitated. No one was rushing to her side. The child was all alone. And in a second she might succumb, as so many were, gagging, eyes rolling, falling to the pavement.

Allison raced to the little girl, grabbed her and held her close, and began to run.

Run while she still could.

CHAPTER 5
Willamette Villas Condominiums

Jim's twentieth-floor condo stretched the full length of the building, so it offered not just a view of the Willamette River, but also of the downtown core only a few blocks away. Cassidy stood close to the glass, careful not to touch it. Careful not to touch anything.

It hadn't even been fifteen minutes since Eric had relayed the news, but already chaos had engulfed the city. Every ambulance, police car, and fire truck within three counties must be on the scene. Cassidy could see there was no way she was going to be able to drive to meet her cameraman. There was no way she was going to be able to drive anywhere. The streets were clogged with cars, so many that some drivers were now driving the wrong way—anything to get away from the center of downtown, where KNWS had its studio.

Cassidy thought about Allison and Nicole. Were they in court today? She couldn't remember. She tried calling each of them, but the circuits were overwhelmed. She asked the universe to protect them, and then tried to let go of her worry. She didn't want to put out negative energy.

Being so far above the scene removed some of its impact. The lavishly decorated condo added to the feeling that she was in another time and place entirely. A quiet place, swaddled by wealth. Behind her, a massive chandelier hung over the mahogany dining room table that seated sixteen. Handwoven Oriental carpets were scattered over the gleaming red oak floors. The condo even had its own library, where leather-bound books lined floor-to-ceiling shelves.

In the stainless steel kitchen, Cassidy used a dish towel to punch the radio button. It was already tuned to KNWS. But there wasn't any local coverage, just a national feed. That made sense if they had had to evacuate the building. Someone could have flipped the switch on the way out. Still using the dish towel, she tried KXL and KEX, but they didn't seem to know much more than Eric had when he sent her out. Something had hit the studios of KNWS—some kind of gas or maybe a bomb—and there were reports that some of the station's personnel had been injured. Maybe Jim wasn't dead, then.

As she listened to the radio, Cassidy found and retrieved what she had come for. How would Jim react if he found out she had been here? Well, she would cross that bridge when she came to it. If she came to it.

The only new news was that police were now evacuating the downtown core. Cassidy didn't need the radio to tell her that. She could see it by looking out the window.

Of course Cassidy wouldn't leave. You didn't get an award-winning story by running away with the stampeding herd. You got it by going where no one else wanted to go. And that meant she had to make her way *to* downtown, not away. She looked down at her four-inch heels. They were not meant for walking blocks and blocks.

She tried calling Andy on her cell, but got another fast busy signal. This was why the station had invested in push-to-talks for its staff. She pressed the button on the side.

"Andy? Are you there? Andy?"

She could barely hear him over the noise in the background. Sirens, screams, shouts. "Where are you? I thought you would be here by now."

"I'm about five minutes away," she said, fudging a little. "What have we got?"

"Some kind of poisonous gas. It sounds like the release was deliberate." Andy made a practice of buying drinks or coffee for every cop in town, so he always knew the inside scoop. "I'm hearing there's one confirmed fatality. Jim Fate, like they were saying at the station."

Cassidy's heart contracted. It was hard to believe. Jim saw himself as the strong one, the one who spoke truth to power, who wasn't afraid to

39

tweak those who deserved tweaking, and to press even harder when needed. Jim loved—*had* loved, Cassidy corrected herself—being macho. That was his personality on air and off. He felt it was his job to take care of anyone weaker—and to prove that no one was stronger. He could drink other men under the table, unfailingly called women "ladies," and always opened Cassidy's car door.

And now he was gone.

"I've got footage of the guys in bunny suits hosing off some woman outside KNWS. Meet me at the corner of Salmon and Broadway. We need to go live with this now."

Cassidy hurried around the apartment, using the dish towel to wipe off any areas she might have touched, not just today, but the other times she had been here. She grabbed a bottle of water, a pair of blue and white Nikes, and a thick pair of socks. For a man, Jim had small feet.

Then she thought of something else. In the bathroom, she opened the medicine cabinet above the floating granite shelf that held a vessel sink. The Somulex bottle was almost full. Jim wouldn't be needing these now.

Before she opened the door, Cassidy put on a pair of oversized sunglasses. In the elevator, she slipped into Jim's Nikes. And when the elevator doors opened, she broke into a run.

CHAPTER 6
Mark O. Hatfield United States Courthouse

This is not a drill," a voice said on a loudspeaker in the crowded stairwell. "Please exit the building as quickly as possible."

"As quickly as possible" did not apply to a woman in her seventies who walked with a cane. Every step was a slow, painful ordeal. Nic felt her stomach clench. They were on the sixteenth floor of a building built for grandeur, meaning the ceilings were unusually high—and the staircases correspondingly longer.

"You go on ahead without me, dear," said the elderly juror, whose name was Mrs. Lofland. "I'll be fine." She smiled up at Nic, the skin pleating around her faded blue eyes.

"I'm not leaving you, ma'am." Nic tucked as close as she could to the older woman. The stairwell was just wide enough that a third person could squeeze past them. And squeeze past they did. There wasn't any panic, not yet, but people were dead serious.

Nic had one hand under Mrs. Lofland's arm and the other on her BlackBerry. With her thumb, she tapped out a note to Leif Larson, asking if he knew what was up. Leif, like Nic, was an FBI special agent. He was also Nic's—well, certainly not her boyfriend, but *something* to her. Something

41

more than just a friend. Even if she still resisted the idea.

Leif's reply came in less than a minute. Nic stared at her screen, glad that it was small enough that even the man pressing up behind them couldn't catch a glimpse of the message.

GET OUT. POSS SARIN 2 BLKS AWAY.

Sarin gas? Oh no. Homeland Security had briefed the FBI on what would have happened in Seattle if the fake janitor had managed to put the gas into the ventilation system, as opposed to spilling it on the carpet. He had died for his mistake, and so had fifty-two other people in the building, as well as five first responders. But if he had succeeded, the number would have been far higher.

Eighty years ago, sarin had been invented in Germany as an insecticide. But the military discovered it worked even better against humans. It was now classified as a nerve agent, the worst of the worst. Extremely toxic. And extremely fast acting.

Sarin was also colorless, tasteless, and odorless. Add a little to the municipal water supply, and kill thousands. Aerosolize it, and it was even more effective. Even just letting it evaporate was enough. In 1995, a Japanese doomsday cult had killed a dozen and sickened hundreds by puncturing containers filled with liquid sarin on Tokyo subway cars.

If the recent terrorist attack had succeeded, Homeland Security estimated that 95 percent of the people in the building would have died, most within minutes. And when it got out through the rooftop ventilation stacks, it would have sunk back down to the ground, because sarin was heavier than air. And there it would have killed even more victims. More than three thousand dead in the first half hour. Thousands more from exposure as they fled. The economic damage would have been incalculable.

All from an attack that would have taken ten minutes to carry out.

They were only on the fourteenth floor now. At this rate, getting out would take more than an hour. Which was still no guarantee of safety, not if the gas were there, invisible and deadly.

Nic wanted to abandon this old lady and run. Push her way through all these people, hold her breath once she was outside, and not stop running until she was blocks away and on higher ground.

Who would raise her nine-year-old daughter if something happened to her? Nic knew it was stupid that she didn't have a will, but she always got stuck on the same question. Who did she trust to raise Makayla? Her parents? They were nearly as old as Mrs. Lofland and starting to show it. Her brothers? They didn't always see eye-to-eye with Nic.

They rounded a corner. Already there were

bottlenecks. An overweight woman in a blue muumuu inched her way down sideways, stepping down with one foot, and then slowly putting her other foot on the same step. Nic wanted to yell out that they had to hurry, but she knew it might only cause a panic. Mrs. Lofland would be the first to be hurt.

People pressed closer together, not talking, concentrating on getting down. The stairway was at times now coming to a complete halt. When Nic looked over the edge, she saw dozens of hands lined up on the handrail.

People kept trying their cell phones, but it was clear they couldn't get through. A few others with BlackBerrys were offering to send e-mails for those around them.

Suddenly Mrs. Lofland's arm jerked out of Nic's grasp, and the older lady pitched forward. Nic grabbed the woman's shoulders with both hands and yanked her upright, ignoring the pain from the healing bullet wound in her own upper right arm.

"I'm sorry, dear. I tripped."

Nic looked down. Some stupid woman had just abandoned a pair of black, very high heels on the stairs, and the old lady had stumbled over one. Nic picked up one and then a few steps later, the other. Not knowing what else to do with them, she shoved them into her bag. The shoes looked expensive. Maybe, if she was lucky, they were her size. Nic realized she was getting giddy. The air seemed stale and close, inhaled and exhaled by dozens, perhaps hundreds, of people before them. But did she really want to smell fresh air if it might also carry the invisible scent of death?

Mrs. Lofland's lips were moving. Was she in pain?

"Are you all right?" Nic asked. "Do you need to stop?"

"No, dear, I'm just praying."

"You don't need to worry. I'll get you out of here, I promise."

"I'm not worried about myself, dear. If it's my time, it's my time. I'm just praying for you and the others."

Normally, Nic would have had to stifle a retort. Mumble to God or mumble to yourself—what difference did it make? But for some reason, Mrs. Lofland's words made her feel better.

They passed an abandoned black wheelchair left in the stairwell. Where was its owner? Nic's eyes strained ahead until she caught sight of a woman being slowly carried down the stairs by four men—young, old, black, white—all united in their common goal of saving another human being.

"Leave me behind," the woman was saying. "Go on without me. The firemen can help me."

Nic didn't hear their answers, just saw them shake their heads.

They had just reached the ninth-floor stairwell

45

when all hell broke loose. Someone below them must have gotten the same message Nic had earlier.

"It's poisonous gas," a man below them shouted, his voice cracking in panic. "They're evacuating all of downtown!"

His words were answered by screams, shouts, and shoves. The crowd had been slowly pushing forward like a herd of cattle. Now it became a stampede. A man in front of Nic fell. She reached out her hand, but in a second he was gone, rolling down, trampled by panicked people. A woman behind them screamed, "I don't want to die here!" before clawing her way past Nic.

Nic grabbed the handrail on either side of Mrs. Lofland. The cane was gone, lost in the chaos. She flattened herself and the older woman against the wall as the crazed crowd surged forward. If she were alone, she thought she could make it all the way down to the exit. But Mrs. Lofland? She would be crushed. The next time she tripped, Nic probably wouldn't be able to pull her back up.

Time slowed down, the way it had at other times Nic had faced death. She saw people's open mouths, but their screams were oddly muffled. All of her attention was focused on finding a way to keep them both alive.

It was clear they weren't going to be able to make it to the exit. But was that really so bad? Leif's e-mail had said the sarin gas was two blocks away. Not here. And if there was no sarin in the building, then paradoxically, the lower they went and the closer they got to being out of this crazy panicked crowd, the more danger they might be in. The gas would seep out through roof vents and then roll invisibly back to the ground—the very ground these people were trying to claw their way toward.

What if they stayed here, higher than the gas could reach? Almost immediately Nic realized the flaw in the idea. Most buildings' HVAC systems vented stale air through the roof and picked up fresh air at ground level. So even if they managed to get back onto a floor, the ducts overhead could still be spewing invisible death. Unless . . .

She thought of a plan. Now all she needed was to get them back out onto a floor.

"We've got to get back inside one of the floors!" she yelled in Mrs. Lofland's ear. "It's the only way." She felt more than saw the older woman nod.

Nic wrapped her right arm around her companion and then let go of the security of the handrail. Almost immediately, they were buffeted by the shoving mass. Using her left elbow, Nic began to create a space where none existed. She made some headway, but the surging crowd pushed them inexorably down two steps, then three, four. The eighth-floor stairwell was now above them. And there was no way they were going to be able to swim upstream.

She had to make it to the far side of the stairwell before they reached the seventh floor. Each time Mrs. Lofland was pushed off balance, Nic hung on for dear life, pinning her to the empty air, until the older woman could get her feet under her.

There. The stairwell door. She yanked it open. Quickly, Nic pulled Mrs. Lofland through the door and closed it behind her.

They were in a typical office space, fuzzy, blue, head-high walls making a warren of cubes. Mrs. Lofland leaned against one of them. Her face was pale. "Don't we need to evacuate?"

"I don't think we would survive if we kept trying to go down." Nic's thoughts whirled. Going—staying—which choice was right? And which choice could kill them?

The old lady's blue eyes were shrewd. "You mean you don't think I would survive."

"There's that," Nic admitted. "But those people might be right. There might be poisonous gas outside. If it's the type of gas I think it is, we're better off *not* being close to the ground—the gas is heavier than air." As she spoke, she pulled out her BlackBerry.

Leif had sent her another message, but she must have been too distracted to notice it. It said: WHERE R U?

Her thumbs flew over the tiny keyboard. 7 FLR. 2 CROWDED 2 LV.

A second later, she had his response. COMING 4 U.

48

When she looked back up from the tiny screen, Mrs. Lofland was staring up at the ceiling. More specifically, at the square air vents set in the acoustical tile. "But doesn't the building bring in air from outside?" she asked.

"Yes," Nic said, unholstering her Glock. "Which is why I am going to do this."

CHAPTER 7
Downtown Portland

In Cassidy's IFB, the earpiece that had been specially molded for her ear, Eric's voice said, "You're on!" She and Andy were standing on a sidewalk, two islands in the middle of a swift-running stream of people.

Cassidy took a deep breath. In the back of her mind, she monitored how the air tasted, how it smelled, and registered nothing that seemed out of the ordinary. At the same time she said in measured tones, "This is Cassidy Shaw, reporting live for Channel 4 from downtown Portland. The scene here this morning is one of panic."

In any disaster, the media served as a conduit for information. You told victims what to do, you provided facts to the general public, and you informed everyone about what was needed and how they should respond.

And of course, ratings would never be higher—which would make the suits happy. Even if commercials had to be temporarily suspended.

Cassidy concentrated on speaking as smoothly as if she were seated behind the anchor's desk instead of watching an entire city melt down around her. On 9/11, people had turned to their TVs for reassurance, listened to Mike Wallace calmly explain what was known and what was not, watched Peter Jennings, his sleeves rolled up and his demeanor unflappable, as he did his best to inform them for hour after endless hour. Cassidy could do no less, no matter that people were tearing past her, running in a blind panic, sirens shrieking all around them.

As a reporter, you had to put up a wall between yourself and the situation. You noted who, what, when, where, why, and how—but at the same time you kept your distance from it, the way a doctor could joke in the emergency room even as the blood of a dying man soaked his scrubs. Cassidy's job was to make sure that the information she gave out was at least of some help to a terrified city.

"We are hearing that KNWS on Salmon Street is the epicenter of the event. There are reports that some kind of gas leak or possibly a deliberate release of poisonous gas occurred there, and we have unconfirmed reports of at least one fatality. People in the downtown core are complaining of dizziness, shortness of breath, and nausea. As you can see on your screen, the ambulance crews and firefighters are working as fast and furiously as they can, trying to get to these people and put them on stretchers and get them to the hospital. It is really a chaotic situation. People are frantically trying to find friends and coworkers."

The images around her were sharp and indelible, but at the same time everything was a blur. Cassidy was working on instinct, trusting her thoughts to organize themselves as she opened her mouth and let the words pour forth.

"Just from where I stand, I can see five ambulances, as well as innumerable fire trucks and police cars. Sirens are wailing, and people are running out in the street, which is completely gridlocked as everyone tries to follow the mayor's earlier order to evacuate downtown. Folks are leaving their purses and their personal belongings behind, just clearing out of the buildings and getting away from the area as fast as they can. Some people are crying, some screaming in panic, some madly dialing cell phones that are no longer working. Some people are coughing, gagging, and stumbling in a daze, but with no evident injuries."

Brad's voice broke in, higher pitched than normal. Viewers might attribute it to excitement, but Cassidy knew it for what it was: fear.

"Cassidy, are you sure it's safe for you and your cameraman to be there?"

She made a show of taking another long breath, even though deep down, part of it was not for

51

show. Still, no alarm bells went off in her brain as she inhaled. The air smelled familiar, if not exactly fresh. "So far, so good. Even so, we still must advise everyone to stay away from downtown. All the major egress routes are jammed." Cassidy was secretly pleased that she could summon up the word *egress* when part of her was screaming that she should just turn tail and get out of there.

Brad said, "Is there any way of knowing if this is a terrorist attack, Cassidy?"

"It could be, Brad. We just don't know. It could be an isolated incident. It could even be some kind of accident. The exact nature of what has happened we're not clear about at the moment. Right now, the police and other emergency personnel are focusing on getting people to safety."

Cassidy saw someone running toward them, dodging cars. A policeman. Andy watched Cassidy's head swivel to the left, and he swung his camera, guessing it was worth the shot.

"You can't be here!" the cop yelled. He was young, his face red and sweaty despite the cold.

Cassidy pulled herself up to her full height, wishing she were still wearing her four-inch heels instead of Jim's Nikes. "We *have* to be here," she told him in a voice that brooked no arguments. "This is history. We are keeping hundreds of thousands of people informed."

The policeman stared at them for a moment,

considering. "Okay," he said and left—again on the run.

Andy gave Cassidy a nod, and she knew that she had earned his respect.

Even though the adrenaline was pumping into her veins at full force, Cassidy made herself continue to speak slowly and clearly. "We want to tell our viewers some things *not* to do. We'll see if we can put these up on your screen.

"First of all, stay away from downtown. If you are on I-5 headed north or south, I'd recommend taking I-205 and bypassing downtown entirely. Traffic is being allowed to travel in some outbound lanes on I-5, I-405, and surface streets. Some people are simply abandoning their cars in the middle of the road, making an already nightmarish traffic situation worse.

"In addition to the streets being gridlocked, cell phone traffic is jammed and landlines are overloaded. If it's not an absolute emergency, please stay off the lines."

Eric had passed some of the information that Cassidy relayed along to her; some came from Andy's sources.

"We are hearing that the hospitals have been overrun with people who have been exposed to whatever this is. There are also injuries from trampling and fender benders as people are fleeing the area. If you are a doctor or a nurse, you should report to the nearest hospital. We will keep you updated with further reports as we get them. This is Cassidy Shaw, reporting live from downtown Portland."

Cassidy let her shoulders droop. She knew they would be back on in a minute or two, that she would need to keep broadcasting until they were forced to leave or this thing sorted itself out. In a second, she might look around for someone to interview, but for now, she just let the chaos wash over her. She realized she was trembling. A block away, she saw a man pushing his way through the crowd, fighting upstream. The only reason she picked him out was because he was well over six feet tall and seemed to be all muscle. The build and the red-gold hair were familiar—it was Leif Larson, the FBI agent, and her friend Nicole's . . . question mark. Boyfriend, friend, friend with benefits? Cassidy didn't know.

Right now he looked like a man on a mission, every inch the Viking warrior.

CHAPTER 8
Mark O. Hatfield United States Courthouse

Why do you need a gun?" Mrs. Lofland asked in a calm voice. Nothing so far today had seemed to fluster her—not being questioned by a judge, not being forced to evacuate, not even seeing a gun in Nic's hand.

"Here's our problem. There could be poisonous

gas at ground level, because it's heavier than air. But if we stay here, then as the building's air system sucks in fresh air from ground level, it will spew it right back out at us. So we're probably not safe here either. I'm thinking if we could break out a window, we could bring in fresh air that's not contaminated."

Nic walked over to the floor-to-ceiling window and looked down. The sidewalk was full of panicked people. Bile rose in her throat when she saw that a few were prone or on their hands and knees, already overcome. Were these the same people who had been on the stairway a few minutes earlier?

She focused on the glass itself. Now that she was away from the chaos, away from the immediate danger of being trampled, her thinking felt slow and muddy. Finally she holstered her gun.

"I can't do it. It's against Bureau policy to fire at anything but an armed suspect who presents an immediate threat. And it's also against my better judgment. The streets out there are just too crowded. The window would deflect the trajectory of the bullet, so it's hard to predict where it would end up. I can't take the chance of injuring someone else." She rapped on the glass. It made a heavy, hollow sound. "This glass is so thick anyway—I'm thinking the chances are good we'd only end up with a little round hole to show for putting other people at risk."

Going back on a floor had seemed like such a good idea, but now Nic could see it was worthless. "If only there was a way to get fresh air in here without hurting someone else." She spun around and looked at the desks behind her. Staplers, telephones, tape dispensers, computers. What she needed was something heavy and pointed. "Maybe we could use something else to break the window. If we started in a corner and compromised the integrity, we might be able to work out from there." She pressed her cheek against the cool glass. Could the resulting shards be fatal to a pedestrian or first responder below? From seven stories up, it seemed possible. A wave of despair swamped her. They couldn't get out, but staying in might be just as bad.

Mrs. Lofland's voice interrupted her thoughts. "Maybe you're looking at this the wrong way, dear."

"What do you mean?" Nic felt an irrational surge of hope.

"Maybe what's needed is not to get the good air in but to keep the bad air out."

In a flash, she saw what the older woman meant. "We could try to find the thermostat, see if that would shut down the air, or at least slow it down. And put something over the vents."

Mrs. Lofland nodded. "The plastic bags in the wastebaskets. We could use them."

Nic looked around. Under every desk, a wastebasket. "Yes. See if you can find scissors and any tape heavier than Scotch tape. I'll look for the thermostat."

She found it around the corner. Ignoring the handwritten DON'T TOUCH! note stuck underneath it, Nic thumbed it to OFF. Would turning off the heat also turn off the fresh air? She had no idea.

On the other side of the space was a small conference room. It was eerie to push open the door and see the papers in front of every seat, the plate of doughnuts, the abandoned cups of coffee, the half-eaten pastries sitting on napkins. Then she looked up. Just two vents. And both of them conveniently located directly above the table.

Nic thought of all the other people crowded into the stairwell. Was she letting them rush toward their deaths? Should she go back out there and try to persuade them to join her? But there was no guarantee that getting back in the building might save them. This scheme of hers was untried, unproven. And the room was too small to hold anyone else and still provide enough air for any length of time.

Nic hurried back and saw that Mrs. Lofland had found a roll of duct tape as well as a pair of scissors. Back in the conference room, Nic stood on the table and taped a double layer of wastebasket liners across each vent. Then she took off her jacket and stuffed it and some of the paper napkins in the crack under the door.

Mrs. Lofland was sitting with her eyes closed and her hand pressed against her chest. Her breathing sounded soft and fast.

"Are you all right?" Nic asked. "Should you put your feet up?"

Mrs. Lofland's skin was pale, but when her eyes opened, they were as sharp as ever. "It will be okay, dear."

By the time she closed her eyes again, Nic realized this wasn't really an answer. And that she wasn't likely to get one.

Nic tried to slow her own breathing, her eyes lingering on the woman's serene face. Was it just a simpleminded refusal to face the facts, or was it a gift that Mrs. Lofland could be so calm in the midst of chaos? She surprised herself by asking, "Are you praying again?"

Mrs. Lofland's eyes opened. "A part of me is always praying. But yes. I'm praying for the people out there. And for you."

"But I think you and I are safe," Nic said.

"That doesn't mean you can't use a prayer." Mrs. Lofland's smile held a hint of mischief. Then she closed her eyes again.

Twenty minutes later, Nic was just picking up a doughnut when Leif's blue eyes appeared in the window of the conference room door.

Calling his name, she jumped to her feet. He tried to open the door, but only managed an inch before it caught. Mrs. Lofland scooted her chair forward, leaned down, and pulled out Nic's rolled-up jacket.

"Is it safe?" Nic asked, feeling her heart beat in her throat. He wasn't wearing a mask.

For an answer, Leif pulled Nic into his strong arms.

CHAPTER 9
Northwest Portland

Forty blocks. That's how far it was to Good Samaritan Medical Center, yet it was still the closest hospital. But Allison would walk all day if she had to. She would walk until her feet fell off. *Dear God,* she prayed, *protect these two precious innocents. And everyone else caught in this nightmare.*

At first she half ran, half walked, the child wailing and clutching her coat collar. Every block or two, Allison made herself stop and turn in a circle, her eyes looking for anyone searching for a lost child. She saw dozens of panicked people, but no one who seemed to belong to the little girl clinging to her. She spared a thought for Nicole and the juror. *Loving God, watch over us . . .* words that were part of the grace she and her husband Marshall said every evening and that she had never meant more than now.

Allison's breath was coming in gasps, forcing her to slow to a fast walk. For a moment, she pressed one hand against her belly, checking in with that little hum she had been feeling for several weeks, the hum of connection. Still there. She shifted the little girl from one hip to the other. The child was finally quiet now, her face wet with tears. Her black hair fell to her shoulders, and in her ears were tiny sparkling stones. Her dark-green coat was a little too big for her, the sleeve edges frayed.

"What's your name, sweetheart?" Allison tried.

The girl's dark eyes stared into hers, but she didn't make a sound. Was she in shock? Or something worse?

"My name's Allison. What's yours?"

She still looked blank. What was the Spanish word for name? Something like *yah-ma*?

"Yah-ma Allison," Allison ventured, pointing at her chest, still moving along as fast as she could. She had managed to put ten blocks between them and what was happening. At least here most people were on their feet. "Yah-ma Allison," she repeated, then turned her finger to point at the girl and raised her eyebrows. "Yah-ma?"

"Estella," the girl answered. At least it sounded like that. She patted her own chest.

"Okay," Allison said. "Estella." Her mood lightened a little. If only she could ask Estella where her mother and father were. If only the girl were old enough to reel off a phone number or an address. Or at least say if she felt sick.

When she came to the freeway overpass, Allison's mouth fell open. Interstate 5 in both directions was bumper-to-bumper as far as the eye could see. A person could have walked down the river of cars and never touched the ground. And they weren't moving at all. Ambulances, cops, and the desperate were using the shoulders, but there were already places where these were choked off too.

By the time they were a half mile from the hospital, Allison was overwhelmingly thankful that she had worn flats. One of Estella's small feet rested just where the bulge of her pregnancy was beginning to show. The weight had been nothing when she had begun her mad dash from downtown. Now her hip and shoulder ached with each step. The girl's head drooped against Allison's shoulder. Either she was used to strangers, or she was tired, or—and Allison didn't want to think too much about this—she was getting sick and no longer had the energy to fuss. They were in Northwest Portland now, an older part of town where the roads were notoriously narrow. Today they were gridlocked, filled with cars whose panicked drivers were convinced they had only a few minutes before they would die. Ambulance drivers cycled through various siren tones and even squawked out orders on their speakers, but there was no place for people to go.

One ambulance simply took to the sidewalk,

scattering pedestrians before it. It didn't seem like the sidewalk would be wide enough, but the ambulance scraped between the building and the parking meters with less than an inch on either side, and then forced its way back into traffic a block later.

By the time Allison reached the hospital, it had been more than an hour since the alarms had interrupted the trial. Thinking about the Bratz Bandits seemed absurd and unreal. Reality was slogging forward with a child like a deadweight on her hip. Reality was looking at the frightened faces around her and wondering if any of them would make it.

Allison had expected the emergency room to be crowded, but what she saw shocked her. Dozens of people stood, sat, or lay in the parking lot and next to the sidewalk. A lucky few were on gurneys. Some children or small adults were even doubled up. The rest sat or lay on their coats or right on the blacktop. Some coughed and moaned; others were silent or talked quietly. One well-dressed woman who leaned against a brick planter called, "Nurse! Nurse!" over and over, but didn't seem to be suffering.

Among them moved a dozen people in scrubs and street clothes, taking pulses, blood pressures, and temperatures. The faces of the doctors and nurses were calm and determined, and just looking at them made Allison feel a little better. They moved quickly, but they didn't appear panicked. And although most wore latex gloves, they didn't seem to be worried about contamination. Here there were no face masks, no moon suits.

And then Allison caught sight of a familiar face—Dr. Sally Murdoch, a pediatrician she occasionally consulted about crimes she was prosecuting. Sally wore an open black leather jacket over green scrubs.

Allison waited until Sally straightened up from talking to a middle-aged woman and then said, "Sally, this child and I were both—"

A hand yanked her back. "Wait your turn!" growled a man in a business suit.

On any other day, she thought, he would have held a door for her, graciously waited for her to get off the elevator, offered her a nod and a smile as they passed on the sidewalk. But this was not any other day.

Allison realized that a half-dozen people were waiting in a ragtag line for Sally. She had the baby to think of, and Estella, but she didn't think even that argument would hold any sway. Sally gave her a sort of smile and a shrug, and Allison joined the end of the line.

Sally spoke to each person in turn, her words a soft murmur, putting a stethoscope to their chests, looking at their eyes and throats, laying a consoling hand on their arms. The businessmen took whatever news she delivered stoically, but the woman ahead of Allison burst into ragged tears.

Allison's heart lurched. She didn't want to imagine what the message had been.

When it was Allison's turn, Sally said, "Who's this?"

"Estella. I think. I found her downtown, crying. I don't think she speaks English. And Sally, you need to know that we were only a block from whatever happened. So we were exposed. Can you help us?" She hesitated, and then said in a rush, "And you should know that I'm—I'm pregnant."

Sally shot Allison a quick glance, then murmured, "Hey, baby girl." She gently touched Estella's knee before she slipped her stethoscope inside the girl's coat. Estella's arms tightened around Allison's neck.

Sally listened intently, and then shook her head. It had to be bad news. Allison felt like her heart would crack.

But then Sally said, "This child is fine. And just from looking at you, I can tell you're fine too. Just like all these people here are fine, except for the ones who got hit by a car trying to run across a street or who ended up with a heart attack from the stress. But everyone else is fine."

"Fine?"

"Fine," Sally said definitely.

"How can you say that?" Allison protested. "I was downtown. I saw it. People were falling to the pavement all around us, gagging and coughing.

And we were right there. We were breathing in whatever they did."

An old man tugged Sally's sleeve. "Please, miss, please, I was downtown. You've got to help me."

Sally turned and pointed at the line. Allison now saw how tired she was.

"Go wait over there with those people. I'll be with you soon." She turned back to Allison. "We've run dozens of blood tests, and they've all come back negative. This has overwhelmed all the hospitals, not just Good Sam. And they're all reporting the same thing—nothing."

"What?" Allison took a step back, startling Estella, who began to cry. "That can't be right. I was there. What are you saying—that all these people made it up?"

"Not at all." Sally sighed. "People were already on high alert because of the terrorist attack last month. You give folks clues like fire alarms and ambulances and emergency crews giving people oxygen right in front of them, and you throw them into a state of hypervigilance. It's the power of suggestion. The same thing happened in Tennessee a few years back. A teacher thought she smelled gasoline. She got dizzy, short of breath, and nauseated. They evacuated the classroom and eventually the whole school. The more ambulances they sent, the more they had to send. More than a hundred people ended up in the emergency room, and dozens were admitted."

"And?" Allison prompted.

Sally shrugged. "They tested and tested—but nothing. Most people who got sick said they smelled something, but they all reported something different—it was bitter; it was sweet; it smelled like something burning. Same thing happened today. People saw the hazmat team, heard there had been some kind of chemical spill, decided this was another sarin gas attack, and began to monitor themselves for symptoms. The air downtown doesn't smell or taste that good anyway, especially not when you add hundreds of idling cars when everyone tried to follow the mayor's order to evacuate. It's called mass hysteria. Otherwise healthy people convince themselves something is wrong."

Allison was still having trouble believing it. "But I was there, Sally. I was there. Something awful happened."

"Something awful did happen—it just didn't affect that many people. The hazmat people tell us there was a small release of some kind of gas at KNWS. Small and contained. One fatality. They're treating a couple of other people who were on scene, but only as a precaution."

KNWS. That rang a bell. "Who was the fatality?"

"They said Jim Fate."

"Jim Fate?" His name sparked the last bit of adrenaline Allison had left. "I was going to meet

66

with him tomorrow. He'd been getting some kind of threats."

Sally raised her eyebrows. "They must have been more than threats. I'm hearing we were lucky that, for whatever reason, he chose to stay in his studio, and it was nearly airtight. It kept this scene"—she swept her arm out to the hundreds of people—"from being a real disaster."

Allison looked closer at the would-be patients. Sally was right. No one seemed in dire straits. "Why do you have all these people in the parking lot—why aren't they inside?"

"It started when we thought they really were contaminated. We couldn't risk it spreading to the entire hospital. Now they're out here simply because we don't have room for them in there. And a lot of them won't go away—they don't believe us when we tell them they're okay. But not one of the people we're seeing has reddened eyes, irritated mucous membranes, or labored breathing. If this had been a real poison gas attack, we would have seen that, at a minimum. And we would be in a world of hurt. We don't have enough protective gear—chemical goggles, face shields, and respirators—even for our staff. We don't have enough nerve antidote kits for all these people. We don't have enough anything. Nobody does."

"If it had been real, what would you have done?" Allison asked, shifting Estella's weight. Her panic was slowly ebbing.

"Triage," Sally said bluntly. "You simply don't treat the weakest and the sickest, the ones who will probably die. You concentrate on the ones you can save, and you say a prayer for the rest."

CHAPTER 10
Good Samaritan Medical Center

Allison had taken a child. *She had taken a child.* At the time, she had thought she was saving Estella's life. But now that she knew there had been no danger, she felt sick when she thought of Estella's family. Somewhere in the chaos, they must be frantically searching for their missing girl.

"What do you think I should do, Sally?" she asked her friend. "This child's poor family must be going crazy trying to find her. Should I try to take her back downtown?"

Sally blew air through pursed lips. "You can't go back there. They're still clearing the area, just to be safe. Even if you did manage to get back downtown, chances are whoever was with her has been moved—either forced to evacuate or taken to a hospital. You might walk her around the parking lot, see if there's anyone she recognizes. But if not, I'd take her home and call Child Protective Services. I'll make a note that you have her in case anyone asks for her. What did you say her name was again?"

"I think it's Estella."

At the word, the toddler lifted her head, and both women smiled.

"Okay. Estella. A healthy two-and-a-half-year-old, by the looks of her. Give me your address and phone numbers in case someone comes looking for her. By this evening, they should have some kind of clearinghouse set up for information."

Allison picked her way through the people sitting and lying on the sidewalk, the flower beds, the parking lot. Now that she knew they were okay, the scene was not nearly as frightening. She saw a few people with bandages and casts, but certainly no one who seemed to be dying.

"Do you see anyone? Anyone you recognize?" she asked, but Estella didn't answer, didn't even seem to be paying attention. More than likely, she only spoke Spanish. Or maybe it was the tone of voice Allison was using. She realized she was talking to the toddler as if she were an adult. Every mother in the world naturally used a singsong, baby-talk delivery, but Allison couldn't even think of how to begin. How was she going to be able to be a mother to the baby she was carrying? Maybe she would just have to fake it and hope that no one caught on.

Finding no one that Estella seemed to recognize or who recognized her, Allison started walking the thirty blocks home. Along the way she tried calling the office, Marshall, and Nicole and

Cassidy, but the cell service was still overwhelmed. So instead she prayed, her lips moving silently. Prayed for Estella and her family. Prayed for the people in the parking lot and the people downtown. For Nicole and the juror she was helping, and Cassidy. For the safety of all the first responders. For all the investigators, that they would be able to get to the bottom of this. And for the friends and family Jim Fate had left behind.

She was plodding along with her head down, her mind someplace else, the sleeping Estella a deadweight on her hip, when she heard a shout.

"Allison! Allison!" The voice was ragged, as if it had been shouting over and over.

She looked up. Two blocks away, Marshall began sprinting toward her. She had never seen him run so fast, at least not wearing dress shoes and a suit. He skidded to a stop as he saw Estella, then threw his arms around Allison anyway, an awkward sideways hug. Estella, jolted out of her sleep, let out a faint protesting wail.

Marshall's breath came in gulps. "I've been looking all over for you." He pulled back to look at her. His jaw was set, his eyes determined, but Allison heard the faintest tremble in his voice.

"I've been trying and trying to call you. I went downtown, but the cops wouldn't let me past the barricades. But it was such a madhouse, I finally slipped in. Only I couldn't find you." He ran one hand through his black hair, which was already

70

sticking up as if he had made the same gesture a dozen times that day. "Oh, Allison, I couldn't find you anyplace."

Tears filled her eyes, the tears she hadn't let herself shed all day. "Marshall, I . . ."

He pulled her close, at least as close as he could, given Estella, and she sobbed against his chest.

His words ruffled her hair. "Let's drive to the hospital, or at least as close as we can get, and then we'll have to walk. I heard they're overrun. We need to get you checked out. You and the baby and . . . who is this, anyway?"

Allison stepped back. "Actually, I've just been to Good Sam. They said I was fine, the baby was fine, and"—she patted the girl's shoulder—"so is Estella."

He bent toward the girl. She offered him a shy smile before turning her head and burying it against Allison's chest.

"I found her outside the courthouse when they were evacuating downtown. She must have been with someone, but I couldn't see them, just this poor little girl crying all by herself. At that time we still thought the air was poisoned, so I picked her up and took her to Good Sam with me."

Marshall cocked his head. "What do you mean, 'still thought the air was poisoned'? Isn't it?"

Allison quickly told him what she had learned from Sally.

Some of the tension went out of his shoulders.

"Thank God. Even if it did bring the city to its knees, it could have been so much worse." He held out his arms. "Here, let me carry her the rest of the way."

Estella's eyes widened. She clutched Allison so hard that her little fingers went white.

"I guess she's not ready for that," Allison observed. The three of them started for home.

When Marshall unlocked the front door, Allison's eyes fell on a note scrawled with a Sharpie and taped on the entryway wall. *Allison, stay here. Looking for you. I love you.*

Tears closed Allison's throat. Marshall had charged out to find her, not knowing if he himself might be struck down. Again the experiences of the past hours washed over her, the terror and fear she hadn't allowed herself to feel. She was home; she was healthy; she wasn't dead or even sick. She and Marshall and the baby—and Estella—all of them safe.

CHAPTER 11
Riverside Condominiums

Cassidy walked in the door of her condo and went straight to her bedroom. *Do not pass go, do not collect two hundred dollars,* she thought as she fell more than lay across the unmade bed. It was all she could do to muster the energy to kick off her shoes. Well, Jim's shoes, really, but he wasn't in any position to ask for them back. She had never bothered to change, knowing that Andy would frame the shot so that it didn't show her feet.

All day, as she reported on the chaos downtown, Cassidy had longed to be home, to be by herself, to have nothing around her but silence. And the Riverside Condominiums were quiet. The builders had broken ground at the height of the real estate mania, when property was appreciating 15 percent every year. Everyone wanted in. They held lotteries to choose who was allowed to buy, and Cassidy had felt very lucky when her number came up. She hollowed out her retirement fund, already imagining the kind of return she would get. Only suckers would hold on to conservative stocks when there was so much money to be made in real estate.

Six months later, the bottom fell out of the market. Roughly half the units in her building remained unoccupied, bought by speculators who had thought they could flip them for a fast profit. A lot of investors had ended up walking away from the debt, giving their units back to the bank. As a result, the building was often eerily silent.

Now that she was finally by herself, Cassidy realized there was a big problem with being alone. There was nothing to distract her from what had happened earlier in the day.

When she closed her eyes, she saw people running past her, heard the screams and the sirens. It was almost like hallucinating, she could see the people so vividly. An old man in a black fedora clutched his throat and fell to his knees. A young woman with a half-dozen silver piercings begged Cassidy to tell her if they were all dying. A boy carrying a skateboard ran out into the street, and before she could even call out a warning, he was hit by a huge blue boat of an Oldsmobile.

Her eyes flew open. *They're not real*, she told herself. *Forget them and go to sleep*. But when she tried, she saw fresh horrors. It was like her overtaxed brain was coming up with new problems to keep the adrenaline flowing.

Even as exhausted as she was, there was no way she was going to be able to sleep tonight. Not without some help. With a sigh, she got up and padded out to her purse. Without turning on the light, she found Jim's bottle of Somulex and shook a tablet into her hand. In the kitchen, she poured herself a glass of wine to wash it down.

"Here's to you, Jim," she whispered, lifting the glass a few inches in the air. "May you rest in peace." And then, with a practiced gesture, she tossed the Somulex into her mouth and swallowed it with a single mouthful of the sharp and oaky red wine.

Cassidy had never been a good sleeper, but events of the past few months had ramped up her problem to the point where she sometimes went an entire night without sleep. It had started when her old boyfriend, Rick, turned jealous and then abusive. After a while, it hadn't felt safe to sleep beside him. And even when he wasn't with her, she worried that he might jolt her awake with a drunken, threatening phone call, or even come creeping into her condo in the middle of the night. Things only got worse when she, Allison, and Nicole had confronted a murder suspect—a confrontation that had ended with the killer dead on the floor and Nic with a bullet through her shoulder. When Cassidy closed her eyes at night, she still saw the blood.

After the shooting, she turned into an ultramarathon insomniac, awake for as long as forty-five hours at a stretch. Nights became endless. She paced her condo, watched TV, flipped through magazines, listened to talk radio, and surfed the Internet. Whenever she tried to sleep, her thoughts raced. She thought about Rick, about how he had hurt her. About her parents and how they had always found her lacking. She thought about stories she wanted to cover, and hadn't. She also thought about Jenna, who was everything Cassidy had once been. Now Cassidy was ten years older than the station's intern—and she was sure that it showed.

And always, always, Cassidy did the math. If she went to sleep in the next ten minutes, then she would get five hours of sleep. But it wouldn't be long until she had to recalculate. The most she would get would be four hours, or three. Worrying about not sleeping kept her from sleeping. By the time it got down to two hours, she would be whimpering, beating her pillow, begging the universe for relief.

Cassidy tried all the remedies in the women's magazines. *Go to bed at the same time each night.* People who suggested that obviously didn't work in the 24/7 world of the news business. *Try a glass of warm milk.* It tasted gross and had no effect. Melatonin, valerian, kava kava, Tylenol PM. She still lay staring at the ceiling. Sometimes a glass or two of wine helped for a short while, but she would wake up after an hour and not be able to get back to sleep.

One evening she complained to Jim over dinner. "I can't sleep anymore. Sometimes I'm awake all night."

"You need to get your doctor to prescribe you some of these." Jim took a bottle from his pants pocket.

"What is it?"

"Somulex." He shook a white, oval pill into her palm. "Here. Take this tonight and see if it helps."

Did it *ever*.

That night, as soon as Cassidy's head hit the pillow, her breathing slowed and softened. It was a deep, nearly dreamless sleep. She couldn't remember sleeping like that since she was a kid.

And people noticed even after a single night.

"You look different," Jenna said the next day, giving her a long, considering look. "Did you change your hair?"

That afternoon, Cassidy called her doctor and got her own prescription. "I can't sleep," she told him. "I'm very stressed-out after everything that's happened. Please, please can you give me a prescription for Somulex?"

It wasn't any harder than that. Cassidy got twenty pills. The label said they were for "occasional sleeplessness." At first, she broke the pills in half and only took them on Sunday nights, the hardest ones.

But if it looked like a big story might break the next day, or she had an important meeting or an event after work and needed to look good—well, there were the pills to help. Over the phone, the doctor had mumbled something about how they could be addictive, but Cassidy decided it was better to have a little addiction and be well rested and alert. Better to be attractive than ugly and exhausted.

It wasn't long before she needed to take a pill every night. If she tried to skip one, she found herself wide-awake. She would lie and watch the glowing green numbers on her alarm clock slowly move forward—3 a.m., 4 a.m., 5 a.m. Finally she would break down and take a pill, even if she only got an hour or two of sleep before her alarm sounded. And some nights she needed more than one.

What was supposed to be a monthly supply of Somulex was gone in under three weeks. When her doctor wouldn't renew her prescription early, Cassidy found a second doctor and had him call in her prescription to a different pharmacy.

The one thing her doctor had lectured her about was the danger of mixing Somulex with alcohol. "If you combine the two, they can depress the nervous system. Maybe even to the point of your body forgetting to breathe."

Cassidy had heeded his warning for a while. But she was working so hard. She needed to unwind. And only a glass or two of red wine allowed her to do that.

Someday she would quit. When her life calmed down.

Now Cassidy stood in the kitchen and felt herself shaking. She had defied death today, but she had also stood in a dead man's apartment and walked home in a dead man's shoes. Five minutes ago she had swallowed a dead man's pill.

And it was doing nothing for her. If only there were an off switch on the back of her head. She would reach around and flip it down and be wonderfully blank.

Instead she took another pill.

Cassidy had never been one to like baths. She was too type A to be anything but a shower girl. But now she remembered the candles Rick had bought her back when he was first wooing her, the expensive bubble bath. In the bathroom, Cassidy ran the water until it nearly reached the edge of the tub, lit the candles, grabbed her glass of wine, and lowered herself into the water. A few minutes later, she began to feel the familiar melting sensation in her arms and legs. The Somulex was finally kicking in.

CHAPTER 12
Pierce Residence

Allison picked up the phone to call Child Protective Services, but instead of a dial tone, all she got was a fast busy signal. Again. The phone lines were still overwhelmed, even though the radio and TV stations were urging everyone to stay off the phone unless it was an emergency. She held Estella on her lap, the useless phone loose in her hand. "I guess she's ours to take care of, at least for now," she told Marshall.

He crouched down on his heels. "Well, that's not such a hardship, is it, sweetheart? Aren't you a pretty thing. And smart. I can tell just by looking at those bright eyes that you're smart."

Estella watched him, her face serious, her

rosebud lips pressed together as if she were waiting for something.

"Maybe try something in Spanish," Allison said. "You know more than I do."

"Which is hardly anything," he said. Then he looked at Estella. *"Hola. Me llamo* Marshall," he said. He reached his hand toward her, fingertip extended.

To their surprise, she flinched, then turned her head and started to cry softly, a repetitive, exhausted sound. Allison pulled the little girl to her chest and patted her back.

"It's like she's afraid of me." Marshall stood up and took a couple of steps back.

"Oh, I don't think so," Allison said, but part of her worried he was right. Maybe not afraid of Marshall, but of another man. Some man in her life. The thought made her heart contract. Had anyone ever hurt Estella? Even uttered a harsh word to her? "I think she's had a terribly long day, and you're just one more stranger looming over her. We've had hours to get used to each other." Turning Estella back around, she still held her close, thinking that the girl might be able to feel her heart beating against her shoulder blades. Maybe she could think like a mother after all.

"Do you think she's hungry?" Marshall asked. Then he turned his gaze to Estella, careful not to come any closer. *"Comida?"* He looked at Allison. "I think that's it, anyway. I don't remember the word for hungry, but I think *comida* means food. *Comida,* Estella?"

Estella licked her lips.

At the sight of her little pink tongue, Allison said, "I think you got her interest." Then a bit of panic set in. "What do we have in the house to feed a child, Marshall?"

They both liked to cook, with the result that their refrigerator was stocked with items like capers, kalamata olives, and roasted red peppers. And what was Estella used to eating? Did they have any tortillas in the house? Or refried beans? And what if all she really wanted was something like a Pop-Tart?

Allison's earlier feeling of confidence was evaporating. Weren't there rules about what you fed toddlers, like no grapes or hot dogs or hard candies, so they didn't choke? And what about allergies?

"We'd better not give her peanut butter," she said. "Or any kind of nuts. What about milk? Do you think milk would be okay?" She looked at Estella. *"Leche?"* she hazarded.

Estella looked interested. So, a glass of milk. Allison wondered if they had any plastic cups.

"I think we've got one of those blue boxes of mac and cheese," Marshall said. "Don't all kids like mac and cheese?"

They all ended up eating the mac and cheese, although Marshall couldn't resist grating half a block of Tillamook Sharp Cheddar into the pan.

Before they took their first bite, he said grace. "God, thank You that You kept us all safe today. Thank You for bringing Estella and Allison together, and help us to get Estella back to her family. And help this city to get back to normal— and for this crime to be solved. Loving God, watch over us."

"Amen," Allison said, and then ladled pasta onto everyone's plate.

In lieu of a booster seat, Estella was perched on the yellow pages. She had only consented to leave Allison's lap when their two chairs were placed side-by-side.

"Nicole and I were supposed to meet with Jim Fate tomorrow. He was getting death threats."

"Guess they were more than threats," Marshall said. "Did he say who they were from?"

"He didn't say much at all." Allison sighed. "And now it's too late to ask."

"Do you think it's terrorism?"

She raised her shoulders. "Who knows? Jim Fate has made a career out of making enemies. It could be personal, it could be political, or it could be anything in-between."

Estella ate well, but was still unnaturally quiet, jumping at any unexpected noise. Eventually, the child's head began to droop. Her eyes were at half-mast. It wasn't yet seven o'clock, but Estella was clearly ready for bed.

Allison tried calling Child Protective Services again. She was surprised when she actually got a dial tone and then again when the phone began to ring. And ring and ring. She was about to hang up when an obviously harried woman answered.

Allison quickly explained what had happened. She could hear the caseworker's sigh through the line.

"I can't get hold of most of my staff. Even if I could, I'm not sure I could find a foster home for this girl right now. The Red Cross is working on a Web site to reconnect missing relatives, but it's not up yet." As she spoke, more phones rang in the background. "Look, I need to put you on hold for a second."

When the woman came back on the line a full five minutes later, Allison said, "Why don't you take the information I have about Estella. Things should be better by tomorrow, and we can keep her for tonight. And you could always call us if you hear from her family."

"Sounds great," the caseworker said, and from her tone Allison could tell she was already moving on to the next set of problems.

After Allison hung up, Marshall said, "Maybe I should sleep in the guest room, and you two can have our bed. I mean, we can't leave her on her own, and I seem to make her nervous."

"Honey, are you sure that's okay? The guest bed isn't that comfortable."

He raked one hand through his hair. "Of course it's okay. A few hours ago, I thought I might never see you again. Sleeping on the guest bed is a small price to pay for having you safe and sound."

Getting ready for bed offered more challenges. Luckily, Estella knew how to use the toilet. Should Allison try to bathe her, change her clothes? But she had to admit that she would look askance at any stranger who undressed or bathed her future child. She set Estella on the edge of the tub and contented herself with removing her little socks and shoes. Using a warm, wet washcloth, Allison knelt down and wiped Estella's face, hands, and feet, murmuring baby talk that felt a little more natural than it had earlier in the day. When Marshall knocked on the door, Allison was marveling over Estella's tiny, perfect toes.

"It's strange to think that in six months we'll have our own baby toes to stare at." Marshall's voice was husky, as if the day was catching up with him.

Allison felt exhausted, from the miles she had walked and from the residue of fear that had hovered over her the whole time. "I don't know if I'm ready." She closed her eyes, suddenly feeling the full weight of the day. Only half-aware of the gesture, she put her hand on her belly.

"I don't think anyone is ever ready." Marshall's hand was warm on her shoulder. "We're just going to have to take it a day at a time, and trust God to give us the wisdom we need."

Allison carried Estella to the bed and tucked her in on Marshall's side. Estella closed her eyes, her breathing already slowing. But when Allison turned to get up, the little girl opened her eyes and sat up, crying out in Spanish. The only word Allison understood was *"Mami!"*

Reluctantly relinquishing the idea of a shower, she slipped into her pajamas and slid into bed. And five minutes later, she and Estella were both asleep.

In the middle of the night, Allison jerked awake from a nightmare where people had again been falling to the sidewalk, but this time bright-red blood bubbled from their lips. She lay in the darkness and heard Estella repeat, *"Mami, Mami, Mami."* Her little voice was sad and hopeless, and it made Allison's heart break.

She reached over and switched on the light by the bed. "Hush, honey. I'm here. I'll watch over you."

But Estella still begged, looking past her, unwilling to pretend any longer that this stranger was her mother. *"Mami. Mami."*

It was a long time before they both fell asleep.

CHAPTER 13
Hedges Residence

Dear God," Berenice Hedges began, and Nic obediently closed her eyes, shutting out the sight of the heaping platters of food. She didn't believe in making her mother angry. Especially when she was starving.

Besides, they did have a lot to be thankful for. Mama squeezed Nic's hand, and Nic passed it on by squeezing her daughter's hand. She heard Makayla's giggle as she completed the circle by squeezing her grandpa's hand.

Nic was alive. Mrs. Lofland was alive, when she could so easily have been trampled to death in the stairway. Nic's family was fine, as were nearly all the residents of the city of Portland. And right now, as Nic waited for Mama to finish praying, she could smell the tureen of milk gravy sitting directly under her nose, the mouthwatering scents of beef and garlic and roux. She was alive and she was hungry, and she was about to eat a delicious meal.

And then there was Leif. Nic had let him hold her this afternoon. Only for a moment. But she had let herself relax against his broad chest, tucked her head under his chin, and felt some of the unbearable tension leave her body.

"Amen," Mama said. At the same time

Makayla's hand shot out and grabbed the serving dish heaped with potatoes that had been cooked along with the pot roast.

"Say excuse me," Nic cautioned, as Makayla heaped potatoes on her plate.

Her daughter grinned unrepentantly. Her braids bounced as she lunged forward for a roll.

"So will Makayla be staying with us for a while?" Nic's father asked. Lloyd Hedges was a tall, slender man with big eyes made even bigger by his narrow face.

"I'm afraid so. They're putting together a task force to figure out exactly what happened." Nic tried to hide her pride at the next bit of news. "I've been appointed the case agent." She had lobbied hard for it, pointing out to John Drood, the special agent in charge, that Jim Fate had reached out to her and Allison just before he was killed.

"Congratulations," Berenice said. "I think." She knew what long hours such an assignment meant.

"Why can't I just stay home by myself instead of coming here after school?" Makayla said. "I'm almost ten. And everybody thinks I'm at least twelve."

Makayla already came up to Nic's nose. She had another striking feature: her unusual green eyes. Even strangers commented on them and sometimes asked where she had gotten them.

No matter how much she tried to pretend Makayla was all hers, there were times when the truth slapped Nic in the face. The green eyes, the height, the paler hue of her skin—all came from Makayla's daddy.

But Nic had sworn to herself that Makayla would never, ever know that.

Or him.

Nic shook her head. "It doesn't matter what you look like. What matters is how old you really are. And in this state you have to be twelve before you can stay home alone. Besides, in the next couple of weeks there are probably going to be times when I don't come home until after midnight. Your grandma will feed you and make sure you brush your teeth and do your homework."

"And say your prayers before you go to sleep," Mama added, giving Nic a significant look.

Nic didn't rise to the bait. She was mostly silent through dinner, her mind going back through everything that had happened during the day. Was it really just this morning that the Bratz Bandits trial had begun? It seemed like a week ago.

She mentally retraced her route down the stairs with Mrs. Lofland, and then back into the court-house. She again saw Mrs. Lofland safely into a taxi—paying the driver herself over the older woman's protests—and then walked with Leif back to the FBI office. It had been a rare sunny day, the kind that made you think that spring was just around the corner. February could be cruel like that.

But as they walked through the nearly empty streets, past abandoned cars and even an empty stroller, Nic only had eyes for Leif.

"Did you ever listen to his show?" Leif had asked.

"*The Hand of Fate*? Not really. Too one-sided for me. He made sure he always had the last word. Not to speak ill of the dead, but the last time I listened to him, he was saying that food companies could be counted on to do a good job of policing themselves because they wouldn't want to kill off their own customers. And that the big-government advocates were using Chicken Little tactics to scare consumers. Well, hello, I am scared. I've got a child to raise. Peanut butter is pretty much 50 percent of Makayla's diet. And that one company had rats and mold and all kinds of things it doesn't bear thinking about. I say, bring on the nanny state." She realized Leif was grinning at her. "What?"

He shook his head, looking amused. "I just don't think I've ever seen you get that riled up."

"And I don't like to feel like that. If I'm going to listen to the radio, I'd rather listen to some jams, not something that's going to raise my blood pressure. But don't worry. Just because I want the food policed doesn't mean I won't do a good job on this."

Leif's expression turned serious. "Don't worry. Everybody knows that if you give Nicole Hedges a case, you had better stand back, because she'll go after it with a vengeance."

Back at the office, Nic had immediately been engulfed in a series of meetings and phone calls and database searches, activities so routine they took some of the edge off the events earlier in the day.

Now her father said, "You're drooping, sweetheart. Do you want to sleep here tonight?"

"Thanks, Daddy, but I'm going to go on home. I've got to get an early start in the morning. I'll bring over some clothes for Makayla on the way in to the office."

"Please, can't I come with you, and then you can bring me back in the morning?" her daughter begged. "I want to get some books and my Game Boy."

"You can just give me a list."

"But I won't remember everything I need. Please?"

Nic was too tired to argue. "Okay, baby. But you can't complain if I wake you up really early."

She helped her mother carry the serving dishes into the kitchen. It would all be packaged into Tupperware, which Daddy might tuck into late at night. Nic envied her father's ability to eat whatever he wanted in huge quantities and not gain an ounce. Spending her lunch hours in the gym and her weekends with a Thai boxing instructor was the only reason Nic's butt wasn't as big as the planet.

She was turning to go back to the dining room when Mama laid a hand on her arm. "There's something you need to know. Makayla was asking questions about her father today."

An icy finger slowly traced her spine. "What did you tell her?"

"That we don't have contact with him. And that she has you and me and your father and brothers, and that should be enough."

"It will have to be enough," Nic said. "Won't it?"

"I'll be praying for you to have wisdom," Mama said.

Nic bit her lip to stifle a retort. Ten years ago she had pleaded in desperation for God to help her, and what had He done? Nothing.

Hoping that Makayla would realize this was no time for asking difficult questions, Nic took her daughter and drove the two miles home.

The first thing she did after locking the front door was to unbuckle her holster and put her Glock in the gun safe. As an FBI agent, Nic carried her Glock to dinner, to the grocery store, and to her kid's third-grade play. The FBI required that agents be ready for duty at all times.

When Makayla was younger, the gun had fascinated her. Nic had told her that she could ask to see the gun as often as she wanted, but only in the house and only when the two of them were alone. And she was never, ever to touch it. Now Makayla took the gun for granted, no more remarkable than her mother's car keys.

In a daze of exhaustion, Nic helped Makayla pack up her things (including a stuffed bear named Fred that Makayla pretended she didn't really care if she brought with her or not), and then got ready for bed. Nic would have to get up at five to have time to drop Makayla off and still drive down to Clackamas County to observe the autopsy.

Two hours later, she was still turning restlessly. Questions ran through her mind. Why had Jim Fate been killed? How would she react if Makayla started questioning her? What would have become of her daughter if Nic had died in the stairwell? And Leif—what was Nic going to do about him?

For some reason, Nic thought of Mrs. Lofland, the way her lips had moved in silent prayer for others, and she felt herself calm a fraction.

CHAPTER 14
Pierce Residence
Wednesday, February 8

Allison woke, but didn't open her eyes. She didn't feel rested at all. Why were her shoulders and hips so achy? Was she sick? And that faint breathing next to her—had Marshall gotten up and the cat sneaked in to steal his place?

Then she remembered. Remembered walking

miles and miles with a toddler in her arms, trying to escape the terror of downtown. Her eyes flew open. And there was Estella, lying on her side facing Allison, watching her with huge, dark eyes.

When Allison opened her eyes, the little girl smiled.

As Allison reached out to hug her, she hesitated. This was not her child. Her own child was growing in her belly. This girl had her own mother someplace, a mother who must be frantic to find her. So Allison contented herself with brushing back her hair.

Something delicious scented the air. Pancakes. "*Comida?*" she ventured, remembering one of the words Marshall had used the night before. "*Comida*, Estella?"

She was rewarded with a small nod and another smile.

Leading Estella to the kitchen by one hand, Allison checked her phone with the other. There were texts from Nicole and Cassidy, saying they were okay and asking how she was. It was too complicated to explain what had happened, so she just texted them both back: FINE. XO. TALK SOON.

In the kitchen, Marshall was pouring batter into the frying pan, with a stack of just-made pancakes on a plate next to him. He reached out and squeezed her shoulder.

"How did you sleep?" she asked.

He shrugged. "Probably about as well as you did. I heard her crying for her mother in the middle of the night."

They both looked at Estella, who now seemed to have forgotten the terrors of the night. Children, Allison guessed, lived in the here and now.

She was just pouring Estella a cup of milk when the phone rang. Marshall answered it. Whatever he heard made his forehead wrinkle. Without thinking, Allison gripped Estella's shoulder, only becoming aware of it when the girl gave a frightened little squeak.

"It's a caseworker from Child Protective Services." He handed her the phone.

She swallowed, and then said, "This is Allison Pierce."

"Hi, Allison. This is Joyce Bernstein. I'm sorry our staff wasn't able to help you last night. It was pretty crazy. Now that things are calming down, we're starting to get up to speed over here. We'll be sending someone by to pick your girl up in about twenty minutes. Thanks for being flexible."

"No problem." Allison kept her voice steady. It was illogical, but it hurt to think about giving Estella back. "So you found her parents?"

"Not yet. But she's not the only child who got separated from her family. It's been a mess. Not only did we end up with a half-dozen other kids who were totally on their own, but three day care centers downtown got evacuated. And with the phones basically being down, no one could get in touch with anyone else. We're only just now getting things straightened out."

It seemed important to have Estella fed and presentable before the caseworker showed up. Sensing that her world was about to change, she clung to Allison, refusing to sit on the telephone book that had served as a makeshift booster seat the night before. Allison ended up feeding her on her lap. Then she wiped Estella's face and hands with a damp paper towel and tried to gingerly brush the snarls from her hair. Only then did she think about her own appearance. She quickly changed out of her pajamas.

All too soon, there was a knock on the door. Marshall answered it, while Allison hung back. She told herself it was hormones that were making this so difficult. Giving Estella to the authorities would be the quickest way to unite this girl and her family.

At the sight of the middle-aged stranger wearing a red sweater and a wide smile, Estella started to cry. She buried her head against Allison's chest, her little hands clinging tightly to her blouse. Allison kissed the top of her head, inhaled her sweet aroma, and then gently began to pry her fingers loose. "They're going to find your *mami*, Estella. *Mami.*"

Her dark eyes were full of confusion and pain.

Even if Allison had spoken Spanish, she had a feeling that Estella was too young to understand why her world was changing yet again. As she got one small hand loose, Allison braced herself. Would Estella scream and flail? But instead, when Allison held the girl out to the social worker, Estella gave her a look of dull despair. It was as if she was resigned to always losing the people she needed.

Allison managed to hold it together until the caseworker had Estella settled in a car seat and was pulling out of the driveway.

Once she was inside the door, she let the tears come.

CHAPTER 15
Riverside Condominiums

Six hours after she had washed down two Somulex with a glass of wine, Cassidy woke with a jolt. It was daylight. She was freezing, shaking so hard from the cold that she could hear her teeth knocking together. Where was she? She was surrounded by low-burning candles, lying naked in a cold bath from which the bubbles had long ago dissipated.

Blearily, she looked at her watch. She had been lying in deep, cold water, basically passed out, for most of the night. What if she had slipped under the surface? Cassidy jumped up, blew out the candles, and grabbed a towel, vowing never again to do anything so stupid.

In the kitchen, she drank one, two, three cups of coffee, trying to shake off the grogginess that made her eyelids droop. Her body ached from sleeping half sitting up in cold water. She turned on the radio. It was tuned to KNWS, but to her surprise what she heard wasn't a national feed.

The person on the air was Victoria Hanawa. Jim's cohost. Cassidy thought about what Jim had told her about Victoria. How much of it had been true? How much of it had been designed to make Cassidy do what he wanted? Jim wasn't above shading the truth and even ignoring facts that didn't fit his theories.

Cassidy had a theory about people who spent their working lives entertaining the public. Actors. Comics. People in TV and radio. Secretly they were all just a tad insecure. No matter how many listeners or viewers they had, it was never enough. Like the philosopher who wondered if a tree falling in a forest made any noise if no one was there to hear it, people who made their living as entertainers—and Cassidy counted herself among them—wondered if their lives had meaning once the cameras or microphones were turned off.

Which is why it made perfect sense that Victoria was processing the horror she had just witnessed by talking about it to an eager audience.

"Hello, Kim in Portland," she said. "You're

on the air with Victoria Hanawa, and of course we are talking about the tragic, tragic death yesterday of Jim Fate, who I had the honor of working with right up until the end. Kim, what memory would you like to share of Jim?"

"I just can't believe he's gone!" A woman's voice, rough with emotion, edged toward hysteria.

"It's almost impossible to believe, isn't it?" Victoria's own voice broke. "Only twenty-four hours ago we were talking about our weekend plans. And now he's gone." She heaved a shaky sigh. "Is there a story about Jim you would like to share, Kim?"

"It's just—just everything. He spoke up for us, you know? The little guy. He wasn't afraid to say what was wrong with this world. Who will do that now?"

"Jim certainly leaves big shoes to fill," Victoria agreed. "Whatever happens, it won't be the same."

"You were there, right, Victoria? You were there when it happened?"

"The authorities have asked me not to say anything about how Jim died. They are concentrating on bringing his killer to justice. They don't want me to reveal any clues they already have. But let me just say this: whoever it was didn't have the courage to look Jim in the eye. Whoever killed Jim was the lowest kind of coward." Victoria's voice strengthened. "But if he or she thought that by killing Jim, they would silence his voice or his thoughts, they were wrong. We will pick up his banner and carry it forward. He cannot be silenced that easily. Jim lives on in each of us."

One by one, listeners called in to agree with Victoria or to build on what she said.

"Jim didn't sound like anybody else, and it was because he was on fire," said Maribel in San Francisco. "He was passionate. He truly believed everything he said."

Zach in Spokane said, "I ran for city council because of Jim Fate. He inspired me to quit complaining about government and go out and do something about it."

"I'm sure Jim would be proud to hear that," Victoria said. "That is the kind of legacy that he leaves behind, and that we can all carry forward. And now we're going out to Phil in Tigard. Phil, what's your reaction to Jim's murder?"

"I didn't tell the guy who answered the phone this, but I'm not sorry."

"What?"

"I'm not sorry he's dead. That Fate guy was a blowhard. He just lapped up attention, and he did anything he could to get it. If he were alive now, he would be loving this. He would be eating it up. That was his goal, to get everybody talking about Jim Fate. Well, you know what? In six months no one will even remember his name. He was just—just flavor of the month. Only it was more like flavor of the day. Just some loud-mouthed jerk who liked to rile everybody up."

"You certainly don't think he deserved to die, do you?" When there was no answer, Victoria's voice sharpened. "Do you?"

"Someone finally took care of him. It's about time."

Cassidy stared at the radio in disbelief. Jim was always talking about people who hated him. But she had thought of it like hating taxes or someone who cut you off in traffic. You didn't really mean it. Oh, sure, you complained to your friends, swore under your breath, or even sent a nasty e-mail that got you the Nut of the Day award, but you didn't go any further than that. You didn't get confused and decide it was something that someone deserved to die for.

She was sure the authorities would get in touch with Phil in Tigard, or whoever it really was. But in her gut, Cassidy knew that this guy would turn out to be no one, nothing. Just someone guilty of the same thing he was accusing Jim Fate of: riling everyone up.

Cassidy carried the radio into the bathroom with her as she tried to make herself look less like a zombie. One by one listeners poured out their horror at Jim's death, their disbelief that he had been murdered, their memories of past shows, and their theories about who was behind it all. Lots of theories. Cassidy paid particular attention to these, because she was developing her own theories. Some muttered darkly about the government, rival talk show hosts, a rather generic "them," and even space aliens.

One man said he thought that Congressman Glover, who had been a nonstop target of Fate's for the past few weeks, must have hired an assassin to "take him out." Another pointed to the family of Brooke Gardner. The young mother had killed herself the summer before after Fate aggressively questioned her about the where-abouts of her missing baby. Cassidy knew a lot about the case because she had covered it too. The thought gave her pause. If Jim had been targeted for his coverage of that story, could she be the next target?

Cassidy thought about it and then shook her head. She was letting paranoia get the best of her. Still, if anyone knew whether she should be worried, it would be Nicole and Allison. Whether it was terrorism or not, they were sure to be in the thick of this. She sent them a quick text mes-sage, suggesting that they look more closely at Glover and the Gardners.

But there was yet one more theory that Cassidy heard, a theory that seemed to leave Victoria at a loss.

"I think it was you," Cynthia from Vancouver told Victoria. "You finally took care of him. You squashed him like the vermin he was."

"Me?" Victoria's voice cracked.

"We've all heard you guys fight on air. We heard how he treated you. He never let you get a word in edgewise. Well, good for you for finally standing up to him."

CHAPTER 16
Portland Field Office, FBI

Nic spent the early part of the morning at Jim Fate's autopsy. The observation suite was crowded with representatives from an alphabet soup of local, state, and national law enforcement as well as public health agencies.

Even though the air in Jim's studio had tested negative for sarin, the examiners took no chances. The forensic pathologist and his assistant wore yellow Tyvek suits and white helmets with their own air supply hoses snaking up their backs. The helmets made them look like spacemen. They also wore rubber aprons, shoe covers, and heavy gloves. Even with all these layers, they worked as quickly as possible, because the CDC had warned them that sarin could penetrate rubber and be absorbed through skin. To minimize the risk, they had begun by washing Jim Fate's corpse—which looked pale and vulnerable and sadly human— with a 5 percent hypochlorite solution.

Of course, washing the body meant there was also a chance that they would wash away hairs, fibers, chemicals, and other trace evidence. But the FBI still had the package the poison had been mailed in. In balancing risk versus reward, safety won out.

As soon as the autopsy was done, Nic drove back to the FBI Portland field office to head up the first meeting of the hastily assembled task force. The conference room was jammed. As a sign of how seriously they were taking this attack, top brass at the FBI had flown out specialized personnel from Quantico and headquarters to assist and evaluate. Senior officials from Homeland Security were also on hand. For now, the outsiders were taking a watch-and-wait approach. If it wasn't sarin, they would turn back around and fly back to Washington. If it was, then they would already be in place to swing into action.

Most members of the Portland FBI's evidence recovery team were also at the table, including Leif, who was the ERT's leader. There were also representatives from local and regional law enforcement, the Oregon Health Department, the post office, and more. Nic was thrilled to see Allison there, which meant she had been assigned as the lead prosecutor, and the two of them would work the case together. Catching Nic's eye, Allison gave her a smile so subtle that to an observer it might have looked like a simple widening of the eyes. For both of them, this was a case that could be the high—or low—point of their careers.

One question was on everyone's mind. Was this an act of terrorism? Or were they looking at a simple homicide?

Nic started off by explaining the findings from the autopsy to the circle of alert faces. "Unfortunately, the immediate autopsy results were inconclusive. Some evidence points to sarin, but some doesn't. For instance, the first responders reported that Fate's face was dry. Sarin pretty much switches all your systems to a permanent *on*, so his eyes and nose should have been running like faucets, and he should have been drooling. But there was no evidence of that."

"Have you thought that maybe Fate died so fast that his tear ducts didn't have time to kick in?" Special Agent Heath Robinson asked.

It was a fair question, but one with a more pointed history behind it. Heath had asked Nic out a dozen times, and even tried to kiss her at a party last New Year's Eve. At the time Nic had told him, truthfully, that she didn't date. Since then she had caught wind of a few whispers about her being a lesbian or a man-hater or both. She was pretty sure that Heath was the source.

"That is, of course, a possibility," Nic said evenly. "It's just one piece of the evidence. Another is that Tony—that's Tony Sardella, the medical examiner," she explained for the benefit of the outsiders—"Tony says the corpse had miosis, meaning the pupils were like pinpricks. That *is* consistent with sarin. Unfortunately it's also consistent with a lot of other poisons. And the lungs were congested, but again that could point to sarin or a dozen other things. The one thing that made Tony wonder was that there was no"—Nic consulted her notes—"no intense postmortem lividity." Lividity was the purplish skin stains seen on the underside of a corpse, where blood settled.

"He says that if it was sarin, the lividity should have been much more pink, but the stains were the typical purple color. Again, not conclusive. We're waiting on the results of the initial tox screens, and we should get those sometime soon. There wasn't enough time for anything to get into his urine, so they're only running tests on his blood."

Nic was beginning to think that the cause of death was going to be solved not with scalpels and saws on the autopsy table, but with microscopes in a lab.

"One thing we do know is that the air in the studio tested negative for sarin. But that test was conducted over an hour after the body was removed. It's conceivable that Fate inhaled most of the dose, and the rest was dispersed when the first responders got there and opened the door to the studio."

"How about his coworker?" Allison asked.

"Victoria—" She consulted her notes. "Victoria Hanawa. I saw her outside the studio, being hosed down by the hazmat team."

"The hospital kept her for a few hours as a precaution, but all tests were negative," Nic said. She looked at the end of the table. "What about the package and its contents, Karl? Any sign of sarin?"

He shook his head. "Initial tests were negative, but we're running a more sophisticated battery."

"What was the delivery device?" Nic asked.

"A modified smoke grenade." Karl held up a printout. It showed a photograph of a black cylinder with a wire trigger loop. "It was in one of those envelopes with a red string you pull to open. The end of that string was tied to the trigger of the smoke canister. So when Fate pulled the string and opened the package, the contents of the smoke canister sprayed directly into his face."

Nic thought they were finally catching a break. "Okay, who uses those—military, law enforcement? Can we trace it?"

Karl had a drooping, lined face that made him look like a hound dog. Exhaustion and frustration only heightened the resemblance. His mouth turned down.

"That's what I thought too. But it turns out that smoke grenades are also used by serious paintballers. They're available all over the Internet. Some sellers only deal with professional per-

106

sonnel who have been vetted in advance. But for every one of those, there are a dozen sites who just want a purchaser to click on a box that says they're eighteen or older."

"What about markings on the canister? Lot numbers, manufacturer's name, anything like that?" asked Dwayne Flannery, a Portland police officer.

Karl said, "There are some numbers on the canister, and we're trying to trace them, but it looks like a lot of this stuff is sold as surplus that changes hands dozens of times. And/or it's sold in big lots that are broken down again and sold individually. I've talked to a couple of sellers. Their record keeping seems deliberately vague, like if they don't keep track of what they sell, then they can't get in trouble for what someone does with it." Karl measured a space with his hands. "The canister itself was fairly small, about the same length as a paperback book. That's one reason they packed them together, so that anyone who handled the package wouldn't get suspicious."

"And then there's the book itself," said Owen Simmons, a Multnomah County sheriff. "Remember that movie *Talk Radio*? It was based on a real case, and later they put out a book. The same book they sent Fate. Alan Berg was a Denver talk show host who was gunned down in his driveway in the early 1980s by neo-Nazis. Maybe it's a sign that we're looking at some kind of extreme right-wing group like The Order?"

"Except Fate was pretty conservative himself," Heath said. "Maybe the left-wingers have decided to play catch-up. He certainly ticked enough of them off."

"Or it could be just one guy, trying to throw us off the scent by putting that book in," Leif said. "Have you ever listened to his show? Probably every day Fate made somebody mad enough to at least think about killing him. He even taunted listeners who threatened him. He had something he called the Nut of the Day award. Maybe one of those guys snapped."

"We're just beginning to follow up on the NOD winners," Nic said. "If you want to call them winners. Unfortunately, the records the station kept about their actual identity are spotty. And in a lot of cases they were anonymous, which let them be even more outrageous." She turned to Rod Emerick, another FBI special agent. "How about fingerprints?"

"No latents on the canister or the book. The envelope had a dozen fingerprints on it. We'll be printing everyone at the radio station as well as the carrier and the sorters at the mailing facility. But whoever prepared this clearly wore gloves. Unless we catch a lucky break, I would say that we're not going to get a match on IAFIS."

IAFIS, or the Integrated Automated Fingerprint Identification System, was the FBI's national fingerprint and criminal history system. It was the largest biometric database in the world, with fingerprints for more than fifty-five million criminals.

"We also recovered one piece of what might be carpet fiber. If we're lucky, we can get a hit on FACID."

FACID, or the Forensic Automotive Carpet Fiber Identification Database, was still being developed by the FBI's Laboratory Division. Once a carpet fiber was analyzed, it was possible to search by fiber type, color, or microscopic characteristics to see if there was a match. That was *if* it came from a vehicle. There was no comparable database for other carpet fibers, as there were far too many. In that case, the only means of identifying it would be to find the suspected source and compare the two.

"And how about you, Sam?" Nic asked the task force's representative from the post office. "What have you been able to find out about the postmark?"

When Sam Quinn spoke, his voice cracked a little. He flushed. It was clear that this meeting was one of the more exciting things that had ever happened to him. "There's been some water damage to the postmark, but it appears to have originated in the New York zip code where the publisher is located. The postage is made up of three stamps that have been canceled as part of a continuous design with the postmark. Oddly enough, the cancellation stamp is also known to collectors as 'the killer.' " His chuckle sounded forced.

No one else smiled.

"That means the gas grenade could have been mailed in New York, possibly from the publisher's mailing room. Or someone could have intercepted the package from the publisher, removed the original contents, and replaced them. The publisher uses a variety of different stamps and envelopes, so they can't tell us if this was one of theirs or not. The publisher tells us they are definitely not mailing out copies of *Talk Radio*—it wasn't even published by them, and the book is more than a decade old—but it looks like they might have a harder time figuring out if they did do some kind of recent mailing to Fate."

"How about the mailing label, Jun?" Leif asked Jun Sakimato, their resident paper specialist. "Did it come from a color printer?"

The public wasn't generally aware, but most color laser printers did more than just print party invites and color-coded bar charts. They also secretly encoded the printer's serial number and manufacturing code on every document they produced. The millimeter-size yellow dots appeared about every inch on the page, nestled within the printed words. While originally put in place to catch counterfeiters, the hidden markings had also helped Jun crack a kidnapping case earlier in the year.

Jun lifted one shoulder. "No such luck. Just a black-and-white printer. But I'm not certain the label actually originated from the publisher. It could have been dummied up. The edges are a little blurry. It could just be from fading or handling or exposure to the elements. Or it could be a fake. It wouldn't be hard to scan in their logo."

It seemed like one dead end after another. *Were they looking at terrorism?* Nic wondered. Her stomach felt like she was standing on the edge of a cliff and looking down at jagged rocks below. First Seattle, then Portland—when would it end? Or was this the beginning of the end?

She shook off such grim thoughts. This *had* to be different from the terrorist attack up north. In fact, it already was different. In Seattle the killers had targeted an office building, not individuals. In Portland, Fate had clearly been the target, as evidenced by his name on the mailing label. In Seattle the killer, a still unidentified Middle Eastern man, had been so clumsy that he had died with his victims. But Fate's killer could have been a thousand miles away when his victim took his final, fatal breath. In Seattle, there had been no warning. But Jim Fate had received threats so unsettling that he had asked for help. Help that she and Allison had been too late to give.

On Nic's hip, her phone buzzed. She looked at the display. Tony Sardella.

She said, "Excuse me," and then got up and walked into a corner of the room. She might as well have put it on speaker—she could hear the table go dead silent behind her. "Yes?"

"Nicole. We've got the results of the initial EMIT screen."

"And?"

"Negative on sarin."

"So if it wasn't sarin, what was it?" She could feel the attention behind her sharpen.

"That I don't know. Most likely, some kind of opiate. I've ordered blood tests to try to quantify and qualitate which one was in play. Could be morphine. Could be something else. But for now, all I can tell you is that whatever caused Fate's death, it wasn't sarin. It's too bad the paramedics shot him up with the wrong antidote. If they had given him Narcan before he was too dead to revive, they might have saved him."

"How long will it take to pin down exactly what it was?"

"These tests take time." Tony sighed, and Nic heard his exhaustion. "Even if we move it to the head of the line, it's still going to take a week or two. Maybe more. You can't speed up a chemical reaction."

"Keep me posted," Nic said. After hanging up, she turned to the alert faces and told them the

112

news. She saw the relief in the circle of listeners. One of the guys from headquarters was already gathering his briefcase and jacket.

"John will want to hold a press conference right away," Leif said. "Let people know that Jim Fate seems to have been the only target and that this wasn't sarin, and that it was more than likely not terrorism."

John Drood, the special agent in charge, had less than six months to go until he bumped up against the FBI's rule that forced agents to retire at fifty-seven. He was having trouble even contemplating letting go. A press conference would be right up his alley, allowing him to stand in the spotlight once more as he reassured Portlanders that there was no reason for worry.

But, Nic wondered, was that really true?

CHAPTER 17
Channel 4 TV

Cassidy drove to work with one eye closed. It seemed the only way she could focus. She kept flashing back to waking up in the tub, her hands floating like starfish.

Yesterday felt like a terrible nightmare. Today seemed just as unreal. Jim couldn't be dead, could he? And all the plans he had talked about had died with him.

"Pull yourself together, Cass," she said out loud.

Once she walked through the station's double doors, she had to hit the ground running. The events of yesterday would spin off into several dozen stories today. Yesterday she had been the disaster reporter. But that wasn't her—or anyone's—normal beat. Today she would be back to being the crime reporter. And it was clear what crime would be number one on everyone's mind: Jim Fate's murder.

Working in TV news meant you had to be able to perform at a second's notice. Today it felt to Cassidy like she would need more like a couple of hours. It wasn't enough to write a good story. You had to be able to look into that camera and convince people that you knew what you were talking about. You couldn't be threatened or nervous or silly or inarticulate. You couldn't fumble your words or lose your train of thought. Yesterday she had managed it, but today it seemed impossibly out of reach.

The last person Cassidy wanted to see this morning was Jenna. So of course, the intern was the first person she saw when she walked into the station.

Jenna looked like she had spent the first part of her day skipping through a meadow and singing. Her tanned cheeks had a rosy glow. Her long hair fell down her slender back like a blonde waterfall. And her unlined face, Cassidy thought sourly, was practically dewy.

"We are all so proud of you, Cass—" Jenna broke off. "Are you all right?"

"I'm fine." Her tongue felt thick.

"Are you sure the air where you were yesterday was okay? You look, um, you look like you don't feel well."

Cassidy hurried to the restroom. In the mirror, she regarded herself with horror. Her hand must have slipped when she applied her eyeliner. On the left side, the line was slender and neat. On the right side, it was so thick that her eye looked like it belonged to Amy Winehouse. Amy Winehouse on her way to rehab.

The thought of rehab brought Cassidy up short. She had never done anything quite as crazy as falling asleep in the tub. But there had been two or three times when an entire package of cookies or cheese disappeared in the middle of the night and she had no memory of what had happened, just the clues of crumbs in her bed and a crumpled package in the garbage can.

Should she have taken her doctor's mumbled warnings more seriously? Was Somulex hurting more than it helped? But the very thought of not having it, of having to go to bed at night knowing that she wouldn't sleep, made Cassidy's hands grow cold and her stomach contract. She had to take Somulex. She *had* to.

Besides, yesterday had been one of the hardest days of her life. She deserved a little slack. So what if her hands had been shaky while she was putting on makeup? So what if she hadn't noticed? Before she went on camera, she would have to redo her face anyway for high-definition TV. She took a travel packet of makeup remover cloths from her purse and wiped both eyes clean. Then she hurried down the hall for the morning story meeting.

She was the last to walk into the conference room. As soon as she stepped over the threshold, everyone jumped to their feet and started clapping. Even though Cassidy knew it was for her, she had to suppress the desire to look around to see who they were really applauding. Jenna was jumping up and down like a high school cheerleader, Jeff Caldwell actually looked teary eyed, and Anne Forster, who covered the business news, was clapping her hands so hard they must hurt. Even Brad was applauding, although his smile looked like someone had hooked the corners of his mouth and yanked them up.

"Great work yesterday, Cassidy," Eric said, "you and Andy, great work! No other station had live footage from the scene. No one else had reporters who were willing to put their lives on the line to report the story at the source. But you were there, and you did the work. And if something like this had to happen, at least it happened during sweeps month!" As people settled back into their chairs—and Jenna on her ball—he added, "We'll

116

be adding the footage into all our promo commercials for the news. 'Channel 4 Action News: there when you need us!' "

He picked up his dry-erase markers. "We need to brainstorm about follow-up stories. Except for sports and weather, everything today is going to tie back to yesterday. So what should we cover?"

"The key question, obviously," Brad said, "is what exactly happened yesterday. Was it terrorism? Or something more personal?"

Eric wrote "Terrorism?" in purple.

"We should also do the whole wake-up call story," Anne said. "If this attack had been more widespread, would Portland be ready?"

"Wake-up?" went on the board in green.

Jenna alone had raised her hand. When Eric nodded at her, she said, "I was thinking that maybe we, like, could do some personal stories about the people who got hit by cars?"

"Vignettes" went on the board in red, with no question mark. Next Eric wrote "Jim Fate" in purple and circled it.

"Since you knew Jim Fate personally, Cassidy, why don't you work on his backstory as well as anything you can find out about who might have wanted him dead and why."

"Now, *that* could be a miniseries," Brad said, and then seemed surprised when nobody laughed.

CHAPTER 18
KNWS Radio

Inside KNWS it was eerily silent. Everywhere was mute testimony that people had fled in panic. Coffee cups lay on their sides in slowly drying puddles, a spill of papers was scattered next to the receptionist's desk, and a purse sat in the middle of a hallway. Nic, Leif, Karl, and Rod—all members of the ERT—were here to gather whatever evidence they could. On the short drive to the station, Nic had been surprised to hear KNWS broadcasting, and even more surprised to hear Victoria Hanawa behind the mike. No one was being allowed in or out of the studio until it had been searched, so the radio station must have found another way to broadcast.

Leif consulted his notes. The others followed him as he walked past the receptionist's desk and took a right turn down the hall. The farther in they ventured, the more Nic was surprised by how cheap the radio station's office looked. The visitors' area had been decorated with leather couches, polished wood, and a vase of hothouse flowers. But once they were past the part that was visible to the public, it looked as if the minimum amount of money had been spent to cram the maximum number of workers into the space. Most of the floor was a rabbit warren of cubicles separated from each other by shoulder-high partitions. Leif led them down a narrow corridor with scuffed walls barely far enough apart for two people to pass each other, and then turned left down a second hallway. On their right was a row of closed doors with unlit red lights that read ON AIR.

Leif pointed at a door near the end. It was ajar, and through it Nic could see a small room separated by a glass wall and a door from the radio studio behind it. The floor of both rooms was littered with discarded medical supplies and spent injectors from the first responders' frantic attempts to save Fate from what had turned out to be the wrong poison. Nic wondered how they would feel once they learned that a simple dose of Narcan might have done the trick.

"That's the studio Fate was in when he died," Leif said. "His office is across the hall and a couple of doors down. Nic, why don't you and Rod take that, and Karl and I will take the studio."

With her gloved hand on the knob, Nic paused to look at the caricature taped to the closed door to Fate's office. Like most caricatures, it featured a giant head supported by a tiny body. The most exaggerated feature was the right hand, which held a microphone. Literally, the hand of Fate. In Nic's opinion, you made your own fate. You took responsibility for what you did and didn't do, and even for what happened to you.

In stark contrast to the tiny cubicles the rest of

the workers occupied, Fate's office reflected the outsized personality of its owner. A painting of a bald eagle hung next to a huge American flag. Farther back sat a cherrywood desk and credenza. Dozens of framed awards and signed photographs of Fate with various famous personalities hung over the desk. A shadow box displayed a camouflage baseball cap touting the Second Amendment.

"Sweet," Rod said as he walked over to the computer.

It was one of the expensive new Macs that Nic could only afford to look at online. When she touched the space bar, the screen sprang to life. She was tempted to click around, but lately the computer forensics lab had been warning about encryption codes and destructive software. So instead she simply shut it down. While she took a seat in front of Fate's desk, Rod unplugged the computer, wrapped it in the pink antistatic bag they had brought with them, and gave it a temporary evidence tag. After they were finished, one of them would drive the computer across the river and deliver it to the lab, where it would be assigned a bar code. You had to maintain the chain of custody "womb to tomb" by documenting who took what, when, and why. Any break in the chain might be a crack big enough to let a killer wiggle free.

It was a little strange to sit in the leather desk chair. The last person to sit here must have been Jim Fate. The pad was compacted a bit to the shape of his larger body. Nic lifted her eyes to the rows and rows of photos and awards. What had it been like to be Jim Fate? Had these tokens of his success reassured him, inspired him, or prodded him to acquire more? Had he liked watching the impression they made on visitors—or was the "brag wall" more for his own eyes, his own needs?

With her gloved hand, Nic slid open the top desk drawer. In it she found the usual loose change, paper clips, pens. Fate seemed to favor the roller-ball variety, black with a fine tip. A half-dozen brochures for a gold investment company featured a grinning Fate on the front and touted the company as "the exclusive precious metals sponsor for *The Hand of Fate*." A little farther back was the good stuff. A flash drive, which she handed to Rod to bag and tag for the computer forensics lab. A business card from a well-known—and female— executive, with "Call me!" scrawled on the back.

She found a credit card receipt for a store called Oh Baby. That could mean nothing or everything, from a present for a coworker's baby shower to one for a secret love child. Nic set it aside to pursue further.

A key card for the swanky Heathman Hotel made the second possibility not quite so unlikely. She showed it to Rod, who was methodically searching the bookcase.

"Some kind of trophy?" Rod speculated. "A night to remember?"

Nic didn't reply. She was looking at a piece of paper she had just pulled from the very back of the drawer. Torn from a trade journal called *Talkers*, it was headlined "Jim Fate Sets Hot Pace Among Talk Hosts." Fate's picture had been defaced with *X*s over his eyes. A cartoon tongue dangled from his mouth. And around his neck was a noose. Whoever had drawn it had taken the time to make it look three-dimensional, shading in the roughness of the rope. Clipped to it was a printed note: "Stop running your mouth. You're going to pay for what you've done.*"

She showed it to Rod. "Allison Pierce and I were scheduled to meet with Fate the day after he died. He wanted to talk about some kind of threats he'd been getting. Maybe he meant this."

"Or this?" Rod answered. He reached past her and slid out another newspaper clipping tucked in the back of the drawer.

Nic had forgotten about this particular story, which had been hot for a few weeks last summer. Someone had scrawled an angry message across the clipping, the ink so thick that at times she had difficulty reading the article underneath.

Mother Who Committed Suicide Knew Nothing of Baby's Disappearance

Two weeks after Brooke Gardner committed suicide after facing tough questioning by a talk show host about her missing 18-month-old son, the boy has been found alive. Authorities discovered the child, Brandon Gardner-Tippets, at the home of his paternal great-aunt, Tami Tippets. Authorities say the child is in good health and that he was taken from his mother's home without her knowledge. Tami Tippets has been charged with custodial interference and could also face kidnapping charges.

On the evening of June 30, Brooke Gardner called authorities to report that her baby boy was missing from his crib. Gardner was divorced from Brandon's father, Jason Tippets, and had primary custody of their son. The divorce has been described as acrimonious.

Although Jason Tippets was said to have initially passed a polygraph that cleared him of involvement, authorities now say they are investigating whether he knew about his aunt taking Brandon.

Nancy Gardner, Brooke Gardner's mother, said, "We told the police and the FBI and everyone who would listen, and so did Brooke, we told them that she had nothing to do with Brandon's disappearance. But no one would listen. Brooke would have done anything to find her baby. But instead of helping her, they acted like she was the guilty one. She wasn't eating, she wasn't sleeping, and she was sick with worry. And finally she just couldn't take it anymore."

Brooke Gardner committed suicide by taking a deliberate overdose of sleeping pills two hours after a live on-air grilling by radio talk show host Jim Fate. Her parents say they have filed a lawsuit against him, claiming their daughter was driven to her death by his badgering questions. They charge that Fate duped their daughter into an interview about her missing son, telling their daughter that it would help find the baby. That interview, which aired on Fate's radio show The Hand of Fate, *was more of a cross-examination, with Fate peppering the 21-year-old woman with questions about why she hadn't taken a polygraph as her ex-husband had. The complainant seeks undisclosed damages.*

Across the clipping someone had scrawled in thick, dark felt pen: "You killed Brooke. Now you need to die too."

CHAPTER 19
Mark O. Hatfield United States Courthouse

It was imperative that Allison keep busy. That she keep her mind off Estella. That she stop thinking of the little girl's dark eyes and her shy smile—and the feeling of prying loose her tiny fingers. Investigating Fate's death offered the chance to drown herself in work.

The first thing Allison did when she got to the office after handing back Estella was to go directly to her boss.

"Dan, you need to know that last week, Jim Fate asked Special Agent Hedges and me to meet with him. He told us he was getting threats."

Dan's eyes widened. "What kind of threats?" He was a slight, dapper man who always cautiously considered the political ramifications of any action. He could also occasionally be persuaded to take a chance.

"Fate wasn't more specific. He didn't want to talk about it over the phone. He was nervous. He didn't even want us to go to KNWS or to meet at either of our offices. We were going to meet tomorrow at a Starbucks." Allison leaned forward. "I want to be the lead prosecutor assigned to his case."

As a federal prosecutor, Allison dealt with federal crimes, or crimes with an interstate connection. In the case of Jim Fate, that would cover any threats made via the Internet, the phone, or the U.S. mail. And if Fate's killing was the result of terrorism, either foreign or domestic, it would also be considered a federal case.

Dan steepled his fingers, then tapped the two index fingers together. "But Chuck worked the Portland Seven case." The Portland Seven was a group of young American Muslim men who had tried to travel to Afghanistan shortly after 9/11 in

125

order to aid the Taliban. "He's got more experience prosecuting terrorism cases."

"But it could be there's no overseas connection. Maybe there's no link to terrorism at all. Fate ticked off a number of people over the years."

Terrorism or not, it was sure to be a high-profile case. Big cases made big names for prosecutors—which could lead to big bucks if they ever decided to switch sides and become defense attorneys. Even if they stayed put, big cases also led to promotions. And good publicity if they ever decided they wanted to run for district attorney.

But that wasn't why Allison wanted this case. She kept thinking of how Fate had reached out to her, and she hadn't been able to find time on her calendar for him right away. If she had canceled another meeting or suggested they meet in the evening, would he still be alive? The least she could do was find his killer.

"What about the Bratz Bandits trial? Weren't you just beginning that when this whole thing started?"

"This morning I had a voice mail saying the girl's attorney has moved for a mistrial."

Dan raised an eyebrow. "On what grounds?"

"Alleged jury tampering." Allison shook her head. "Condorelli says he has one potential juror ready to swear that she heard two other potential jurors during the evacuation discussing how they should get together on a book deal when the trial was over. Of course, it's all bogus, but that means the trial will be postponed at least until they get a new jury pool." She leaned forward. "Looking for Jim Fate's killer needs to be our top priority. This country was founded on the principle of free speech. And I have a feeling that whatever the reason behind this was, whoever did it wanted to shut Jim up."

Dan said nothing for another minute, just continued tapping his fingers together. Finally he looked up at Allison. "All right. It's your case."

Allison spent the first part of the morning meeting with the task force at the FBI Portland field office. She was glad to see that Nicole had been assigned as case agent. She knew the two of them would be sure to get to the bottom of this case. While everyone around the table had the same goal, they also brought their egos. Personally and professionally, they wanted themselves and their particular branch of the alphabet soup associated with the winning outcome. But Nicole kept everyone in line. Allison enjoyed watching her take center stage as she directed the meeting—and delivered the news that it wasn't sarin.

After the task force met, Allison returned to the federal courthouse and opened a grand jury investigation for Jim Fate's murder. Since the investigation was just at the beginning phase, this would only be a formal opening.

The grand jury was Allison's investigative arm. Even when it wasn't in session, in its name she could issue a search warrant or a subpoena. The grand jurors never knew what she might ask them to investigate—everything from murder for hire to hate crimes against a local mosque to men who trolled the Internet for teenage girls.

"Good afternoon," Allison said to the twenty-three private citizens who made up the grand jury, and received smiles and nods in return. It was one of the two grand juries in Oregon that served at any given time. These grand jurors were in the fourteenth of the eighteen months they would ultimately serve together, so they had had time to become friends with each other—and with Allison. Over the past year she had celebrated birthdays with them and gushed over photos of babies and pets.

"Today we're going to open the case of Jim Fate, the radio talk show host who was murdered yesterday. Together with the FBI, we have started the investigation. I will report on the findings as soon as they are available."

At the sound of Jim Fate's name, there were nods of recognition. Grand jurors weren't banned from watching all media, which meant they often had a passing familiarity with any headline case she brought them. Jim Fate, of course, was in a category by himself. Thanks to what had happened only the day before, even people who never listened to talk radio now knew his name. But now that the jurors knew they would be considering his death, they would try to stay away from any fresh news about it.

While a grand jury might consider dozens of cases over the course of a year, they never saw a single one through until the end. Instead, they served only to investigate various criminal cases and formally indict any suspects. In some cases, they voted not to indict. Because they weren't asked to determine guilt or innocence, only decide whether charges should be filed, the grand jury's standards were looser than those of a trial jury. A trial jury couldn't convict without believing beyond a reasonable doubt, but a grand jury could indict just on probable cause. And the grand jury didn't even need to be unanimous: only eighteen of the twenty-three needed to agree. It was an old joke among defense lawyers that it wouldn't take much effort to persuade a grand jury to indict a ham sandwich. But it was a little-known fact that prosecutors sometimes advocated for the grand jury not to indict.

"While this wasn't sarin gas," Allison told them, "it could still be terrorism. Maybe someone who wanted to stop Jim Fate from broadcasting his opinion."

"You mean opinions," said Gus, a retired hardware store owner. "That man had lots of them."

"Hmm, sounds like someone else we know,"

said a juror in the back. The other jurors laughed. Including Gus. Even Allison managed to crack a smile.

After opening the grand jury, Allison walked back to the FBI's Portland field office, a dozen blocks away. Her feet still ached from the day before. She wasn't hungry, but she made herself buy a gyro from a street cart. No matter how she felt, she had to think of the baby.

Everywhere were signs of the panic that had gripped Portland the day before. She saw a half-dozen lost scarves looped around street trees, an abandoned stainless-steel coffee mug set on a win-dowsill, misplaced hats now settled on top of parking signs. Portlanders were, in general, an honest lot. She thought about Estella, who was more important than any scarf, mug, or hat. Surely by now Child Protective Services must have reunited her with her family. Surely Estella was now cuddling with her *mami*, all her fears quieted. Allison wanted to call the caseworker, but she told herself that the girl was being taken care of. Estella wasn't her problem anymore. But Jim Fate was.

When Nicole came out to escort her back, Allison found herself giving her friend a hug. Even more surprisingly, Nicole unhesitatingly hugged her back.

Nicole said, "Cassidy just called. She wants the three of us to go to dinner tonight."

130

"Tonight?" Without even considering it, Allison shook her head. "I just want to go home. Go home and go to bed."

"Same here. But Cassidy was pretty insistent. She's already made reservations at McCormick & Schmick's Harborside. And you know—Jim Fate asked her to hook him up with us. We need to find out what she knows about the threats and who might have made them."

"Can't it wait?" Allison asked. Even as she said the words, she realized that it couldn't. They needed to know as much as possible as soon as possible about what had happened to Jim—and why. She sighed. "Well, at least we'll get to eat something rich and chocolatey."

"I hear you on that," Nicole said. As they walked back to her work space, she called Cassidy on her cell phone and agreed that they would meet at seven.

Nicole's cubicle was piled high with teetering stacks of paper, with more folders stacked on the floor. Allison picked up a heap of papers from the visitor's chair, then didn't know where to set them.

"Oh, give them here," Nicole said impatiently. She turned them at an angle and set them on an existing pile.

As she sat down, Allison said, "I *have* thought of one bright side to this case."

"There is one?" Nicole rubbed her eyes. "I'd like to hear it."

"Usually when we work a murder case, it's hard figuring out who would be mad enough to kill someone. We're not going to have that problem with Jim Fate."

"Yeah, it would probably be easier figuring out who he *didn't* tick off." Nicole stifled a yawn. "We found two threats in his desk." She handed Allison two printouts. "This one with the sketch of the noose is from a magazine article that mentioned a number of controversial things Jim did."

Allison looked at the second piece of paper, feeling a pang as she remembered reading about the sad case. " 'You killed Brooke. Now you need to die too,' " she read aloud. "Well, that's pretty clear. Just like Cassidy said, we need to look at Brooke Gardner's family and friends. And given that horrible commercial that's been running non-stop, Quentin Glover too. And that's probably only the beginning. I've ordered six months' worth of transcripts of the show so that we can look for other people he might have ticked off."

"You can listen to them all online," Nicole said. "I already checked."

"Yeah, but I'd have to do that in real time. It's too hard to jump ahead with a recording. Whereas on paper, it's a lot easier to skip over the parts that don't have any bearing."

Nicole made a face. "Do you have any idea how many people we could end up having to investigate? The killer could be an individual or a business owner or a politician Fate slammed on air. That's already a pretty big group. Then you add in people who might have had issues with his success, like rivals, stalkers, coworkers, anyone he climbed over on his way up."

Allison said, "And there's all the usual suspects: family, friends, lovers, and enemies." As a starting point with Jim, as well as every suspect in his murder, the FBI would check the basics: the phone book for numbers and addresses, public utilities records to find out who paid the bills and how often, Department of Motor Vehicles for driver's license data and registration records, and National Crime Information Center indices for prior convictions. With such a wide circle of suspects, this alone would mean an incredible amount of work. Allison added, "Plus there's Fate's NOD award. I'll bet that really torqued some people."

"Yeah, in retrospect maybe it wasn't such a good idea that he taunted the people who were the most angry at him." Nicole stifled another yawn. "For tomorrow, I've lined up the use of the radio station's three conference rooms. I figure you and I will take the people who worked closest with Jim, and I've got two teams to take the rest."

"You look like you didn't get any sleep," Allison said sympathetically. "Maybe we should have dinner with Cassidy on another night."

"No. We need to talk to her. But yeah, I am

pretty tired. It was everything that happened yesterday. You know what it was like. Everyone in that stairwell really started believing that we were all going to die, and it wasn't pretty. I ended up trying to shelter in place with Mrs. Lofland—that older lady from the jury pool—on the seventh floor of the courthouse. It was Leif who tracked us down and told us things were okay. I was so glad to see him that I actually gave him a hug."

"Really?" She kept her tone neutral. Nicole rarely talked about her personal life, and Allison didn't want to scare her off by seeming too interested.

Allison, Nicole, and Cassidy had attended the same high school, but they hadn't been close and they hadn't kept in touch. By the time they got reacquainted at their tenth reunion, Nicole had a daughter, Makayla. No father was ever mentioned—and Nicole never, ever dated. Allison just figured that the father had been bad news.

Nicole shook her head. "I shouldn't encourage him. My life is too complicated. There's no room in it for a man. I've tried to make that clear, but Leif says he's happy to just be friends. But you know that when a guy says that, he doesn't really mean it."

"Well, I guess there are two possibilities. If Leif really *does* mean it, then you're okay. But say you're right," Allison ventured. She hoped she wasn't pushing Nic too far. "Say he doesn't mean it. Leif's a good man and a good agent. And he just might be good for you too."

It was always a pleasure to work with Leif. There was a solidity to him that was calming. And it was clear that those blue eyes of his missed nothing.

"But I don't need a man," Nicole answered. "I don't need anyone."

CHAPTER 20
Willamette Villas Condominiums

While Nic was brainstorming suspects with Allison, her cell rang. At the sound of Leif's voice in her ear, telling her that they now had a search warrant for Fate's apartment, her cheeks heated up. Her body was too eager to betray her.

After promising to call Allison if anything important turned up in the search, Nic gathered with the rest of the ERT in the FBI's parking garage.

At Fate's condominium building, they met the building manager and took the elevator to the twentieth floor.

Leif let out a long, low whistle when the manager unlocked the door and swung it open. "I think I went into the wrong line of work."

Nic felt a smile rise to her lips, and then quickly let it drop. She didn't want anyone on the team guessing anything about her feelings.

Fate's living room ran the width of the building. The wall facing the river was nothing but windows. Nic checked out the view. She could see a half dozen of Portland's bridges, as well as the dark, gray waters of the Willamette itself.

The team took a quick tour. It was beautiful, if not to Nic's taste. It looked like an old, rich white guy's place, all leather and gleaming dark wood and Oriental carpets. As a concession to the modern age, the living room also held an expensive-looking sound system and a huge flat-screen TV. The kitchen had a sharper edge to it. Everything was shiny stainless steel, down to the countertops, and so clean you could have performed surgery in it, using one of the ranks of Wüsthof knives.

Rod opened the refrigerator, and Nic peered over his shoulder. The door held capers, gherkins, cocktail onions, and Thai chili sauce. On the shelves were three lemons, bottles of seltzer and tonic, five take-out cartons, and a pint of half-and-half that was bulging suspiciously.

The side-by-side freezer was equally empty, containing only a bottle of Grey Goose vodka, a stack of frozen entrees from Whole Foods, and a half-dozen bags of Jamaican Blue coffee beans.

"I'm surprised he doesn't have those coffee beans that are excreted by meerkats or whatever," Heath said. "Supposed to be the best in the world. They say it lends them a unique flavor." He smacked his lips.

136

Nic kept her face impassive.

Leif gave them their assignments, and they spread out. He took the bedroom, often ground zero for any investigation, the inner sanctum, where the best secrets were concealed. Nic got Fate's office, Heath the dining and living rooms, Karl the library, and Rod the bathroom.

Just as they had in Fate's office, Nic boxed the computer up for the electronic forensics lab. On the desk were two microphones and a couple of sets of headphones that she had to disconnect from the computer.

Next she took a quick run through Fate's three-drawer oak filing cabinet, but there was nothing that stood out. Tax returns, clippings about himself, product manuals, bank statements. No cards, no photos. No love letters or hate mail either, but these days, both of those would probably be on the computer. Anything that seemed like it might need closer scrutiny went into lidded cardboard file boxes for closer review.

Nic thought of something and looked around the walls. They were decorated with a couple of large art photographs, one a close-up of peeling bark and another of a sunset turning the ocean pink. But what had caught her eye was something that wasn't there. Here there was no brag wall. No trophies. No visible signs—other than every possession being top-of-the-line—of Fate's success.

In the desk, Nic hit pay dirt. She walked into the

bedroom to show it to Leif, who was checking underneath a drawer to make sure nothing had been taped there.

As she waited for him to straighten up, she noticed the strong V of his back. Even through his jacket, she could see the shape of his shoulders. To distract herself, she looked closer at the book that lay facedown on the bedside table. It was about the Civil War. When Jim Fate had set that book aside, he hadn't known that he would never pick it up again. One day she might be just going about her business, leaving things unfinished, but planning to pick them up again—and then she would suddenly be gone. And in Nic's view, dead was dead. Fate wasn't a soul who might be going to heaven or hell. He wasn't a ghost, and he hadn't been reborn as a dragonfly or a dog. He was just gone.

It was a hard reality to look in the eye, and Nic was glad when Leif got to his feet and said, "What have you got?"

"Look at this." Nic held out the envelope she had found in Fate's desk drawer. The contents and the envelope had been printed on a computer. She was nostalgic for the time when each typewriter left its own unique marks on a piece of paper, but those days had already been dying out even before she joined the Bureau.

Leif slid out the piece of paper inside and read it aloud.

"'I know where you live. I know what you look like. You're going to pay for what you've done.'" Leif looked more closely at the envelope. "And whoever sent this showed him that they meant it. Because this was mailed to his home address." He slipped it into an evidence bag, and Nic went back to finish the office.

When they had finished their search, Leif gathered the ERT for a quick rundown of what they had found. It wasn't much. Leif had discovered a woman's earring underneath the bed. Hammered silver, it looked handmade, not mass-produced. It was shaped like a Chinese character.

Rod gave voice to a thought that was just coming clear in Nic's mind. "Could it be Japanese?"

Leif said, "You thinking of Victoria Hanawa? I'll ask Jun if he knows what language it is."

Heath laughed. "Maybe it will turn out like all those people who think they're getting tattooed with the character for *wisdom* in Chinese, and it turns out to be the character for *idiot.*"

"How about the living and dining room?" Leif asked. "Did you find anything in there?"

"Just tens of thousands of dollars of equipment, all of it top-notch. He had a couple hundred DVDs. No porn. Everything from old John Wayne movies to the latest thrillers. Nearly all of them feature one man up against the odds and fighting for justice."

It was an interesting insight, reminding Nic that even Heath occasionally had something useful to say.

Rod said, "There wasn't much of interest in the bathroom. The only drugs had prescription labels on them. It looks like Fate had high blood pressure and high cholesterol. Oh, and in one of the drawers I found a box of condoms. A few of them were gone."

Karl said, "Lots of books, but that's about it."

A frown creased Leif's face. "This whole place is more conspicuous for what it doesn't have than for what it does. No photos of family or friends. No cards. And it's all very clean. Like it's going to be photographed for a magazine shoot. It feels . . . impersonal."

"It feels lonely," Nic said quietly, and Leif shot her a surprised look. She had kind of surprised herself.

"Maybe this was the place where he went to retreat from the world," Karl said.

"Maybe," Nic agreed. But part of her wondered if Jim had felt more at home sitting behind his mike and watching the phone lines light up, knowing that thousands of people were hanging on his every word.

When the team left, an older woman with hair dyed a purple-black was standing in the hallway. All of her clothes were shades of lavender, violet, and magenta. She eyed them with interest.

"Hello, officers. Are you here about my erstwhile neighbor, Mr. Fate?"

"Yes, ma'am," Leif said.

"I wanted to impart to you that I saw something the morning that Mr. Fate was killed. Or rather, I saw someone."

"What did you see?"

She paused, obviously enjoying the fact that she had the team's full attention.

"I saw a woman depart his apartment."

Leif's voice sharpened. "Did she leave with him?"

"He had left four hours prior. This young woman looked like those movie stars you see in the tabloids. The ones who are pretending that they don't want anyone to recognize them."

"What do you mean?"

"She had a black coat, blonde hair, and big, black sunglasses. Who wears sunglasses in Oregon in February? Indoors, no less."

"Have you seen her before?" Nic asked.

She started to shake her head, and then hesitated. "Well, that might not be true. Something about her was familiar. I know I haven't seen her in this building before. But it seems to me that I *have* seen her. Maybe at church or at the supermarket or at the Multnomah Athletic Club."

"Would you recognize her if you saw her again?" Leif asked.

"I might."

"You said you haven't seen her leave Jim's condo before," Nic said, thinking of the condoms and the woman's earring. "But have you seen other women leave here before?"

She gave them a coy look. "A few. Not as many as you might speculate."

Nic thought of half-Japanese Victoria Hanawa. "And were they all blonde? All white?"

Jim's neighbor shook her head. "Mr. Fate," she said, "had eclectic tastes."

CHAPTER 21
McCormick & Schmick's Harborside Restaurant

While they waited for their table, Allison was quickly moving from hunger to nausea, a continuum that her pregnancy had shortened considerably. Swallowing hard, she pressed her fingers against her lips.

"Here." Cassidy put something in Allison's other hand. "Eat this."

It was a granola bar studded with nuts and chocolate chips. Her stomach rumbled, but she hesitated. "Isn't it kind of rude to eat something they didn't sell you?"

Nicole shook her head. "Girl, you could starve to death before we got anyone's attention." She shot a rare grin at Cassidy. "Did that come out of your magic bag?"

Cassidy hefted her huge, black leather tote.

"You know it. If I ever get stranded on a desert island, I'll be fine as long as I have my purse."

It was a standing joke that Cassidy's purse held everything anyone might need: safety pins, sewing kit, makeup, food, bus tickets, greeting cards, and of course, food. Allison wouldn't be surprised if there were a small tent and a ham radio in there as well.

Surreptitiously unwrapping the granola bar, she scanned the room. People were five deep at the bar, laughing, shouting, flirting, and, by the looks of things, drinking hard. Everyone was giddy. Only the day before, so many had been convinced that they were dying. But only a dozen people had been hospitalized, injured in the mad panic. And now Portland, having so narrowly escaped disaster, was more than ready to party.

As Allison remembered how people had collapsed all around her, a wave of relief washed over her. *Thank You, Lord, for watching over us.* She grinned at her two friends.

"What?" Cassidy shouted above the noise.

"It's nothing," Allison said as Nicole leaned in to hear. "I'm just glad that we're all okay."

Fifteen years earlier, the three of them had graduated from Catlin Gabel, one of Portland's elite private schools. Then they had barely known each other, although they had known *of* each other. Nicole had stood out by virtue of being one of the fewer than a half-dozen African American students. Cassidy had been a cheerleader. And Allison had been a fixture on the honor roll and captain of the debate team.

At their high school reunion, their common interest in crime—Cassidy's in covering it, Nicole's in fighting it, and Allison's in prosecuting it—had drawn them together. When Nicole was transferred to the Portland office, Allison had suggested they meet for dinner, and a friendship began over a shared dessert called Triple Threat Chocolate Cake. In its honor, the three women had christened themselves the Triple Threat Club. And whenever they got together to talk about their jobs and their private lives, they made it a point to share the most decadent dessert on the menu.

"To the Triple Threat Club!" Cassidy said, raising her gin and tonic.

Nicole echoed her words, bumping their glasses with hers of red wine.

"Long may it reign!" added Allison as she tapped her glass of orange juice against her friends' glasses. When she tipped her glass back, Allison caught a glimpse of the TV screen over the bar. "I can't believe they haven't taken that commercial off the air," she said, pointing. The other two women turned to look.

The political ad began with a video, shot at an angle, of Quentin Glover talking with his mouth full, a half-eaten hot dog in his hand. Slumped and slovenly, he obviously had no idea he was being filmed. As he gestured to an unseen listener, a piece of food fell from his mouth.

But it wasn't that image that had made Allison think they would have pulled the ad by now. It was the voice-over, which she had heard so often in recent weeks that she could have recited it from memory. The announcer was saying, "Radio talk show host Jim Fate was Quentin Glover's best man. Now even Fate says we shouldn't reelect Quentin Glover."

The noisy bar quieted as Jim Fate's own voice, recorded from his show and laced with indignation, came on. "Quentin Glover has now been indicted on charges that he lied about receiving hundreds of thousands of dollars in gifts from a manufacturing firm. Some of the goodies he allegedly received include a car and a second home at Sunriver. Now, people, you know I find it hard to believe that the guy who was cheating on his wife was 100 percent honest."

On the screen, the words THOUSANDS OF DOLLARS IN GIFTS, GOODIES, and CHEATING ON HIS WIFE appeared.

"I'm not saying our congresspeople have to be perfect," the voice of a dead man continued, "because I myself have weaknesses. But our standard is that just because you are popular doesn't mean you can get away with committing felonies. And if this week it's perjury, and next week it's theft, and the week after that it's having somebody beaten up, then one day America may well end up a sleazy country like Iraq, where the corruption is unending."

An angry man appeared on the screen. He wore traditional Middle Eastern clothing: a long, white robe; a white kaffiyeh head covering; and a black circlet to hold it in place. With one hand he hoisted a machine gun. In the other was a stack of money.

Only two days earlier the commercial, paid for by a group called Clean Up Oregon Politics, had been annoying or amusing, depending on your political leanings and how many times you had already seen it. Now people muttered and shook their heads at the sound of Jim's voice. The three women looked at each other, and Allison knew they were sharing the same thought: exactly how angry had that commercial made Quentin Glover?

Just then the hostess came up with a smile. "Sorry for the delay, ladies. Your table is ready now."

"This was worth the wait," Allison said as she settled in next to the window overlooking the river. The tables, set in tiers, all offered a view, but the ones next to the window were the best.

After they ordered, the three women took out notebooks and pens. Normally when they met, it was as friends, with work being just one topic of conversation. But this was work, taking place over dinner.

146

"Let's start at the beginning." Nicole turned to Cassidy. "Allison and I need to know everything you know about Jim Fate. Leif got this photo of him at the radio station. We'll be using it for the canvas. Is this a current likeness?" She set a photo on the table. Usually they dealt with candid snapshots, not eight-by-ten glossies.

Picking it up, Cassidy regarded it critically. "This is a bit out-of-date. He's had a little work done in the last couple of years. Botox, some resurfacing. Most of these old acne scars are gone. Although I don't know why Jim bothered. They just give a man character."

"So you knew him pretty well," Nicole observed. She rested her glass of wine against her cheek, partly obscuring her mouth. In high school, Nic had had a prominent overbite. A few of the crueler kids had dubbed her Mrs. Ed. Somewhere in the intervening years, she'd had her teeth straightened. With her dark, smooth skin and slightly slanted eyes, she had always been pretty. Now she was beautiful. Still, old habits died hard.

Cassidy shrugged and set the photo down. "You know. Portland's a big town on a small scale, so we cross"—she corrected herself—"crossed paths a lot."

"Where did all this path crossing take place?" Allison asked.

"Press conferences, fund-raising dinners, that kind of thing."

The waitress set down a basket of bread and carafes of olive oil and balsamic vinegar. Cassidy busied herself pouring the oil and vinegar into a small, white dish.

"We both worked in the media, albeit in opposite ends." Cassidy dabbed a slice of bread into the mixture. "Is it true that he refused to leave the studio when he knew he had been exposed to the gas?"

Allison said, "That's what we're hearing. He stayed inside so that the others wouldn't be exposed."

"He died a hero. He would have liked that." Cassidy's eyes sparkled with tears, but she managed a smile. "Except for the dying part. Would he have lived if he'd opened the door?"

Nicole shook her head. "No. At the autopsy this morning, they said he would have needed an immediate dose of an opioid antagonist. And maybe even that wouldn't have saved him."

Cassidy's perfectly groomed brows drew together. Her eyes were an arresting teal blue— the result, Allison knew, of colored contacts. "That's what I don't understand. I was at the press conference John Drood held this afternoon. So it wasn't sarin gas?"

Nicole said, "No. The results of the autopsy point to some kind of opiate. We won't know which for a while."

"What *do* you know?" Cassidy asked. Sometimes

Allison and Nicole would give her tips that she wouldn't have heard anyplace else, allowing her to scoop the competition. In return, Cassidy occasionally brought her own findings to them.

"Something interesting did turn up today," Nicole said, "but you can't air this. Not yet. A neighbor told us she saw a blonde woman leaving Jim's condo yesterday—and it was probably *after* Jim was already dead."

"Really?" Cassidy's eyes widened. "Do you have any idea who it was?"

Allison wondered if she was jealous.

"That's the thing. There were no signs that he was living with anyone," Nicole said. "Do you know if he was dating anyone?"

Cassidy shrugged one shoulder. "Remember, you're talking about a guy who started his own Internet dating service for conservatives: Let Fate Find You a Date. Jim dated any beautiful single woman in Portland he could get his hands on."

Matter-of-factly, Nicole said, "So that would include you."

Allison winced at her bluntness, but she had had the same thought.

"I didn't say that." Cassidy flushed and looked away. "Besides, it wasn't anything serious. Jim plays—played—the field."

"How about his cohost, Victoria Hanawa?" Allison asked. "Do you think she was having a relationship with Jim?"

"You mean, had they dated?" Cassidy asked. "Of course. A couple of times. But was Victoria his girlfriend? No. Jim always said he liked to keep his work life separate from his private life. Of course, this is the same guy who always used his name to get a good table at a restaurant."

"What was Jim like, anyway?" Allison asked. "Especially off the air."

Cassidy looked up, remembering. "Shrewd. Intelligent. Street-smart as well as book smart. Some of his fans called him The Great One. He pretended not to like it. Jim's charming when he wants to be, cranky when he doesn't. Like pretty much anyone who works in the media, he can be a gossip. He likes—liked—power. Liked getting people to do things for him." Cassidy's description bounced back and forth between past and present tense as Jim became alive for her again. "Fastidious. He liked everything tidy. At the same time, Jim's macho. That is one man who would never back down. Never."

Allison looked at Nicole as Cassidy finished. They were sharing the same thought—Cassidy knew Jim a lot better than she had admitted.

"But why would someone kill him?" Allison asked. "We need to figure out if it was personal or some kind of domestic terrorism. The anthrax attacks targeted the media and the government, so there's a precedent."

"I don't even really think of people like Jim Fate

as members of the press," Nicole said. "It's not like they report the news. They report their opinions."

"In the anthrax case, the first person to die was a photo editor at a supermarket tabloid," Allison pointed out, "not a Tom Brokaw type. It was only later that they sent anthrax to ABC, CBS, and NBC. Cassidy, Jim told you he was being threatened. I talked to him, Nicole and I had set up a meeting for the day after he died, but he wouldn't give me any details. We need to know what he told you."

They stopped talking for a minute as the waitress brought their food: New York steak for Cassidy, king salmon for Allison, and arctic char for Nicole.

After the waitress left, Cassidy said, "He never said who he thought they were from, or even what was in them. He just said he was getting threats and asked for your phone numbers."

"Do you know how they were delivered?" Nicole asked. "Through the mail, dropped off at the station, phone . . . ?"

"E-mail, I think. And in the mail. But mostly e-mail." Cassidy cut a piece from her steak. She had ordered it rare, and Allison averted her gaze from the juices collecting on the plate. Some days she craved red meat; on others the very thought repulsed her.

Nicole said, "Did Jim try to find out what IP address they were sent from?"

"An IP address?" Cassidy took the last piece of

bread from the basket and used it to mop up the juices from her steak. "That shows what computer you're using, right?"

"IP addresses are how we caught all those sick pervs who chatted me up when I was working Innocent Images," Nicole said.

Innocent Images was the FBI's cyber crime squad's effort to take down online predators. Nicole had spent hours pretending to be thirteen. Not surprisingly, Nicole's work on Innocent Images did not seem to have improved her view of men. Allison didn't know what had happened in the years since high school, but Nicole was now wary, even dismissive, of nearly all men. Only Leif had seemed to crack that hard shell.

"Each time you go to a Web site, your computer's IP address is recorded on its servers," Nicole said.

Cassidy said, "So once you have the address, then you know who sent something, right?"

"For most of the guys we tracked on Innocent Images, yes. They weren't that sophisticated. But sometimes it's not that simple. Say a computer is at a business. That business might share a handful of IP addresses, making it hard to link an e-mail to a single person. Or you can go to a library or Internet café, and send your e-mails from there. And if you really want to get tricky, there are programs called anonymous proxy servers that can hide your address."

"Isn't that illegal?" Cassidy asked, raising one eyebrow.

"No, it's not. Unfortunately." Nicole took a sip of wine. "But with a subpoena, we can get the information from the proxy server. Usually."

The waitress came over to their table just as Allison was taking her last bite of buttery salmon. "Is anyone going to want a dessert?"

"Of course," Allison answered with a smile. "We need your famous chocolate mousse. With three spoons."

After the waitress dropped off their dessert, Cassidy said, "All I know about the threats is that when Jim talked about them, he looked scared. And if you knew Jim—he was never scared. Nothing could rattle his cage."

"We found some threats at his home and office," Nicole said.

Cassidy bit her lip. "Are any of them related to Brooke Gardner?"

CHAPTER 22
McCormick & Schmick's Harborside Restaurant

By the way her friends straightened up at the mention of Brooke's name, Cassidy knew she had hit pay dirt. She took advantage of their distraction to sneak an extra spoonful of mousse.

"Why?" Nicole asked. "Did he say anything about Brooke Gardner to you?"

Cassidy swallowed and then said, "He told me the family was angry at him. He felt bad about what had happened, sure, but at the time anyone would have put money on the idea that she had killed her own child. I mean, how many times have we seen that scenario? Kid disappears, and then the too-young mom says the babysitter took her, or she just turned around and the baby was gone. Only it always turns out that the story doesn't add up."

"Except that this time it did," Nicole said dryly.

Just looking at her made Cassidy feel guilty. "We both covered that case. Everybody did. The parents even called me right after Brooke killed herself." She remembered how sick she had felt, listening to their message. "They left me a voice mail calling me a jackal."

Allison picked up her pen and made a note. "Did you save it?"

"No. But I do have transcripts of the story Jim did on her." She pulled her tote onto her lap and found the copies she had made earlier for each of them.

FATE: Now, a mother's worst nightmare. She tucks her 18-month-old into his crib, settles onto the sofa in the very next room for a video. When she returns to check on him, the baby is gone. Today, the search is on for 18-month-old Brandon Gardner-Tippets.

HANAWA: That's right, Jim. Police are telling us that Brooke Gardner put Brandon into his crib around 7 p.m., and when she went to check on him an hour later, he was gone and the window was open.

FATE: Joining us right now is Vince Rudolph, a private investigator, to give us his thoughts on the case. Vince, what say you?

VINCE RUDOLPH, PRIVATE INVESTI-GATOR: First, Jim, let me say that *The Hand of Fate* is doing a huge service to this baby boy by putting this information out there. People need to go to your Web site and look at Brandon's picture and forward it to their friends. The facts need to be turned over and over, and people need to think back to that day. What do they remember? Did they see anything out of the ordinary? Or did they see this baby, maybe with someone else? Your show provides a huge service by focusing on those things.

FATE: Whatever help we can provide, we are glad to do so. Also joining us today are two very special guests, the mother and father of missing 18-month-old Brandon Gardner-Tippets. On the line with us we have Jason Tippets, Brandon's father. Welcome, Jason. You just told us that you cooperated with police, and they checked everything out and cleared where you were that night. Now, do you think it's possible someone could have leaned in the window and taken your baby, and he just slept through it?

JASON TIPPETS, MISSING BOY'S FATHER: I find that one hard to believe, because Brandon is a very, very light sleeper. I mean, if you move him while he is asleep, he automatically wakes up.

FATE: Interesting. With us also is a special guest, Brooke Gardner, Brandon's mom, who is divorced from Jason Tippets. This is a mother who is simply watching TV in the next room, she goes in to check on her son, and he's gone. Brooke, thank you for being with us. Now, Brooke, where is the crib in relation to the window?

BROOKE GARDNER, MISSING BOY'S MOTHER: The crib is directly underneath the window. As soon as I saw Brandon was not in the crib, I looked through the room and in the closet. I didn't know what to think. I thought maybe he had climbed out of his crib. He had done that once before.

HANAWA: Was he sleepy that night? Was he ready to go to bed, or did he want to stay up?

GARDNER: He was very tired. We had had a long day. And my son is not a light sleeper whatsoever. You can move him from room to room, and he'll still be asleep. And on top of that, he is very friendly and outgoing. He can walk into a room full of strangers and make friends with people.

HANAWA: Now, Brooke, what did you do first after you opened the door to his room?

GARDNER: Like I said, I looked all around his room, I looked in the closet, and then I checked the bathroom and my room, which are right down the hall, which he could have gotten to without me seeing him. And after that, I looked in his room again and realized the window was wide-open. It wasn't obvious at first because there are curtains in front of it.

FATE: Brooke, the window—you said that when you put him to bed, the window was up about three inches. What position was the window in when you saw it again?

GARDNER: At that point, it was all the way open.

HANAWA: Is there any way Brandon could have climbed out that window?

157

GARDNER: Even if he stood on tippy toes, he couldn't have reached the edge.

FATE: I'm struggling with how somebody gets into a room, takes a little baby, and somehow struggles out the window with that baby. It seems kind of inconceivable.

GARDNER: When the investigators came in to do the visuals and everything, when they leaned in through the window, they could reach the crib. God forbid if Brandon was up or something like that. Nobody would need to crawl in the window.

FATE: Brandon's father, Jason Tippets, you're on the air. Have you taken a polygraph?

TIPPETS: Yes, sir.

FATE: You pass it?

TIPPETS: They don't say whether you pass or fail, but they said the response was favorable.

HANAWA: What questions did they ask you on the polygraph?

TIPPETS: Like if I knew where Brandon was, if I had anything to do with it, just the kind of questions that they would ask in a case like this.

FATE: Let's ask Brooke Gardner, Brandon's mom. Brooke, have you taken a polygraph?

GARDNER: I've spoken to the investigators, and as far as the investigative techniques are concerned, you know, polygraph, stress test, physical searches, interviews, etc., my family and I have fully cooperated with local law enforcement and—

FATE: Have you taken a polygraph?

GARDNER: Locally, they don't have enough necessary experience, and that's why the FBI was called in to begin with. I've been instructed to only speak with them, with their unit, and anything that they release to the media or public is up to them. Now, as far as—

FATE: Have you taken a polygraph?

GARDNER: Like I said, I mean, anything that I do is in cooperation with them. I'm doing everything they want me to. But as far as details and everything, I'm leaving everything up to them.

FATE: Right. Have you taken a polygraph?

GARDNER: I've done everything they've asked me to.

FATE: I want to go out to Vince Rudolph again. Vince, what do you think about this case?

RUDOLPH: Don't forget, there are 50 sex offenders within 5 miles of this house. They're interviewing them, reinterviewing them. The authorities don't have tunnel vision. But I'm telling you, Jim, one and one is not adding up to two on this case.

FATE: What do you mean by that?

RUDOLPH: Time of day, between 7 and 8 o'clock, and you have his mom in the next room, watching TV. What happened when this baby saw a strange person? Why didn't the baby scream? I'll give you one possibility that I know the police are looking at. What if that baby wasn't in the crib to start with? So if I'm the lead investigator, I'm going to interview everybody. Father, mother, relatives, I want to know if there is any drug use, I want to know everything that's going on, on both sides. I understand this was a bitter, nasty divorce, but these people need to get on the same page. Father says the child is a light sleeper that would cry and scream. Mother says the baby's a heavy sleeper that wouldn't put up a fuss. You have to answer a lot of questions for me if I'm the investigator on this.

FATE: Explain, Brooke. I'm sure you have an answer. Brooke Gardner, Brandon's mom.

GARDNER: Jason doesn't even live with us anymore, so what does he know about how Brandon sleeps? I'm his mother. I know how Brandon would react.

FATE: What about those people who say that you are not being emotional enough about this, that you should be crying and in hysterics? That you are not acting the way a mother who has lost a child should?

GARDNER: Well, they aren't in my shoes, are they? If I spend time crying my eyes out, then I can't find Brandon.

FATE: Most people would be emotional about this—the abduction and possible murder of their child. Yet there is not a quiver in your voice.

GARDNER: I cry when I'm alone. I cry when I go to bed. I don't sleep.

RUDOLPH: People need to think back to that day. What did they see? Did they see a strange car outside? Did they see a parent taking the baby away? Did they see the baby get taken by someone, or did they see the baby in another

161

location? Jim, thanks to the attention *The Hand of Fate* show is bringing to this case, it's going to be really hard for facts that don't line up— kind of like we're hearing in this case—to not be spotlighted. And when we can focus in on those things, they just might give us a clue to where this little guy is.

As Cassidy read Jim's words again, and the stark accusations behind them, she felt sick. Her own coverage of the story had been scarcely better, although a transcript wouldn't have been as damning. She had conveyed her doubt of Brooke's story with a raised eyebrow and a sarcastic emphasis on certain words. "Brooke Gardner *says* . . ." She hadn't been the young woman's chief accuser, but she had certainly joined in the chorus. There were times her job felt like that of a vulture, waiting for something to die so she could swoop in and pick over its bones. And maybe if it wasn't quite dead yet, she could help it along. As had been the case for Brooke, who had killed herself rather than face continued accusations that she had murdered her son.

Allison was the first to look up. "Did Jim ever say how he felt when he learned the truth?"

"Jim?" Cassidy shook her head. "Jim's philosophy was that the past was past. That you couldn't change the past, so you just had to move on." Cassidy thought of something they might not

162

know. "Jim used to be a news reader. It was kind of an accident that he ended up as a radio talk show host. He used to say it was his fate. His little idea of a joke." She wished she could get used to the idea that he was dead.

"Do you believe in that?" Nicole asked. "That people have a certain fate, no matter what they do?"

"You mean, is everything predestined? Like Jim would have died yesterday no matter what he did? Sometimes I think that. Maybe." Then Cassidy thought of how hard she worked. What would be the point if no matter what she did, the same fate would befall her? "But I guess I hope it's not."

"Henry Miller said, 'We create our fate every day we live,'" Nicole said.

Both women looked at her in surprise.

"Hey," she said shrugging, trying to hide a smile. "I was an English major, remember?"

"I know another quote about fate." Allison finally looked like she had shaken off all the cares of the last few days. "Although I don't know who said it."

"What is it?" Cassidy asked.

"'Fate chooses our relatives, but we choose our friends.'" Raising her glass, Allison looked at each of them in turn. "To friends."

"Present—and absent," Cassidy said, as she tapped her glass against the others.

The plan was to interview Jim's coworkers one by one on their own turf, where they would be more comfortable and forthcoming. None of these people was a suspect. Yet.

But Nic had a feeling that by the end of the day they would be looking at one or more of them more closely. Jim Fate was a polarizing figure. For every person who loved him, there were probably ten others who loathed him.

And some of those people might work at KNWS.

First up was Chris Sorenson, the call screener. Allison opened the door and waved him in. Chris was about five foot nine, with medium-brown hair and a face that was neither fat nor thin. Only his large, green eyes, fringed with dark lashes, saved him from being completely unremarkable.

The color hit Nic like a fist to the gut. She drew in a sharp breath, reminded herself that the past was past. Only this man's eyes were the same color—nothing else.

"Are you the one who sits in that little room next to Jim's?" she asked, trying to drag her mind back to the here and now. When he nodded, she said, "Do you think you could show us how the whole setup works?"

He nodded again, and the three of them walked down the hall. A few employees watched curiously as Nic took down the yellow POLICE LINE DO NOT CROSS tape. She let Chris and Allison in before taping it back in place, ducking under, and closing the door. Someone had picked up the clutter of medical supplies, but everything else looked much the same as it had the day before.

In the control room next to the studio where Jim had died, a man gave them one look through the glass before going back to adjusting his dials and gauges. "That's Greg," Chris said. "He runs the board, you know, adjusts audio levels, takes network feed and traffic reports. We have two other studios, so he's working with someone down the hall."

"Can he hear us?" Allison asked.

"Not unless we want him to."

"And you sit here?" Nic pointed at a small desk that held two computer screens and a telephone with multiple lines. It sat underneath a square window that looked into the radio studio. "And Jim was—where?"

Chris slowly walked into the radio studio until he had his back against the wall, facing the window. "Right here. A host always needs to see his call screener." With a faint shiver, he stepped out of Jim's spot. He moved around the table. "This is where Victoria sits. She has her back to me."

"For a long time it was just you and Jim, right? How did you get this job?"

"I was working at another station, but I always liked Jim's show. Usually I'm so tired of people talking that I only listen to music in the car and at home, but for Jim's show I made an exception. Then one day he fired his call screener." Chris chuckled and shook his head. "Live and on air. Typical Jim. As soon as my shift was over, I drove over here and applied. I ended up talking to Jim directly. I guess he liked what I had to say, because two weeks later, I started working here. And that was four years ago."

"Were you a little anxious," Allison asked, "knowing that your predecessor had been fired?"

Chris shrugged. "Jim always said you either like this business or you get out. I like it. And I like Jim." He pressed his lips together. "Liked Jim," he said softly.

"How do you decide who gets to talk to Jim?" Allison asked. "Or do you put almost every caller on the radio?"

"No, I have to choose. My job is to figure out who would be good on air and who would be horrible." Chris ticked the requirements off on his fingers. "I want people who are on topic. Who are coherent. I don't want people who are going to freeze up when they hear Jim Fate use their name. Some people don't make any sense. Some can't

166

get to a point. And some use colorful language that the FCC would frown upon."

"What if someone does swear once they're on-air?" Nic asked.

"There's a short delay before anything is broadcast. See this button?" He took two steps back into Jim's space and pointed. "Push it once, and it cuts off the last three and a half seconds. Press it twice, you get seven. That's the most you can get, but that's usually enough. And then the computer stretches out their words like taffy until the time's made up." He bunched his fingertips, touched his hands together, and then pulled them apart.

Nic moved back to the doorway to look at Chris's phone. "Do you have caller ID?"

"Sure." Chris nodded. "It comes in handy when Jim bans someone from calling in for two weeks. Of course, the hard-core ones will just borrow someone else's cell phone. But I can still tell. I remember voices really well."

Nic made a note. "How much hate mail would you say Jim got?"

"Oh, dozens every day. Maybe more. Largely anonymous. Jim would pick out the most outrageous one for his NOD award."

"Was he ever afraid that someone was going to do what they threatened?"

"Jim?" Chris looked surprised. "He thought it was funny."

"Do you think one of those people killed him?" Allison asked.

Chris's answer was immediate. "No way."

"Why not?"

"Because the people who get mad, they get mad in the moment. They shoot off an e-mail right away and get it out of their system. Killing Jim like that took planning. It wasn't a crime of passion."

Nic nodded in agreement. Fashioning a deadly gas grenade was not a spur of the moment act. "How many calls can you take at any one time?"

"An hour of talk radio is actually forty-one minutes after you take away the weather, traffic, news, commercials, and promo. So in an hour, you might be able to take twenty calls. Jim always said there was no point in having more than six waiting on the phone lines. And if he had someone on air who couldn't get to the point, he would get impatient and dump them."

"I'll bet that made some people unhappy. All of a sudden they are talking to a dial tone."

"Oh yeah," Chris agreed. "Then they would call back and really ream me out. Like I was the one who cut them off." His green eyes flashed from Allison to Nic. "But it would be ridiculous for someone to kill Jim over *that*."

"People have been murdered over spare change." Nic shrugged. "How about people who have been angry about shows Jim has run about them?"

"I got several calls from Brooke Gardner's parents right after she killed herself. But I never put them on. It wouldn't have made Jim look very good, especially after their grandson turned up. And then recently Quentin Glover has been calling, yelling that Jim has to back off, that Jim is ruining him, that Jim's going to be sorry if he doesn't shut up."

"Really?" Nic and Allison exchanged a glance.

"I guess at one time they actually used to be friends, back before Glover got caught with that mistress. Jim went to college with Glover's wife, Lael. The affair turned Jim against him. It didn't matter to him that Lael took Glover back. Once Jim's made up his mind, it stays made."

"Do you have any regular crazy callers?" Nic asked.

Chris looked up at the ceiling. "Maybe Craig. He's a regular caller and also a nut. He always disagrees with Jim. Jim could come out against Satan, and Craig would call to say he's wrong. He's always got his Bluetooth on, and he's always in his car. Jim has even had him come into the studio every now and then. It's good for entertainment on a slow news day. It generates calls."

"Anyone else?" Allison asked.

"Jim has more than his share of crazy fans. One guy we always see lurking around the background every time we do a remote broadcast. He's pretty distinctive—he always wears a leather hat with

169

this wide brim. We just call him Leather Hat Guy. He paces back and forth and watches us, but sooner or later he'll get close enough to snatch whatever junk we're giving away: refrigerator magnets, key rings, window decals."

"Do you know Craig's last name?" Nic wrote as she spoke. "Or how about the Leather Hat Guy? Do you know his name? Has he ever called in to the show?"

"No, no, no, and not that I know of." Chris shifted from foot to foot. "But they're both just lonely guys who have to turn on the radio to hear any other voice besides their own. There's no way they would kill the guy they think about so much. I mean, for some people, it's like their lives revolve around the show. They get upset if Jim takes a day off."

"Who fills in when that happens?" Allison asked.

"Victoria, but for a lot of listeners, it's not the same. Some people don't like to listen to a woman, to be frank. They say her voice is too shrill or that she's not serious or smart enough."

"Do you think that?" Nic asked. "That Victoria doesn't have the voice or the smarts that Jim had?"

Chris looked away. "She doesn't have the same edge Jim does, that's for sure. Jim's all about getting in someone's face. People want the arguments, the excitement. They want a knock down, drag out fight. And Victoria doesn't offer that. Not on the radio, anyway."

Allison took a new tack. "Maybe whoever targeted Jim was someone in his personal life. Tell us a little about that."

Chris lifted his empty hands, palms up. "I don't know much. Jim wasn't the type to kiss and tell."

"What about him and Victoria? Did they ever date?" Nic asked.

Chris opened his eyes wider, the picture of innocence. "I don't really know."

"Come on, you look through that window right there at the two of them for hours at a time," Nic said in a tone that implied she already knew the answer. "You can see how they talk to each other, how they look at each other, how much they touch."

"Exactly. Do you think Jim is going to do anything while he knows he's got me and the board op guy and maybe the reporters and the station manager watching him? No way. Besides, if Jim had any relationship at all, it was with his listeners. They were a lot more real to him than people he actually saw day to day."

"What about the other people who work at the station?" Allison asked. "How did they get along with Jim?"

After a long pause, Chris said softly, "Maybe you should talk to Victoria."

"We'll be talking to her later." Nic cocked her

head. "What do you think we should talk to her about?"

"Ask her how well she got along with Jim." He looked away.

Nic hated coyness. "Look, we need you to tell us whatever you know."

He straightened up. "Okay, for each show Victoria goes in with three or four folders, one for each segment. They have research she wants to have handy, points she wants to make, stuff like that. And as the show goes along, her papers tend to get spread out." He pointed at Victoria's place. "See that Talk button? A couple of times, her folders ended up on top of it. She didn't know it, but I could hear everything she and Jim were saying. And what I heard was them arguing."

Nic looked up from her notes. "What about?"

"Victoria was maybe a little starry-eyed. You know that saying about people not really wanting to know how sausage is made? She didn't really understand how the talk business works. That there's a give-and-take."

"What kind of give-and-take?" Nic asked. "And who's giving and who's taking?"

His mouth twisted, as if he would have been happier to continue winking and nudging. "Okay. Jim had LASIK eye surgery awhile ago. So for a few weeks he talked up the surgery, kept saying how easy it was and how he wished he had done it years ago."

172

Nic saw the light. "And he got that LASIK surgery for free. In return for talking it up."

Chris nodded. "Exactly. Jim always said one hand washes the other. But Victoria doesn't understand that sometimes you have to do things to keep the sponsors happy. It's not always about news value. You don't do a live remote from the opening of a big chain store because it's news. You do it to help out on the advertising side of things. The wall between advertising and editorial came down a long time ago. It's all just content, and if it gets you listeners and advertisers, then you know it's working. Victoria liked to talk about the freedom of the press, but no one just hands you a microphone and says, 'Go for it.' Nothing is for free."

"So you're saying Victoria didn't understand the business side," Allison said.

Nic knew Allison well enough to know that she sympathized with Victoria.

"Yeah. She was always talking about fairness and transparency." Chris's eyes flicked up to the ceiling. "Like they would have hired her if she wasn't a thirty-one-year-old woman who was easy on the eyes and half Asian. They hired her to get the ratings up and to bring in more young women listeners."

"What will happen now?" Nic asked.

Chris shrugged. "For right now, she's host. And the station might keep her on, if the ratings stay high once everyone has gotten over wanting to talk about Jim's death. She acts like she's just taking the baton from Jim's fallen hand or whatever. But now she gets to take the show in a whole new direction. And that never would have happened if Jim hadn't died."

CHAPTER 24
KNWS Radio

As a prosecutor, Allison knew never to interview a potential witness by herself. If she did, and the witness said something different on the witness stand, she couldn't take the stand herself to counter him. She couldn't be both prosecutor and witness, which is why she needed Nicole.

More than that, she and Nicole made a good team. Allison was skilled at building connections with people, whether they were victims, witnesses, or even perpetrators. While it wasn't as simple as good cop, bad cop, Nicole brought completely different strengths to an interview. She sat back and listened with all her being, which made some people feel off balance. They could tell they were being put under a microscope.

The next person to be interviewed was the program director, a tall, thin man in his midfifties. "I'm Aaron Elmhurst," he announced when he opened the door. He reached out to shake their

hands as Allison and Nicole introduced themselves.

Aaron looked awful—his eyes were shadowed,
and it looked like he hadn't shaved since Jim died.
"Just let me know what I can do to help," he said.
"We need to catch the guy who did this to Jim and
string him up. And not the fast way either, where
your neck gets broken when you fall. I want him
to feel what it's like to strangle to death." He sat
down across from them and pressed his fingertips
against his closed eyelids.

Allison needed answers, not tough talk. A few
softball questions might help Aaron calm down
and focus, not on revenge, but on facts. And who
knew? Every now and then a softball question got
hit out of the park.

"I wanted to ask you how KNWS managed to
broadcast yesterday when the station was shut
down. Did you use one of those live remote trucks
you see at events?"

Aaron dropped his hands, and some of the tension in his face smoothed out. "No. A live broadcast comes right back through the studio, so that
wouldn't have worked. We've got a transmitter
site out in Damascus, and the engineers put
something basic together. Greg—that's the guy
who runs the equipment—he grabbed a sound
board and a couple of microphones before he
left."

"Pretty quick thinking," Nicole observed,

making a note. Later she would write up a report and share it with Allison.

Aaron shrugged. "If you work in live radio, you have to be quick on your feet. Thank goodness Greg was. He flipped the switch to the national feed, so we were never off the air. And locally, we were back up with a cobbled-together program within four hours. We came back here last night after you guys gave us the all clear, but there was never a gap in broadcasting. If you're off the air for more than sixty seconds, you're history. Listeners will change the dial, and you might never get them back."

"So what does a program director do?" Allison asked.

"Just like it sounds. I direct the programming. I'm responsible for hiring, firing, and overall supervision of staff. It's everything from controlling the on-air sound to the really important stuff, like deciding who gets stuck working on Christmas." He managed a weak smile.

"And how long have you known Jim Fate?" Allison asked.

"His name's not Jim Fate."

"It's not?" Allison said. She and Nicole exchanged a look.

"It's Jim McKissick. That rolls right off the tongue, doesn't it? All those s's don't sound too good hissed into a microphone. When I hired Jim twelve years ago, I told him to change his name.

Not only was it wrong for radio, but it was already associated with the other station in town where he'd worked."

"Did he leave that station so he could get his own show on yours?" Nicole asked.

Aaron snorted. "He left that station because he got a pink slip. Him and all the other on-air folks. A big chain of radio stations bought it up. That's their standard operating procedure. Buy a station, fire all the talent, and then use one guy sitting in Texas or Nebraska or whatever to do shows for towns in a half-dozen different states. It's called voice tracking, but what it means is it's all robots and computers and prerecorded, and the only real people in the studio are the traffic reporters. They try to customize the program to make it sound as if the host is actually local, but when you listen, they can't even say the names of nearby towns and roads."

Allison tried to lead him back onto the path. "You said Fate's real name was Jim McKissick?"

"Yeah. I told him he needed something punchier, something unique to our station. I didn't want people thinking we were taking somebody's leftovers. Of course, who was I kidding? That's all our station was at that point. Leftovers. That was back when we were one of those stations that plays classic hits from the sixties, seventies, and more!" Aaron boomed out the last few words like a hammy announcer, then sagged back in his chair. "This was way before he was 'Jim Fate with *The Hand of Fate*, heard in thirty-eight states.' I thought I was doing Jim a favor when I hired him, but it turned out that he was doing me one."

"What do you mean?" Allison asked.

"It was kind of an accident, but Jim has ended up being this station's bread and butter. When I hired him, our Arbitron ratings were in the toilet, and we were hanging on by the skin of our teeth."

Allison winced at the mixed metaphor, but Aaron didn't notice.

"At that time, Jim did pretty much what you would expect for the kind of station we were back then. Took requests, did a little bit of patter between songs—nothing that anyone would remember the next day, let alone the next minute —and read the news at the top and bottom of the hour.

"Then one day the lead story was about an old lady who had been dropped by the nursing home staff on the way back from the bathroom. But they didn't fess up about what they had done. Instead of taking her to the doctor, they just put her back in bed and tried to convince her that it had all been a bad dream. Yeah, right. A bad dream that left her right leg broken in two places. Eventually gangrene set in. When they finally took her to the hospital, it was too late, and she died."

Allison was sickened. "That's awful."

"Jim thought so too. After he read the story, he

made a few choice comments about it on air. It was definitely *not* part of the script. I remember sitting in my office and thinking I was going to have to give him a talking-to during the next break. At that time we were the go-to station for any dentist or office building that didn't want to shell out for Muzak. They knew we could be counted on to play unobjectionable thirty-year-old hits that everyone had heard a million times before and that no one paid any attention to. I was worried we might have lost our toehold in the one niche we had.

"But instead people started calling in. And they weren't mad about what Jim said. They wanted to talk about it. I think that was the first time in the station's history that anyone wanted to talk about anything that we played or said. Before, they didn't even notice. So when these people started calling, we put a few of them on the air. Then more people called in. And the whole thing snowballed. The more people listened to Jim, the more he talked. That was one man who was never neutral about anything. He always had an opinion, and the more anyone tried to argue with him, the stronger it got. You could never get Jim to back down. Never. It was great. Talk radio thrives on conflict.

"Well, that was all it took. Three months later, *The Hand of Fate* was a real morning talk show. We ended up completely changing our format.

No more classic lite hits. Now we've got a guy who does financial advice, a garden lady, two guys with a sports show, a couple that gives dating advice, and a shrink who yells at people to get their act together. And Jim and his show. Less than a year after he made those first comments, he was airing on a dozen local networks. Now he's syndicated. *The Hand of Fate* airs on 120 affiliates, and Jim's my golden boy." Aaron heaved a sigh. "Was. Was my golden boy. Now I don't know what we'll do."

Allison said, "I heard Victoria Hanawa filling in for him yesterday."

Aaron shrugged. "She doesn't have that out-there quality that Jim does. Did. She's more the voice of reason. And that's not necessarily the voice you want to tune in to. Reasonable isn't as entertaining. It doesn't really matter to me what someone says on the air. It doesn't have to be right or wrong. It just has to get people to listen. In the end, it all boils down to the ratings. The higher the number, the more we can charge for commercial advertising time. And that's the only thing that keeps us in business."

Thinking of Cassidy, Allison said, "I have a friend who is a TV reporter, and she says the same thing. It's all about ratings."

"Exactly," Aaron said. "And even then it's not enough to have a huge number of people tuning in to your show. They have to represent the right

180

demographic group if the station's going to make money. Most ad agency media buyers target the twenty-five to fifty-four age bracket. And women aged twenty-five to thirty-four are pure gold. They're the ones who control the purse strings. That's one reason we brought Victoria in last year. Jim's listeners tend to be older and male. Victoria was supposed to help us skew more toward people like herself."

"You said supposed to," Nicole observed. "That didn't work out?"

Aaron sucked air in through his teeth. "Our numbers haven't risen that much. And Jim didn't really cotton to the idea. He felt it was—hmm . . . something of an intrusion. He didn't exactly make things easy for Victoria. But she's a real trouper. You've probably heard that she stayed even when Jim ordered us to leave. She risked her own life to be with him for those last few minutes. It was . . ." Aaron's voice cracked, and he paused for a minute, his lips pressed together as he struggled for control. "It was horrible to look at him and know that he had to be dying and that you couldn't help him. When I left, he already looked awful. And when I looked back, Victoria had her hand up against the glass, and Jim was on the other side, pressing his hand against hers, with the glass in between."

Aaron put his hand over his eyes, and they watched as his shoulders heaved with a silent sob.

He finally straightened up, his eyes wet and red.

"Why would Victoria take the risk of staying?" Nicole asked. "Were they more than just coworkers?"

Aaron blinked. "I don't know, and I don't want to know. I mean, technically, Jim wasn't Victoria's boss—I was. Sure, it was Jim's show, but when it comes to talent, I'm the one who hires and fires. Jim has always had an eye for the ladies; that's all I can tell you."

Allison and Nicole made eye contact. Allison knew they were thinking the same thing. *In other words, yes.*

"Did Jim have any enemies?"

Aaron shrugged. "He ticked people off on a regular basis. But mad enough to kill him? Killing someone for being a blowhard or for riding roughshod over a caller—that's pretty hard to fathom."

"How about Quentin Glover?" Nicole asked.

"I'm sure he wasn't happy, but he's facing an indictment. He's got too much on his plate to be worrying about Jim Fate."

Allison said, "What about Brooke Gardner?" The transcript had been pretty damning, once you knew the truth behind it. "She killed herself after appearing on the show."

Aaron's face darkened. "The story is not that simple. That's why her family settled out of court. That girl had a whole raft of problems."

"What do you mean?" Nicole asked.

"She had a drug habit and let a number of men come and go through that apartment. Her ex was trying to get custody. She was afraid all that was going to come out."

Allison didn't let it show on her face, but she was revising her opinion of Aaron. He seemed like the kind of man who went with what was expedient, who toted up the balance sheet before making any decision. How much of his grief was about Jim's death—and how much was about losing the golden goose? That gave her an idea.

"Did you have keyman insurance on Jim?"

Aaron looked blank. "What's that?"

"It's a kind of insurance that a company can take out on someone key to the business. Then if that person dies or is incapacitated, the insurance pays the company."

He raised his shoulders. "I don't know. You'll have to ask our accountants. We do carry liability insurance against lawsuits. That's what paid off when Brooke Gardner's family decided to settle."

"How about the other staff?" Nicole asked. "How did they get along with Jim?"

He pursed his lips. "Pretty well. No more arguments than at most workplaces."

"There were arguments?" Nicole raised an eyebrow.

"Well, not really arguments. People learned it was better not to get into a discussion with Jim.

183

He had that way of never stopping, never letting go. He would just talk over you until you gave up."

After they told Aaron he could go, Allison turned to Nicole. "What do you think?"

"I'm thinking we might want one of our accounting specialists to go over the books. If you read between the lines, it sounds like the station might have been in financial trouble. They brought Victoria in, but it didn't help."

"And if they did have keyman insurance," Allison said slowly, "then Jim might have been worth more dead than alive."

CHAPTER 25
KNWS Radio

Back in the interview room, Nic looked at Allison and shook her head in mock amazement. "Okay, for suspects we now have station management, the Gardners, Representative Glover, Craig, NOD winners, and now Victoria. And don't forget Leather Hat Guy."

Allison laughed. "Maybe for this next interview we should concentrate on finding out who *couldn't* have killed him."

"Who's up next?" Nic asked as she massaged a knot on her inner thigh. Because she was still recovering from being shot in the shoulder, her Thai boxing instructor was focusing on the lower half of her body. Thanks to the training Nic had begun at Quantico, she was already good with her fists, but Muay Thai also used shins, knees, and elbows as weapons. The past weekend she had been too slow to block a kick and learned first-hand exactly how much pain the nerve that ran from the groin to the knee could produce.

Allison looked at the schedule. "Next up is an intern who was assigned to work directly with Jim. Willow Klonksy."

"Willow Klonsky? Doesn't exactly sing, does it?" Nic wondered which part of her name the girl would take after. Hippie chick Willow or plodding peasant Klonsky?

The answer turned out to be neither. Slender and model pretty, Willow was dressed in a black skirted suit, ivory blouse, and a single strand of pearls. Her makeup was flawless, her dark hair pinned up in a French twist. She looked like she was about to pose for a stock photo that would be labeled "young businesswoman." But when she shook hands with Nic, her palm was damp.

"I understand you're an intern here," Nic said, taking the lead. "Is that a paid position?"

"I get college credit," Willow said in a low voice. "I'm a senior in the broadcasting program at Reed."

Nic revised Willow's age down five years. She raised an eyebrow. "No offense, but you don't really look like a Reedie."

Reed was a top-drawer private college that attracted extremely bright kids with Birkenstocks, progressive ideas, and a liberal attitude toward drug use.

Willow offered them a smile, her first. It changed her face, softened some of the edges. "I don't necessarily dress like this when I'm not at work." Her tone became more serious. "And I don't necessarily take part in all the after-school activities you hear about."

"So you're working here for free?" Nic asked. Maybe white girls whose parents had lots of money could afford to do glorified volunteer work while they attended a college that cost tens of thousands of dollars. Every hour Nic hadn't been studying while she was in college, she had been making milk shakes, mopping floors, entering data into a computer. She barely remembered her courses. Every now and then her parents had been able to give her a twenty or two, or sometimes just a bottle of shampoo.

Willow leaned forward. "You don't understand. I am so lucky to be here. There were more than two hundred applicants for this position. Being an intern is about the only way to get around that whole catch-22: 'Can't get a job without experience, can't get experience without a job.' Because I've worked here, I'll be able to show on my résumé that I *do* have relevant experience."

"What are your duties?" Allison asked.

"They told me I would be booking guests, doing some research and editing, sound gathering, audio production . . ." Willow let her voice trail off.

Nic said, "And in real life?"

Willow raised one shoulder and smiled. "About what you would expect. I answer phones, and sometimes check the newswires for stories. But I'm mostly a gofer. I go out for coffee and sandwich runs."

"So how did Jim Fate like his coffee?" Allison asked.

Willow replied without hesitation. "Twenty-ounce latte with four shots, extra hot, no whip, with three sugar packets. He was very firm about that. No Splenda or Equal. It had to be sugar."

"So Jim was a man's man, huh?" Nic said. "Not afraid of a little sweetener?"

A smile quirked Willow's mouth. "Jim wasn't much afraid of anything."

Nic wondered if that trait had gotten Jim Fate killed. "How long have you known him?"

"I met him when he interviewed me and the other finalists for the job. But I've been listening to him since I was in middle school. In fact, he's the main reason I decided to major in broadcasting. He spoke the truth without fear."

Willow was so earnest that Nic practically expected her to put her hand over her heart.

"What was Jim like to work with?" Allison asked. "Was he a good boss?"

"He liked to explain to me how radio worked, what listeners wanted versus what they said they wanted. He liked to tell me why something was wrong, and how it should be changed."

"Sounds like pretty one-sided conversations," Nic observed. She had worked for a lot of people like that in her time. Some of the older guys at the Bureau still treated her like she was wet behind the ears.

"But that's what I'm here for," Willow said earnestly. "To learn about how things really work in the real world."

"What are your plans now?" Allison asked. "Will you stay here?"

"I don't know." Willow sighed. "Aaron says I can stay. But my dad wants me to quit. He's worried that it's not safe here. He keeps asking me, what if someone sends another package? Aaron says they are going to contract with a company that will X-ray any package before it comes to the building, but my dad's afraid something will slip through, or that some crazy guy will just show up at the front desk and start blasting away with a machine gun."

Nic could understand that. If this girl were her daughter, she would already be gone.

"Did Jim Fate have any enemies?" Allison asked.

Willow's answering smile seemed faintly patronizing. "You must not have listened to the show very much. He made a lot of people mad. I saw some of the letters Jim threw in the trash after reading them. People would say that they hoped he would get cancer or that lightning would hit him or that God would strike him dead."

"Given that Jim made people so mad, were you surprised that he opened the package? Why didn't he have you screen things for him?" Nic asked.

Willow shrugged. "Jim always opened his own mail. He made that clear to me the first day."

Allison asked, "Isn't that just the kind of thing you have a gofer for?"

Her cheeks pinked. "He got a lot of, um, things, in the mail. Personal things."

Nic raised an eyebrow. "Personal things?"

Willow looked down at her lap. "One time I saw him open a package, and a pair of lace panties fell out. Maybe he just wanted to check out everything on his own so he could decide what to do with it without everyone knowing about it."

"It sounds like he was a player," Nic said.

Willow's smile was rueful. "Kind of. I guess I didn't pick up on *that* when I was in middle school."

Allison said carefully, "If you don't mind me saying so, you're very attractive. Did Jim ever express an interest in you?"

Her lips twisted with disgust. "Jim *Fate*? He's old enough to be my father! In fact, my dad's only two years older than him."

"But you didn't really answer the question," Allison pointed out. "Just because Jim Fate was older doesn't mean he didn't have eyes in his head. Did he ever flirt with you, ask you out, touch you inappropriately?"

"Flirt? Jim flirted with any woman from seventeen to seventy. But if I had thought there was anything more there, I would have cut him off right away."

Looking at Willow's curled upper lip, Nic had no doubt she was telling the truth.

"Now, you were there when Jim died, is that right?" Allison asked.

"Yeah." The girl swallowed. "Aaron was talking to me and Chris—that's the call screener. There was a break for the top-of-the-hour national news feed, and Victoria got up to get her tea. The next thing I knew, Jim was pressing the Talk button and telling us we had to leave, that there was sarin gas."

"You've heard that it wasn't sarin, right?" Allison asked.

"Yeah, but at the time, I think all any of us could think of was that we were all going to die. You could tell Jim was trying to hold his breath. It was awful. His eyes were all wide and pleading, just staring at us through the glass."

"But Victoria stayed, right?" Nic said. "She stayed with him until the end."

"That certainly took a lot of courage," Allison added.

Willow raised both shoulders slightly. "That's the one thing I wanted to tell you. Maybe Chris or Aaron won't mention it you, but I thought it was strange."

"What's that?" Nic's antennae quivered.

"Even though I don't open his mail, once it's been sorted, I take it all in to Jim, and he opens it during the breaks. And that's what I did yesterday."

"Yes, yes," Nic said, trying to hurry her to the good part.

"But that package—the package with the poisonous gas—wasn't one of the ones I gave him. It was Victoria who gave it to him right before she left the studio to get her tea."

"What are you saying?" This could change everything. Nic remembered what Chris had said about Jim and Victoria arguing. "Are you saying that Victoria knew what was in there? That she gave it to him deliberately? That she's the one who caused his death?"

Willow's face crumpled. "I don't know. Maybe the mail sorter *did* put it in her box instead of his. But I mean—everyone knew they had had some kind of fight. They were barely speaking to each other. But, you know, Victoria is so nice! I can't see her being a—a murderer."

Nic tried to picture it through Victoria's eyes if she had been the killer. Imagined handing over the package and then walking as quickly as you could away without breaking into a run. Knowing that as soon as your coworker tore it open, he was dead. And that maybe whoever else was in the room with him would be dead as well.

But if Victoria were the killer, then she would have known just how much gas was in there. Maybe it was only enough to kill one man. And couldn't she have had a backup plan? Nic remembered what Tony had said. Had Victoria had a loaded syringe of Narcan hidden in her pocket or purse, ready to give herself the antidote if she accidentally inhaled some of the gas too?

But why had she stayed behind, stayed with Jim as he died? Was that the act of a killer?

Then Nic thought of another possibility. Maybe Victoria had decided that pretending to care would be the best alibi she would ever have. Had Jim spent his last few moments on earth drawing comfort from his killer?

CHAPTER 26
KNWS Radio

After Willow left, Allison said, "She dresses pretty nice for someone who works behind the scenes." She wondered if Willow came from money. Probably, since she was going to Reed.

"You know what they say," Nicole said. " 'Dress for the job you want to have.' She doesn't want to always be going out to get coffee or sandwiches."

"Yeah, she's got that hungry look," Allison agreed. "Kind of like Cassidy. But there's something else. Didn't you get the feeling we were just looking at the surface?"

"Well, she *was* wearing a lot of makeup."

Allison pushed Nicole's shoulder. "That's not what I meant. I don't know. It's just that she seemed artificial somehow."

"She's—what? Twenty-one or twenty-two years old." Nicole shrugged. "At that age, she's just pretending to be an adult."

There was a knock on the door, and then Victoria entered the conference room. Victoria's mixed heritage had resulted in a strikingly beautiful woman. She was tall and slender, with high cheekbones, tip-tilted eyes, and dark, straight hair that fell past her shoulders. Allison wondered how much of a coincidence it was that Victoria and Willow—the two women who worked most closely with Jim—were both so good-looking.

Victoria's black eyes were shadowed, and in her left hand she carried a crumpled tissue. "I want to help you catch whoever did this," she said as she sat down across from them.

"I was surprised to hear you on the radio yesterday morning," Allison said.

"Haven't you ever lost yourself in your work? When I'm on air, I don't have time to think about myself. Talking about Jim was like having a therapy session I didn't have to pay for."

Although she nodded sympathetically, Allison wondered just how high the ratings had been. "Tell me about the day before yesterday," she said.

"It started out like an ordinary day." Victoria blinked, and the next second tears were in her eyes and her voice was rough and sarcastic with suppressed emotion. "It was basically like every other day, only one minute I'm watching Jim die in front of my eyes, and the next some guys in white hooded suits are dragging me out of the building and spraying me down on the sidewalk with a fire hose." She dabbed at her eyes.

"I know how difficult this must be for you," Allison said, patting Victoria's free hand. "Why don't you tell us about a more normal day. How would that go?"

"Sorry." Victoria wiped her eyes again. "Jim and I would usually come in three or four hours before the show began. Chris helped too. Good talk radio takes prep. We would look at the *Drudge Report*, the *New York Times*, the *Oregonian*, the wire services, clips from TV shows that had run the night before . . ." Her voice trailed off. "And then we would start to build the show. Jim always says there are three rules for great topics. One is picking a question that could be reasonably answered from at least two points of view. Like, should we build more nuclear power plants or more windmills? The second rule is, will the audience understand it? Like, should we have a national sales tax or a national income tax? And the third is, does it engage the listener? You have to tell them what's in it for them. Will they get higher taxes or better schools or free broadband or what? If you do it right, then they're eager to call in." Victoria massaged her temples. "And then we would make a show sheet. We scheduled a new topic roughly every half hour. Jim liked to over-build every show. To have more topics, more information, than he could possibly use."

"Who decided on the topics?" Allison asked. She rubbed her own temple, mirroring Victoria, to build a bridge of nonverbal rapport. When Victoria tilted her head, so would Allison. If Victoria winced, Allison would do the same. Everything Victoria said, Allison affirmed with a nod or a subtle smile. Without words, she was telling her, *You and me, we're in this together*.

But underneath, Allison carefully weighed Victoria's words and actions. People either lied by commission, or they lied by omission. Did she cut her eyes to one side, stutter, stall, add emotion that she really didn't feel, vouch for her own veracity? How many lies had Allison heard preceded by the words *I swear to God?*

Victoria said, "Jim was always the one who chose the topics. Oh, he asked me what I thought, but in the end it was his decision. He was a little bit more old-school than me."

"What does that mean?" Nicole asked.

"I look at the research. And yeah, people want topics they can talk about when they come to work. But there's other information they want before that. When they listen to the radio, they want to be grounded. Jim thought that kind of stuff was a waste of time."

"What do you mean, grounded?" Allison leaned forward.

Victoria's face became more animated. "The first thing people want to know when they get up in the morning is, is my world safe? Did we drop a nuclear bomb in Iraq? Was there an earthquake in the middle of the night? After they get that information, then they want to know what time it is, even if they have a clock. Somebody on the air telling them the exact minute it is lets them know they're still on schedule. So in between talking about stories and taking calls and interviewing folks, I would mention how many minutes past the hour it was. That might seem like just a way to kill time, but it's what listeners really want to hear. Once they are oriented, then they're ready to call in and talk about the big story of the day. But Jim felt it wasn't a good use of airtime."

"It sounds like Jim had a lot of opinions." Allison gave her a knowing smile.

"You're right about that. I even have a bell to ring when he's going a little crazy, you know, to tell him he needs to shut up."

Allison was surprised. "And he was okay with your doing that?"

"He gave me the bell." Her smile faltered.

"How long have you worked with Jim?" Nicole asked. Allison could tell by Nicole's narrowed eyes and the set of her mouth that she continued to have reservations about Victoria.

"I was hired about a year ago. Aaron told me I would be billed as Jim's cohost. That's not exactly true. If our names are in print, Jim's is ten times bigger than mine. Aaron keeps saying I have to prove myself." Victoria rolled her eyes. "You try getting a word in edgewise. There's a reason Jim has succeeded in talk radio. It's like survival of the fittest. Only in talk radio, it's survival of who-ever can keep talking. He who talks the loudest and the longest wins."

"It must have been difficult, playing second fiddle to him," Allison observed.

Victoria's smile looked like it had been ordered up. "Ninety-nine point nine percent of the time, Jim and I got along great."

"But I saw a transcript of a time where you didn't agree with him, and he cut your mike." Allison tried to pin her down. "That must have been hard, having him just cut you off like that."

"That was just part of the game." Victoria shrugged. "People like it when we argue, so some-times we pretend and give it to them. Look, the Jim you heard on the radio wasn't really Jim. Not completely. You're not *you* on air. You're more like an actor playing you. Before the show starts I always take a deep breath and picture the person I'm playing. She's like me, but she's louder, funnier, braver, stronger. But she's not really me. Just like Jim wasn't the same outside of this studio. When Jim and I were off air, we got along great."

Nicole stepped in to play bad cop. "That's not what we've heard from your coworkers. They told us there was tension between you two. Do you want to tell us about that?"

Victoria snorted. "Tension? You get two people in the room, and only one of them can be on air at a time, of course there's going to be a little tension. But as Jim always told me, it's *The Hand of Fate*, not *The Hand of Hanawa*. And maybe we had some different ideas about what was best for the show. But that wasn't personal. That doesn't mean I would *kill* him."

"What do you know about the threats he was getting?"

"Jim got as many as a thousand e-mails a day. A lot of those were threats. He relishes—relished—them. It meant people were talking about him."

"But something must have changed." Allison lowered her voice. "This isn't to be shared outside of this room, but he approached us about some threats that were bothering him. He died before we could talk to him. Do you know what these threats were? Why they were different?"

Victoria bit her thumb, looking thoughtful. "He showed me a couple of them recently. He hadn't done that before, so I don't know if they were worse or different from the ones he normally got. One said something like, 'You jerk—you think you can get away with what you're doing, but you can't. If you can't shut your mouth, I'll shut it for you.' And another one showed his head with a noose around it. It said, 'We are measuring your neck for the noose.' "

"Did he tell you who he thought had sent them?" Allison asked.

"No. But he's made a lot of people mad over the years. If you were lying, covering up, especially if you were rich and arrogant, then Jim wanted to take you down. He's certainly made enemies." She lowered her voice. "And not just out there in radio land. There are a lot of people here who fought with him."

"So who fought with him here?" Nic asked.

Allison wondered if Victoria would nominate herself, but instead, after a long pause, she said, "Chris, sometimes."

"Chris?" Allison was surprised. She hadn't detected any tension when Chris was talking about Jim Fate. Was Victoria lying, trying to throw them off the scent?

"Jim was always screaming at Chris. He would yell at Chris if one of the callers turned out to be nutty or turned nervous or inarticulate once they

199

were on air. Jim would start screaming, 'What's the problem, Chris? Can't you just give me people I can work with?' Sometimes by the end of the shift, Chris would jump if you touched his shoulder when you were walking by him.''

"What about you?" Allison asked, her eyes never leaving Victoria's. She was looking for a blink, a twitch of the lips, any kind of tell that would betray Victoria's thoughts. "We understand that you might not have agreed with Jim blurring the line between ads and the show.''

"Did Chris tell you that? Jim and I are both two strong-willed people, that's all. Look, maybe when I started working here I had to surrender a few of my principles. But the show isn't about principles. It's about ratings. You know what Jim said to me? He said, 'This isn't journalism. This is showbiz, and don't you forget it.' ''

"What about the flip side?" Nicole asked. "Did you and Jim date?"

She snorted. "Where did you hear that? I swear, all anyone does here is gossip. Oh, we went out for drinks a couple of times after work, but that's all. It wasn't anything serious. If you knew Jim, nothing was serious with him. Not really. He could argue about something like his life depended on it, but he stopped caring about it as soon as we went to break.''

Allison said, "Why did you stay when he was dying? Jim ordered everyone to leave, and they

200

did. But you—you stayed. Even knowing it might be dangerous."

Again, Victoria's dark eyes brimmed. "I think part of me didn't believe it was really happening. And if it wasn't real, then there was no risk to me. Have you ever been in a car accident?"

When Allison nodded, she said, "It's like that. Time slows down, and you don't believe it's really happening. You watch the bumper crumple, and then the hood buckles, and your face starts heading toward the dash, and you still have time to be surprised when you hit it. So part of it was just this feeling of unreality." Victoria took a long breath that shook at the end. "And part of it was that I just couldn't bear to turn around and run away. You could tell just by looking at Jim that he was dying. His eyes—I'll never forget the look in his eyes. Desperate, pleading, naked. I couldn't leave him. At that moment, we weren't two people who sometimes fought for control of the mike. We were two human beings. And I couldn't leave him to die alone."

"Weren't you worried about the gas getting to you too?" Nicole still looked skeptical.

"The studio is soundproof. There's weather stripping and magnets around the door, so it's virtually airtight. The air gets so stale in there sometimes. So I knew I was probably safe as long as he didn't open the door."

Allison and Nicole spoke at the same time.

201

"Were you surprised that he didn't?" Allison asked.

"Were you afraid that he would?" Nicole said.

Victoria shook her head. "I honestly believe he thought he could hold out until the paramedics came. Jim was never afraid of anything. Not until—" Her voice broke. "Not until the last."

She turned her head and laid her cheek on the table, sobbing, while Allison patted her shoulder and muttered reassurances.

Allison looked up. Nicole hadn't moved. And she was watching Victoria with narrowed eyes.

CHAPTER 27
Channel 4 TV

Holding a venti-size coffee the way a drowning man might clutch a piece of floating debris, Cassidy was shuttling through B-roll footage of old press conferences, trying to find some tape of Jim Fate. B-roll was footage without a sound track that could run while viewers listened to Cassidy or one of her interview subjects.

Normally it was easy enough to get B-roll footage. For example, the cameraman might want to shoot a sequence of the subject working at his desk. What if the person had no plans to work at his desk? No problem. Change his plans. What if he had no desk? No problem. Use someone else's desk. What if the subject wasn't working that day? No problem. Change his schedule.

And usually the subject agreed. It was for TV, after all.

But Jim was dead, meaning Cassidy had to rely on whatever footage already existed. Now all she had to do was find it. All the footage at the station was logged, which technically meant that someone had recorded what was on the tape and the time it appeared. Logging was supposed to save you time in the long run, so you could come back to the B-roll and find exactly what you needed without having to watch hours of tape.

The problem was that Jim Fate had only appeared in this five-year-old footage incidentally. If he was here at all. But Cassidy was pretty sure she remembered him asking some pointed questions.

As she took another sip of coffee, she used the knob to shuttle forward. At this particular press conference, the governor had introduced stricter state standards for handling "downer" cows that were too sick or weak to stand on their own. The idea was to make the risk of mad cow disease entering the food chain even smaller. The crowd of activists had cheered and applauded.

And if Cassidy remembered right, Jim had immediately denounced the governor's plan as alarmist, saying the legislation would be so costly it would put small, family-run farms out of business and make meat unaffordable for most low-income consumers. The two had argued, with the governor red in the face and Jim full of venom and vinegar. Jim being Jim, in other words. At least his public self.

Cassidy had sometimes seen a different side of Jim. More mannerly. More seductive. The last time she had seen him had been at dinner two weeks earlier. He had asked her to meet him at the RingSide, Portland's venerable steakhouse. A red-meat kind of place for a red-meat kind of guy. The RingSide featured big drinks, big prawns, big wedges of iceberg lettuce, and of course, steaks three inches thick. The waiters dressed in black suits and starched white shirts, and the walls were hung with autographs of famous athletes.

"You did a marvelous job on the Katie Converse story," Jim said after ordering for both of them. "You found a million angles. You always made it fresh and interesting."

"Fat lot of good it did me," Cassidy said as she settled her snowy-white napkin on her lap. "Station management promised me an anchor chair. Now they're saying I don't test well. When I had TV stations all over the country calling me."

"But that was then." Jim took a sip of his water. He had stopped drinking two years earlier, although callers sometimes accused him of falling off the wagon. "And this is now, right? And we all know that, in TV and radio, yesterday doesn't matter."

"Yeah." Cassidy raised her glass of gin and tonic to her lips. The bitter taste matched her mood. "Now that I've turned everyone down, Channel 4 has said they are going to bring in some pretty little wind-up doll who was Miss Connecticut, some kid who can sing 'The Star-Spangled Banner' and do a mean baton twirl, but who doesn't have any understanding. She's got no depth, no . . . no context!"

And Miss Connecticut was about twelve, although Cassidy didn't bring that part up. Now that Channel 4 was broadcast in high-def, she was conscious of every laugh line, every imperfection. And the older she got, the more there would be. On the way to the restaurant, she had stopped to get gas, and the gas station attendant had called her ma'am. Ma'am, not miss. And Cassidy had looked at his pimply face and realized that she was nearly old enough to be his mother.

"Look, I want you to think about something." Jim's blue eyes drilled into her. "Think about coming to work with me."

Was he serious? "What? On *The Hand of Fate*? Why would I want to do that? I'm a serious broadcast journalist."

Palming his chest, Jim mimed taking a bullet. "Ouch, Cassidy! You just shot me down without even hearing me out. Are you saying that my show is frivolous? I've seen the kind of stories your station has been running. The last broadcast

I saw showed a water-skiing squirrel. Is that really news? You may be a serious journalist, whatever that means, but you're also a woman who has opinions and who never gets a chance to air them."

The waiter slid their plates in front of them. Jim picked up his knife and fork and began to attack his steak with the same ferocity he brought to the microphone.

"I do get to." Cassidy crossed her arms, realized she looked defensive, uncrossed them, and picked up her own silverware. "The shots I choose, the quotes I use—it can all go a long way to telling the story I want to tell. Just because I don't come right out and say what I think doesn't mean I don't try to shape it."

He gave her an indulgent smile. "But if you join *The Hand of Fate*, you won't have to disguise how you feel. You can just come right out and say exactly what you think and why. And people *listen*. And if you join the show, they will listen to *you*." He cleared his throat. "Besides, Cassidy, maybe you and me—we could be something more."

He was definitely teasing—wasn't he? "We tried that, Jim—remember?"

They had been lovers for a short time the year before, long enough for Cassidy to realize that they had the wrong things in common. Both of them, at heart, were hustlers. Both of them were looking out for number one. And then she had met Rick, and he seemed to be everything Jim wasn't: romantic, impulsive, adoring. Jim hadn't protested when Cassidy said she had met someone new. Somewhere in the depths of her purse she still had the key to his condo he had given her the first night they slept together, back when they both thought their relationship might be the real deal.

"That was then," Jim said. "This is now."

Deciding that she had better stick to one gin and tonic, Cassidy followed Jim's example and took a sip of her water. "I'm done with men, Jim. You might have heard what happened to me with the guy who followed you." Thinking of Rick, she remembered the flowers. The bruises on her wrists. The apologies. And then the night he had pulled a gun on her.

"And the station *is* letting me tell my story. I'm doing a special report on domestic violence just before Valentine's Day. It's a pretty big deal." Cassidy suspected they had thrown her a bone after not living up to their promises, but it was still airtime that was hers and hers alone. "After what happened, I've decided to take a break from men."

Jim never took anything seriously. "You know I'd be gentle," he said, and gave her a wolfish grin. He had ordered his steak rare, and with every bite he sliced off, the pool of bloody juices on his white plate grew.

"Not interested," Cassidy said, although she was. In a way.

"Even if you're not, you and me, kid, we could go places together. Strictly on a professional level. We would make a great team. We could bill it as Beauty and the Beast."

Cassidy was beginning to think Jim was serious. "Aren't you forgetting something? Or should I say some*one*? What about Victoria Hanawa?"

He snorted. "That's not working, and it never has. Not from day one."

"What are you talking about?" Cassidy didn't want Jim to see that there was something about the idea that intrigued her. "You guys have great chemistry."

"Don't give me that. It's not great chemistry when someone's main contribution is to laugh or say, 'Oh, Jim!'"

She gave him a skeptical look. "Or do you mean it's not great chemistry when someone doesn't go along with what you're saying? I heard about you cutting her mike when she disagrees with you too much."

He lifted his open palms, as if to show he had nothing to hide. "Look, the problem is that Victoria and I are too much alike. We're always fighting for the microphone. The result is barely listenable. What the show needs is two different kinds of people. One person like me: someone with a million ideas, even if, I admit, they might not all be good ones. And someone like you, who, once you give them an idea, always comes back and says something funny or thought-provoking or just generally wonderful. I've seen you do it time and again on Channel 4. You can think on your feet. You can put disparate facts together and tell a coherent story. Cassidy, together you and I could be magic. If not personally, then still professionally."

She broke his gaze and looked down at her plate. Half of her steak was already gone. How had that happened? She would just have to leave her baked potato untouched. Everyone always said the camera added ten pounds. She couldn't afford to look fat. Not now. Not when she had to sit next to Jenna in story meetings.

"Yeah, but it would still be *The Hand of Fate* show, right?"

He shrugged. "You can only have one top dog."

Jim was like a force of nature. Cassidy didn't relish getting caught up in the whirlwind. "No, thanks. I'm my own person. I'm not meant to be anyone's order taker."

"But what are you at Channel 4? You're not coanchoring with Brad, even though they promised you. And I see they're even giving airtime to that young thing they've got there—Juno or whatever her name is."

"Jenna." Cassidy said her name reluctantly. Jim had a knack for finding her painful places and then poking them.

"At KNWS I have an intern, but you won't see me confusing her youth and beauty with talent. Channel 4 is getting desperate because they know their average viewer is eighty plus. I mean, look at the ads you guys run during the news. It's all motorized scooters, Viagra, and 'you can't be turned down for our insurance.' So in a desperate bid for attention, TV news is now all about eye candy. Radio still has some gravitas." Jim slid a fork piled high with baked potato, sour cream, chives, and bacon bits into his mouth. He obviously had no qualms about his waistline.

"I'm surprised you can say that with a straight face. I've heard your program. It can be pretty one-sided. You work someone over until they're the consistency of mush."

"Okay—how about this aspect? You never have to worry about aging out of the radio market. Whereas on Channel 4, one day it might be Jenna sitting in the anchor chair, right next to Miss Connecticut. And you'll be out on assignment. Someplace where it's raining and it takes you three hours to drive there. One way."

The sickening thought of Jenna in the anchor's chair was not as far-fetched as it might have sounded even a month ago. "I don't know," Cassidy said slowly.

Working in TV was like a drug. You got addicted to the action and the recognition. But the business was so small that once you lost or left an important job, it was difficult—if not impossible—to go back. But did she want to jump into something new, or did she want to wait until she was pushed out?

"Tell you what. Why don't you come by my condo after dinner?"

He certainly had a one-track mind. Oh, well, at least she still had it, as far as Jim Fate was concerned. Cassidy lifted one eyebrow. "What—and see your etchings? Haven't you already shown me those?" She allowed herself one bite of baked potato. One bite had never killed anyone.

"No. A couple of months ago I put in a small studio setup. Just try practicing with me, and I'll record it and give you a CD. Once you hear for yourself how great we can be together, you'll know why I want this."

"I don't know, Jim." The second forkful slid into her mouth before she could stop it.

"That's not a no. Come on. Just give it a try. And if you don't think it's right for you, then no blood, no foul."

"Mm, maybe." She ate another bite of baked potato. Weren't potatoes a vegetable? And didn't she need to eat more vegetables?

Forty-five minutes later, she was sitting in Jim's condo, wearing headphones and staring at a black mike. "How are we going to do this?"

"It's easy." Jim smiled at her. One earpiece of his headphones was pushed back, as was hers.

"This is your microphone. Stay about six inches away, and speak directly into it. All you need to remember about radio is: no last names, no brand names, no phone numbers over the air. Other than that, speak normally."

Cassidy's palms were damp, and her stomach felt sour. She hadn't felt this anxious in a long time. With Rick, sure. But not when it came to work. She was good at her job. And this was just like her job, only minus a camera.

"Just follow my lead. I'll start talking about something, and you chime in." Jim slid his headset back into place, flipped a switch, and then leaned toward his mike. "Now, I don't know how many of you have read it, but there's a B-list actress who has just come out with a book that says aliens are living among us. What do you think, Cassidy?"

There was no audience here but Jim and the microphone. Still, she heard the faint tremor in her first few words. "Well, I'm not sure I believe in aliens." Her voice steadied. "But I will say her theory would go a long way toward explaining a few of our politicians."

Jim laughed, a little theatrically, and shot Cassidy a thumbs-up.

They went on for about twenty minutes, Jim riffing on current topics, and Cassidy following his lead. Then Jim copied the file he had made and handed her a CD.

"Just listen to this in the car on the way home. And tell me you don't think we could blow everyone else out of the water."

She looked at her watch. It was nearly midnight. She had to get home. Get home to her Somulex. All of a sudden the water she had drunk in between sips of gin and tonic in a bid to stay sober caught up with her.

"Could I use your bathroom?"

"Of course."

The nearest one was off Jim's opulent and masculine bedroom. The bed was made with the same red and gold silk coverlet she remembered from last year. Nothing was out of place. Nothing had ever been out of place any of the times she had been here before. Jim must either be a neat freak or have a housekeeper. Cassidy's guess was both.

When she came out of the bathroom, Jim was waiting for her. He put his arms around her. His mouth was covering hers, his body insistent, his hands on either side of her head.

For a moment, Cassidy's body answered him. For a moment, her body betrayed her, as it had so many times before. And then she twisted her head and pushed on his chest.

She stepped back. The sound of their breathing hung in the otherwise silent room. "No, Jim. I can't do this again. Not now." She had always been a sucker for blue eyes and black hair. She had always been a sucker for pretty much anything in trousers.

"Can't you see? It's like yin and yang. You and me, we would fit together like puzzle pieces." For a second he pulled her to him, demonstrating, and then slowly released her.

"That might be true. Maybe. But I don't think I want to go back there."

"Let's just leave that door open for a while, then, why don't we? We can be whatever kind of partners you like." He walked with her out into the foyer, helped her into her coat. It was funny to see him acting like such a gentleman now. Cassidy kind of liked that there were two sides to Jim, and he wasn't ashamed of either one.

His face turned serious. "Look. There's another reason I wanted to talk to you tonight."

Cassidy wondered what it could be. He had already offered her a job and a place back in his bed—what else was there?

"If I remember correctly, you have friends in law enforcement."

She kept her face smooth. "I went to high school with Allison Pierce and Nicole Hedges. Allison is a federal prosecutor now, and Nicole is a special agent with the FBI."

"Can you give me their cell phone numbers? I'd like to get in touch with them."

"Why?"

Jim shook his head. "I'd rather not say."

"I'm not handing out their personal numbers if I don't know what it's for. They would kill me if they got a call from the show and ended up being broadcast."

"This doesn't have anything to do with the show. Well, it probably does, but not the way you're thinking. I don't want them as guests. I want their advice. I've been getting some threats."

"Don't you get a lot of threats? Whenever I turn on the program, you're handing out that NOD award."

"These are different," Jim said, and wouldn't elaborate much further.

Finally, Cassidy wrote down their numbers and gave him a kiss on the cheek before she left.

It was only later that she realized one of her earrings was missing.

CHAPTER 28
Portland Field Office, FBI

The cop sitting next to Allison in the FBI conference room had recently eaten onions. Raw ones, she guessed, as he exhaled again. Her stomach pressed up against the bottom of her throat. As if lost in thought, she cupped her hand over her mouth and tried to concentrate on the neutral smell of her own skin. In another ten days she would officially be in her second trimester, and

215

Dr. Dubruski had said the bouts of nausea might fade away.

The task force had thinned considerably since sarin gas had been ruled out. Yesterday, the big-wigs had flown back to DC. Now it was down to local representatives.

"What have you learned about Jim McKissick?" Nicole asked Rod Emerick.

"Well, a lot more than about Jim Fate, that's for sure." Looking down, Rod began to read from his notes. "James Robert McKissick. Only child. Dad a drunk. Mom died in a car accident when he was nine. Dad was driving, but wasn't charged. It's not clear why. A few months after that, the state took custody after a teacher reported seeing welts on the kid's back. Dad died of liver failure about two years later. Meanwhile, the kid was bouncing from foster home to foster home. Reading between the lines, there may have been some physical abuse."

Allison imagined what it had been like. Jim must have envied his classmates their living mothers and sober fathers, their siblings, their certainty of their place in the world.

Rod continued, "Fate went to college on scholarship. He worked at three other radio stations, including one in college, before joining KNWS. He's been there for about twelve years. He had an excellent credit rating, no outstanding bills, and a nice-sized 401(k). He

216

owned a BMW and a condo in Willamette Villas. There's been no unusual outgo of money in the last year, so it doesn't look like he was paying blackmail. His medical history was unremarkable—some trouble sleeping, and his cholesterol was a little high."

"How about his personal life?" Leif asked.

"Well, as you might have guessed from what we heard from his neighbor, it was, hmm . . . *robust* might be one word you could use to describe it. He dated a number of women. And he took photos, of some of them, at least, with a digital camera we found in his condo."

"What were they wearing?" asked Officer Flannery.

"Or what *weren't* they wearing?" Heath Robinson chimed in with a leer.

Allison shot Nicole a resigned look. She didn't know how Nic could stand to work with Heath. Nicole's face was impassive. Even though her expression hadn't changed, Allison saw that her friend's face had gone strangely flat, as if she had withdrawn deep into herself. Talking about photos must have dredged up memories of her work with Innocent Images. Online predators often used pornography to convince young girls that having sex with them would only be natural.

"The shots were actually kind of tasteful," Rod said. "Nothing hard-core. Negligees or strategically placed sheets." He looked over at

Nicole. "Oh, and Nic—that receipt you found for Oh Baby in Fate's desk? Turns out that's an upscale lingerie shop, not a baby store. He bought someone a, a—" He stumbled over the word. "A bustier." He pronounced it *buhst-ee-air*. No one corrected him.

"Speaking of kids, were the women in these photos all adults?" Allison asked. "Did anyone look underage?"

Rod shook his head. "All what I would call age-appropriate eye candy. Late twenties to early forties."

"How many in total?"

"There's some question as to whether a couple of shots are of the same woman or not. My best guess would be nine."

"Any familiar faces?" Allison braced herself to hear Cassidy's name.

"Negative. And we isolated just their heads and showed them to the neighbor who saw a woman leaving his apartment the morning Fate died, and she didn't recognize any of them either. None of the photos were of Victoria Hanawa or any of Fate's female coworkers."

"Could you tell if the women knew they were being photographed?" Nicole's voice had a raspy edge.

"It was all pretty much 'smile for the camera.'"

"I can't believe anyone was that stupid. Let alone nine of them." Special Agent Karl Zehner shook his head. "In five minutes, he could have sent those photos all over the Internet."

Rod shrugged. "They must have trusted him."

"How about that hotel card from the Hilton?" Allison asked.

"They say the cards are automatically repro- grammed for each visitor, and they can't say when or who used it last," Karl said. "I'm guessing it was just a memento."

Nicole turned to Riley Lowell, who worked at the computer forensics laboratory. "What'd you find on Fate's computer?"

"No big surprises. But what was really useful was the memory stick you found in his desk. He had saved copies of a lot of threats that he had gotten by e-mail. Some of them weren't threats per se, just people who were angry at him." He patted a stack of paper. "I've made printouts for you so you can prioritize which ones you want us to try to get IP addresses on."

"And then there are the people Jim knew in real life," Leif said. "Nic and Allison, you guys han- dled the bulk of the interviews this morning. What do you think?"

Allison looked at Nicole, but when she didn't say anything, Allison went first. "I can see a number of angles. One is that if you read between the lines, ratings for his show have not been as strong as they wanted. They added Victoria Hanawa in the hopes that she would bring them more young female listeners, but it didn't work."

"So the solution was to rig up some kind of poisonous gas and kill Fate at work?" Karl's face wrinkled in disbelief. "Shoot, wouldn't it be a lot easier just to fire him, or both of them, and bring in someone new?"

"You would think so, but I just got off the phone with the station's insurer," Allison said. "They carried keyman insurance on Fate. Now that he's dead, they'll be getting five million dollars."

Karl whistled, but Leif said, "This still feels personal to me, not corporate. In every interview I conducted today, it seemed like Fate had managed to tick off that person at least once."

There were nods around the table.

Nicole said, "Victoria disagreed with him about the direction of the show. And she said that Chris was bullied by Jim on an ongoing basis."

Rod nodded. "A couple of people I interviewed mentioned Fate picking on Chris."

"I think we need to look closely at Victoria," Nic said. "To me, she seems a much more likely suspect than Chris. Victoria certainly had the motive. Fate didn't listen to her ideas. He mocked her and cut off her mike. He didn't appreciate her suggestions for changing the show. And there could have been some kind of relationship that soured."

"There weren't any photos of her on his camera," Karl said.

"All that means is that she's smart enough not to

get talked into posing. And as for opportunity—we already have a witness saying that Victoria is the one who handed the package to Jim. She claims she found it in her box."

"What about the person who normally sorts the mail?" Rod asked. "Do they remember seeing the package?"

Leif said, "The mail room guy doesn't remember putting that package in Victoria's box. The thing is, he handles at least a hundred packages a day. He says he doesn't remember any of them, unless maybe they're so big they don't fit in the box at all."

"Just because the guy had access to the package doesn't mean he'd have the motive to kill Fate," Rod said. "Do we know yet what kind of opiate was used? Would Victoria Hanawa be able to get any? Would she have the know-how to modify a smoke bomb?"

"Tests have been negative so far for heroin, morphine, and Percocet," Nicole said. "Now the lab is testing some of the less common ones. But we won't have the test results back for several days—maybe longer if they don't get a match."

Rod looked dubious. "I still keep coming back to the idea that it would have been incredibly risky to hand him the package and then hang around. Would Victoria have the guts to stay?"

Nicole shrugged. "What better way to provide herself an alibi than to stay with him until the end

221

and then cry crocodile tears while she takes over his program?"

"I'm not sure I would agree," Allison said. "If you want to look at people who had a beef with Jim Fate, the line would be down the block. So Victoria Hanawa and Jim Fate didn't always see eye to eye. But is that enough reason to kill someone?" She knew that it actually was, that almost anything could be reason enough in the right person's twisted mind. "Victoria didn't evacuate the building. She stayed even though she knew that something in that room was killing Fate. She stayed even though he ordered her to leave. She says it was so he wouldn't be alone."

The idea nearly brought tears to Allison's eyes. She remembered what it was like, thinking she might be dying, anonymous, surrounded by strangers in the street. To have someone there, comforting her, steadying her, would have been so welcome.

Nicole would not be swayed. "Yeah, but what happened after everyone else had evacuated? What if Hanawa stayed so she could take evidence? With no witnesses. Or only one witness. And she knew *he* wouldn't be able to say anything."

Leif asked, "How about people who were listeners, or who had been on the show?"

Smoothly shifting gears, Nicole said, "I think the family of Brooke Gardner has got to be at the top of the list. After all, their daughter killed herself after having been on the show and basically having him accuse her—falsely—of killing her own child. And Fate did receive a threat directly linked to her death."

Allison added, "And there's Congressman Quentin Glover. We've all seen that commercial. And the transcripts show that Fate was hammering him day after day, calling on him to resign. Chris told us he has gotten several angry phone calls from Glover, and that he and Fate were once personal friends."

"There's no greater enemy," Rod said, "than an old friend."

CHAPTER 29
Southeast Portland

Leif drove easily, one hand on the wheel, the other resting lightly on the emergency brake, only a few inches from Nic's left thigh. After calling earlier in the day, they were driving out to interview Brooke Gardner's parents, who lived in outer southeast Portland.

For the past few weeks, Nic had begun carrying Leif around in her head. Every morning, when she put on a blouse or selected a pair of earrings, she wondered what he would think when he saw them. If she read an interesting article in the paper or watched an intriguing segment on the news, Nic imagined sharing it with him. Pushing her grocery cart through WinCo, she wondered if he liked sharp cheddar or had a favorite brand of Ben & Jerry's.

A few weeks earlier, they had met for Saturday breakfast. Makayla had spent the night with Nic's parents. Before she agreed to meet him, Nic made it clear to Leif that it wasn't a date. That they were just friends. And he had kept it light, not touching her, or looking at her in a certain way, or even saying anything that a coworker wouldn't say.

But now, sitting beside him, aware of his every breath, she wondered if she was making a mistake, the way Allison and Cassidy kept saying. Something had shifted inside her in that crowded stairwell, when she had been convinced that she was only a few minutes from death.

Leif's voice interrupted her musing. "What are you thinking?"

Nic wrenched her mind back to the case. "I think we're missing something. But I can't think what." She looked out the window. Twenty years ago, this had all been fields. Now it was strip malls, strip joints, and used car lots.

"Let's hope it comes to you. Because right now, the way I see it, the problem isn't that we don't have enough suspects. It's that we have way too many."

The Gardners lived in an aging apartment complex that covered a couple of blocks. Leif kept to the posted five miles per hour as they wound through the narrow streets curving around dozens of identical gray two-story buildings.

They found the unit they were looking for toward the back of the complex. As soon as Leif knocked, the door swung open. A man and a woman—Stan and Linda Gardner, Nic presumed—stood in the doorway. They were both blond, both a little overweight, and neither of them looked that much older than Nic.

But there was a third person with them, one she hadn't expected. A toddler straddled Linda's hip. After Leif and Nic introduced themselves, Linda said, "And this is Brandon." He gave them a shy grin that showed his small, white teeth like freshwater pearls, then turned and pressed his face against his grandmother's bosom.

The Gardners invited them in, and then settled into a worn, beige plaid couch. Leif took the tan recliner while Nic sat on the matching ottoman, which was the only other piece of furniture in the room.

"Do you know why we're here?" Nic asked.

"I would guess this has something to do with what happened to Jim Fate," Stan said. He regarded them steadily.

Leif opened up the file he had brought and held up a plastic evidence bag. Inside was the newspaper clipping about Brooke Gardner's death—and the threat scrawled on top of it—that Nic had found in Jim's office. The Gardners looked at it without any sign of curiosity or alarm.

Leif said, "We were able to use new technology to get fingerprints off this. And guess what? They match someone in this room. And it's not me, and it's not Special Agent Hedges. Or Brandon, for that matter."

There were no prints on the clipping, so it was a lie, but it was a legal lie, one that often encouraged the guilty to immediately admit the truth. They had successfully used the same technique before. Two months earlier, Leif had told a robbery suspect that he had sent the mask the robber wore into the lab, which had been able to get a "facial print" off the mask. The robber had at once admitted his guilt.

Stan shook his head. "I didn't write that."

Linda said, "I did."

They all, even Stan, turned to look at her.

"It was right after they figured out"—she looked down at her hand stroking her grandson's fine blond hair—"that Brandon was alive. My only child was gone, and it was all Jim Fate's fault, and Brandon's father was threatening not to let us ever see our grandson again." She made a sound of bitter amusement. "Grandparents basically don't have any rights in Oregon. With just a few careless words, Jim Fate destroyed my entire family. He hounded my only child to death solely for the sake of getting more listeners. And he never even apologized. There were times I *did* want him dead. But I never acted on what I was feeling, other than to send him that note." She took a shaky breath. "And we've all come to terms with it since then."

"How *could* you come to terms?" Nic asked. She couldn't buy it. "I've got a daughter. If someone caused her death, I would never, ever forgive them. I would probably hunt them down and kill them myself."

Leif shot her a sideways look. They were supposed to be playing roles, but she figured he knew the truth when he heard it.

"And maybe one of us would have." Stan raised his empty hands. "Except we probably would have just gunned Jim Fate down in the parking lot and then stood there and waited to be arrested. No sense in running and hiding when you've got nothing to live for. And no sense sending him some package not knowing who else would be in the room when he opened it. Our beef was with Jim Fate, not anyone else. Six months ago, I would have gladly looked into his beady, blue eyes and put a bullet right between them. Linda and I used to talk about it. About how we would do it. The only thing that stopped us was this little guy here." He reached out with one square hand and cradled Brandon's left foot, clad in a tiny blue Nike. "If we killed Jim Fate, we risked never seeing Brandon again."

The boy gave him a smile, which made Stan grin in return.

Linda said, "Look, a couple of months ago, we got four hundred thousand dollars from our settlement with KNWS. Maybe the money is what brought Jason—Brandon's dad—around, I don't know, but now we're back in his good graces. We babysit Brandon every day while Jason is at work. Sure, I know, it's free child care for him, but I get to see my little baby grandson every day. Brandon is just a wonderful, wonderful boy. And he reminds me so much of his mother."

While Linda directed her words to them, she simultaneously played a game with Brandon, poking him under his arm or in his round tummy. Now he let out a delighted giggle. She raised her eyes to their faces. "So, no, we didn't kill Jim Fate. By the grace of God, we didn't do it."

As they were getting back into the car, Leif asked Nic, "What do you think? Do you believe them?"

"I think I do, actually. I think we need to look someplace else."

Leif raised one eyebrow. "Would you still think that if I told you that they have a nephew who is a paintball enthusiast?"

The news made Nic raise her head, like a dog catching a scent. Paintballers used smoke grenades. Was she going soft, getting distracted?

228

Why was she making decisions based on emotions and not facts? "Knowing that, I'm going to have to reserve judgment. Has anyone questioned the nephew yet?"

"It's happening as we speak." He shot her an amused look. "You're second-guessing yourself now, aren't you?"

His crooked grin made her stomach do a slow flip.

"If it makes you feel any better, I think you're right. I think those two were telling the truth. They wouldn't risk losing their grandson."

What was she thinking, continually letting this guy slip past her guard? Nic kept herself to herself for a reason. In a careful voice she said, "I don't think I've had a chance to thank you for tracking me down during the gas leak."

"Well, that hug you gave me was a good start."

Heat flooded her face. "That's the thing, Leif. I shouldn't have done that. And going out to break-fast with you a couple of weeks ago was . . . Well, I don't want to say it was a mistake, but I think it sent the wrong message."

"Wait a minute. This isn't going to be one of those 'Let's just be friends' speeches, is it? Because A, you already gave it to me. And B, I already *am* your friend. At least I like to think I'm your work friend. But Nic, I can't lie to you—I want to be more. I want to be your friend outside of work too. And I even want to be more than that.

I won't deny it. But if all you feel comfortable with is friendship, that's fine. And if you don't want either of those things, if you just want me to be your coworker and that's all, then I'll accept that."

Leif raised an eyebrow, and she guessed that it cost him to keep it light. "And I won't even let you know how much you are missing."

"What if I don't know what I want?" Nic said softly. Those weren't the words she had intended to say, but they came out anyway. "What if some days I want one thing, but the next I want something different?"

He lifted his hand from the emergency brake, gave her left hand a brief squeeze, then let go. "All I can tell you, Nic, is that whatever you want, whatever you're ready for, whenever you're ready, I'll be here."

CHAPTER 30
Keller Auditorium
Friday, February 10

Jim Fate's funeral was held at the Keller Auditorium, only a few blocks from KNWS. Every one of the nearly three thousand seats was filled. As in so much of her life, Cassidy was present in two capacities: as a participant and as a reporter. She was expected to write a story about the funeral as soon as it was over. Andy, along with dozens of other cameramen from media outlets all over the country, was relegated to the balcony.

Eric had told her that more than half of the "Heavy Hundred"—a list of the top American talk show hosts ranked by *Talkers Magazine*—were expected to be in attendance. As she walked into the lobby, Cassidy saw a few famous faces, but thanks to the nature of radio, many of the attendees were anonymous enough that only their bodyguards and the outlines of bulletproof vests under their dark suits gave them away. Making up the bulk of the crowd were hundreds of people who, Cassidy guessed, were just fans of Jim. Although he would never have used the word "just" to describe them.

Entering the auditorium, Cassidy caught sight of the gleaming mahogany coffin onstage. It was hard to imagine that Jim was in that wooden box. How could someone so much larger than life be in there? The thought made her feel panicky, and she pushed it away. She would definitely need Jim's Somulex tonight. To the left of the coffin was a podium, and to the right was a string quartet. While she could see them moving their bows over their instruments, the crowd made too much noise for her to hear them.

Was Jim's killer somewhere in the auditorium, mingling with the others drawn here for their own reasons? Cassidy knew that police would be photographing license plates and videotaping people as they walked through the doors.

She waved at Allison on the far side of the room. As she looked for a seat, she saw Nicole sitting toward the back and gave her a smile. Nicole answered with a single nod. *Does that woman ever loosen up?* Cassidy wondered. Sometimes when she was with Nicole, especially on the rare occasions when Allison wasn't around, Cassidy was painfully aware that she was just too much—too talkative, too disorganized, too loud. Next to Nicole's dark pantsuits, even her clothes seemed too bright.

Cassidy plopped her much-maligned tote into one of two empty seats. But eventually a woman stood in front of the seat and glared at Cassidy until she was forced to set the tote on top of her feet. *If you need a tissue*, Cassidy thought, *don't look at me*. She got more glares from the woman when she pulled out her notebook and began to take notes.

Cassidy ignored the frowns and sighs. She had a theory. Act as if you were allowed to do something, or deserved something, or that it was only natural—and after a while people would begin to believe it.

The ceremony began with a minister reading the Twenty-third Psalm, and then praying for all those Jim had left behind. For a minute Cassidy hoped that Jim, wherever he might be now, could see the full house. She knew it would mean a lot to him.

After uttering a few vague platitudes, the minister turned the mike over to a tall, stooped man, who cleared his throat nervously.

"Hello, I'm Aaron Elmhurst. I'm the program director for KNWS. I had the privilege of hiring Jim Fate twelve years ago. I thought I was doing him a favor, but it was really the other way around. It wasn't long before he found his voice and turned our little station into a powerhouse. A lot of you out there probably want to know how he did it. What was his magic? I'll let you in on a little secret." He leaned closer to the mike. "I have no idea."

There was scattered laughter.

"Jim could take the kernel of a story and turn it into a provocative show you couldn't stop listening to. He had such a way with words. A way of cutting straight to the point that was as sharp as a razor blade. I mean, sure, sometimes you would say, 'Holy cow! That's not what you expect to hear on the air.' But that was what made you listen to Jim." Aaron paused to wipe his eyes. "This might come as a surprise to those of you who only knew Jim from his on-air personality, but Jim mentored and inspired so many people. And he was loved by so many. He may have had a bombastic personality on air, but he was a very compassionate and caring human being in his private life."

Cassidy wondered if they were thinking of the same Jim. She had liked Jim, liked him a lot, but they had had something in common. They both realized that they had to look out for themselves. That no one else would do it for them.

Aaron ended by saying, "And if any of you would like to come up here and share stories about Jim, please do so now." There was a pause, as everyone waited for someone else to go first.

Finally, Victoria Hanawa made her way to the stage. Cassidy watched her closely. This was the woman Jim had wanted her to replace. She was tall and slender and painfully erect. Her high cheekbones were sharp under her skin, her eyes dark shadows.

"I was with Jim those last few moments. As you've all heard by now, he died a hero. He knew he had been poisoned, but he refused to expose anyone else." She forced a smile onto her face. "But I'm not here to dwell on how he died, but on how he lived. And how he worked. Jim did his homework. But there were days I would come in with carefully researched pieces, and he would show up with something he had read in the *National Enquirer* the night before and light up the board for hours."

Appreciative chuckles rippled through the room.

"What I liked best about Jim was that he wasn't afraid to tell it like it was. And if anyone dared to disagree with him?" She pretended to hesitate.

"Can I say *rant*? Is that too strong a word? There's a reason people called him The Talkmaster or The Man Who Will Not Shut Up."

Now laughter rolled through the audience. Victoria leaned closer to the mike.

"Can I get a 'Hey now'?" she asked, echoing one of Jim's catchphrases.

"Hey now!" came the response from all sides. Even Cassidy found herself calling out the phrase.

Victoria's smile faltered. "I keep thinking of arguments I want to have with him. But now I won't." She burst into tears. "Jim, I wasn't through with you yet."

Aaron took her arm as she left the podium. By now there was a line waiting to speak.

Willow Klonsky, Jim's intern, said, "I dreamed my whole life that I would work with Jim Fate. But I never dreamed that my life would be saved by him."

A nationally known radio talk show host said, "People say that Jim Fate was hated by some. Just look at how many of us are here. I think we put the lie to that."

Chris Sorenson, Jim's call screener, said, "I hope that wherever Jim is, there's a mike there. Because taking it away would be like cutting off his air. He *needed* to be talking to strangers from behind a microphone."

Another west coast radio broadcaster who had reached national prominence said, "You know what? Jim would have loved this. He would have been here telling better stories than we are. If he were here, he would be interrupting us, talking over us, but we wouldn't mind because he would be so darn interesting."

The crowd, which had been in tears moments earlier, chuckled. And so it went, speaker after speaker, some famous, and more often as the service went on, not so famous. Cassidy took fewer and fewer notes. Instead she found herself contemplating the reality that Jim was gone and she would never see him again.

She didn't realize she was crying until a hot tear splashed on her bare knee. Jim hadn't even made it to forty-two. He died with a million dreams and plans. Someday she would die too. And what did she have to show for her life? A bubble of pain expanded in her chest, making it hard to breathe. She wished she could crawl back to her apartment, take another Somulex, and pull the covers up over her head.

Aaron was the last to speak. "Jim Fate was a patriot, a man who stood up to special interests, a man who wasn't afraid to speak truth to power." His voice grew strangled as he struggled not to cry. "Someone has tried to silence your voice, Jim, but you live on in our hearts. Rest in peace, gentle warrior."

CHAPTER 31
Keller Auditorium

As the funeral ended, Allison rested her hand on her belly, wishing she was far enough along that she could feel the baby kicking. Dr. Dubruski had told her that it would be at least another month before that would happen. She wanted the reminder that life went on, that there were miracles to balance atrocities.

"Before we meet with Glover tomorrow, I think we should press Victoria harder," Nicole said in a low voice when Allison met her in the lobby. "Move from informational to confrontational."

"Now?" Victoria's emotion had seemed honest. Then again, Allison's emotions were right up against the surface. She needed to be more dispassionate.

"Now's the best time. This service brought Jim back to life for everyone who attended—including her. They're holding a smaller gathering for Jim at KNWS. Let's talk to her there."

A half hour later, the three of them were sequestered in a small conference room. "Look, we know this is a bad day for you, Victoria," Allison said.

Her eyes were swollen. "You can say that again. I just buried my friend."

"Your *friend*?" Nicole said, putting a sarcastic

spin on it. "Why do you keep lying to us?"

Victoria's head flew back as if she had been slapped. "What are you talking about?"

Allison let some of her tiredness show. "Look, you don't have to pretend with us. This is just us, talking. And who's more likely to snap—someone who sees Jim every day, someone who has to put up with all the things he does, or a listener who can simply turn the dial any time he gets fed up?"

Victoria scrubbed her face with the palms of her hands, smearing her mascara. "No, no, I can't believe what you're saying."

Nicole said, "Let's look at the facts, Victoria. Jim may have liked to stretch them, but everyone tell us you're a stickler for the truth." She held up one finger. "Fact number one: *you* are the one who gave Jim the package that killed him." When Victoria started to object, Nicole said sternly, "Let me finish." She held up two fingers. "Fact number two: you two argued all the time." Three fingers. "Fact number three: we've heard from several people that for the last couple of weeks you weren't even speaking to each other when you were off air."

Victoria opened her mouth again, but Allison spoke first, not looking directly at her. She kept her voice flat, as if she were simply stating facts that they had already agreed upon. "Jim was condescending. He hogged the mike and talked over you when you managed to get a word in edgewise.

And when you did talk back, he simply cut your mike so you couldn't talk at all. He never wanted you to be part of the show. What happened could even have been some kind of temporary insanity, brought about by his constant badgering."

"No. What are you saying? No." Victoria shook her head, her eyes wide.

"You sent him anonymous threats," Nicole said. "You were trying to get him to quit so you could take over the show. But when that didn't work, you decided you needed to get him off the air permanently. So you rigged up a way to kill him, put it directly into his hands, and then made sure you left the room before he pulled the string."

"That's crazy. That package was in my box. If I hadn't looked at the label, I might have opened it myself."

"Look, if you tell us what really happened, we'll make it easy on you," Allison said soothingly. "Everyone will understand why you snapped. Jim wouldn't stop harassing you. The evidence of how he treated you is all on tape. Any reasonable person would understand."

"Are you on any kind of painkiller?" Nicole asked. "Got a relative who is?"

"Stop it right now! Stop it! You two are crazy. I did not kill Jim." Victoria put her hands flat on the table. "It is true that Jim and I didn't always see eye to eye. But I didn't kill him."

"What did you disagree about?" Allison asked,

watching Victoria closely. She had seen killers cry at their victims' funerals. But in truth, they only felt sorry for themselves.

"When I started here, I believed in the ethics of broadcast journalism. And Jim just laughed at me. Editorial, ads—it's all blurred together now. There's no difference. Jim was always shilling for the people who gave him Botox shots. It was embarrassing. And how about the contests he was constantly running? Do you really think they always give the concert tickets to the ninth caller? Or does Chris pick the one who sounds the most excited, or the one who fits the demographic that the station wants?"

"But those are old arguments," Nic said. "And what we heard was that something new happened between you two recently. Something that pretty much made you stop talking to each other. So what was it?"

"I *was* angry at him. You're right about that."

"Why? What happened?"

After a long hesitation, Victoria said in a rush, "I found out that he was grooming someone to take my place. But as Jim would say, it wasn't personal; it was business. I would never kill anyone over that. Especially not like that. Watching Jim die and knowing there was nothing I could do to help—it was the worst moment in my life."

"Do you know who it was?" Allison asked.

"He wouldn't say." Victoria stood up. "Now, if

you'll excuse me, I'm going to go back to the gathering and remember why so many people hung on Jim's every word."

"What do you think?" Nicole asked after Victoria had left.

"If she hadn't stayed behind with him, I think she would be my number one suspect."

"Yeah," Nicole agreed. "I'm beginning to think she doesn't feel right for this. And neither do the Gardners. But—"

Allison's phone rang, and she held up a finger to ask Nicole to wait. "Hello?"

"Hey, Allison, it's Joyce over at Child Protective Services. I thought I'd give you an update about the little girl you found downtown during the evacuation. We were finally able to locate her family."

"What? Are you saying Estella has been in foster care this whole time?" Allison's heart sank as she wondered what it had been like for her, all alone with a new set of strangers. At work, Allison had managed to put the girl out of her thoughts. It all seemed like a dream, anyway, picking up a toddler and running through the streets while the city went crazy around her. Now it was as if Estella were again clinging to her trustingly, looking up at Allison with her dark eyes.

"It turns out Estella's mother's not in the country legally, so she was afraid to come forward."

"Oh." Allison let the news sink in. "So what happens next?"

"We'll give the child back to her and let them go on with their lives. We're not ICE." ICE was Immigration and Customs Enforcement. "Estella was born here, so she's a citizen, which means she doesn't fall under ICE's jurisdiction, anyway. Her mother may be subject to deportation, but it's not our job to start that process. We're all about reuniting families, not separating them. And the girl seems well cared for."

"Have you met the mom?"

"Just this morning. Her name's Ana. She asked about you. She is overwhelmingly grateful that you tried to help her daughter. She kept crying and grabbing my hand and praising God. She wants to thank you. I told her I needed to check with you before I gave out any information."

Allison didn't have to think twice. "Give her my phone number, my address—anything she wants." Part of her had been hoping she might see Estella again. "So what's the mom's story?"

"Ana got a tourist visa eight years ago, but then just stayed on. It's only one of the reasons we didn't hear from her until now. She also doesn't speak much English, and she doesn't have Internet access. She works as a cleaning lady for private citizens. She never married Estella's father, who doesn't have contact with the girl. Estella's babysitter—who is also her cousin—was with her

242

downtown when the two got separated. The cousin's not legal either." Joyce sighed. "The same kind of situation happened on 9/11. Several dozen undocumented immigrants died in the Twin Towers: deliverymen, busboys, janitors, construction workers. It took a long time to figure out about them too. Relatives were reluctant to come forward."

"What happens if the authorities do catch up with Ana?"

"Mexicans without papers are automatically deported. Some people think these kids are 'anchor babies,' but it doesn't work that way. It doesn't matter that the kids are citizens. Three million American children have at least one parent who is illegal. But if you're here illegally, whether your kids are legal or not, you'll still be deported if you're caught. And if that happens, the only way your children can stay in America is if you leave them with someone who is a citizen. And the kids can't appeal for their parents to become citizens until they themselves turn twenty-one."

In Oregon, nearly every person holding a leaf blower or a broom had a brown face. And then there was all the produce that was grown in the state. Cherries, apples, potatoes, pears, strawberries, peas, beans—none of it could be grown and harvested without the help of illegal immigrants. Allison didn't know what the solution was. Some people said Americans didn't want such back-breaking work, others that they would willingly take the jobs if they paid more, still others that the farmers couldn't afford to pay ten dollars an hour.

And in the middle was a sweet little girl who hadn't had any say on where she was born.

CHAPTER 32
Mark O. Hatfield United States Courthouse
Saturday, February 11

Congressman Quentin Glover didn't come to his meeting with Allison and Nicole alone. Michael Stone, Portland's most high-profile lawyer, was at his side. Allison was careful to keep her face neutral. She had tangled with Stone before.

Stone was the go-to guy for people with deep pockets who were in deep doo-doo. If you were accused of paying to have sex with a child, or if you were a doctor fighting a malpractice case that had left a mother and baby dead, or a parent whose teenager had shot a cop, then Stone was the guy you wanted sitting at the defense table. It was rumored that he never took a vacation, never took a day off, never even slept.

Stone was as famous for his expensive suits as he was for his high-profile clients. Today he was dapper in charcoal pinstripes. His black shoes were like individual works of art. In her two-inch heels, Allison was eye to eye with Stone's intense, ice-blue gaze.

Quentin Glover didn't cut nearly as impressive a figure. He had a ring of graying brown hair and a potbelly ill concealed by what appeared to be an off-the-rack suit.

"How you ladies doin'?" Stone said as he shook their hands, his teeth gleaming against his tan face. After they had all murmured pleasantries, Allison led them into a conference room that overlooked the Willamette River.

"We appreciate your coming in to talk to us, Congressman Glover," she said after everyone was settled. "We're talking to many people who knew Jim Fate, in the hope that they can help shed some light on what happened to him."

"Whatever I can do to help." Glover offered them a smile that left as quickly as it had come.

"Why don't you start by telling us about your relationship with Jim Fate," Nicole said.

Stone gave Glover an encouraging nod.

"He went to college with my wife, Lael. When I met him, we clicked. We were good friends for years. We went out to dinner, golfed, even went salmon fishing together. Even after everything that's happened, I'm shocked that he's dead. It's pretty unbelievable."

"You said you 'were' friends," Allison observed.

"It's no secret that we had had a falling-out." Glover shook his head ruefully. "In fact, anyone who has seen those ridiculous commercials or listened to Jim's show in the last few weeks would probably be surprised to learn that we had ever *been* friends."

"And what caused this falling-out?" Nicole asked.

"What Jim would tell you about that and what the truth was are two entirely different things." He sighed.

Allison was sure that every word, every hesitation, had been rehearsed with Stone. "What do you mean?"

"A couple of years ago, it came out in the media that I had had a brief relationship with a female aide." Glover cleared his throat and looked away. "I came clean about it and asked forgiveness from my constituents and my wife. I was reelected, and Lael forgave me." He shook his head. "Jim never did. As a result, he's tried to make out that a few simple paperwork errors my accountant made were some kind of elaborate kickback scheme. He's been harping on it so much that the real media have picked it up, and now even the House Ethics Committee is involved. When it's totally ridiculous. I paid every bill that was ever presented to me. But Jim didn't care if the allegations were true or false. He had already turned against me. Jim always liked my wife. Maybe more than he should have."

This was a new angle. Allison said, "I've been looking over the transcripts from *The Hand of*

Fate. In the last forty shows, he mentioned your name in thirty-two of them. How did you feel about that?"

Glover shrugged. "We all have our roles to play. I guess Jim decided to forget that he was ever my friend. He tried to build himself up by tearing me down. Anything for ratings. Of course, Lael doesn't speak to him anymore. It's been stressful, not just for me, but for my whole family."

"And Quentin's mother just passed away from cancer," Stone added.

Glover gave a sharp shake of his head. "I don't want to bring that up. I'm not looking for any sympathy."

"I'm so sorry," Allison said. "Was your mother in a lot of pain?" It was just a hunch, but she followed it. Sometimes it paid to trust your gut.

He snorted. "With bone cancer? Of course she was. Even the pain patches didn't touch it." He started to say something more, but Stone cut him off.

"I'm sorry, we've wandered off course. We're here to talk about Jim Fate."

Pain patches. And the medical examiner had said that Fate had died from some kind of opiate. As soon as this interview was over, Allison would request a subpoena to conduct a search of everything connected to Glover. It would take about an hour to prepare and get it to the judge, and she didn't want to give Glover time to destroy evidence.

She put her hand to her brow, making a face as if she were in pain. She needed an excuse they wouldn't question. But Stone was shrewd. He would sniff out a lie in a second, so she had to tell something close to the truth. "Would you gentlemen mind if we postponed this interview?" Allison said. "I'm not feeling well."

Nicole's face showed nothing. Only her eyes narrowed, almost imperceptibly.

"Are you all right?" Stone put on a look of concern.

Allison took a deep breath. "The doctors have been running some tests." She thought of how they checked her blood sugar at each prenatal visit. "I haven't disclosed this to anyone, so I'm relying on your discretion."

Both men nodded, losing focus, Allison hoped, on exactly what they had been talking about when the break in the interview occurred.

"I hope everything turns out okay." Glover seemed genuinely worried.

"I hope we can reschedule," Allison said, "and continue this at a later date."

"Of course, of course," Stone said, while Glover nodded.

Once the two women were alone in Allison's office, Nicole raised one eyebrow. "Running some tests?"

"It wasn't a lie." Allison felt a little defensive.

"Uh-huh." Nicole nodded, tweaking her a little. "And it should keep them from thinking about what we just learned. Glover's mother was on a pain patch—and I think that's usually some kind of opiate." Dialing a number from memory, she pressed the button for the speakerphone.

"Tony, it's Nic. And Allison Pierce is here with me. Hey, have you figured out what killed Fate yet?"

His voice floated up to them. "Are you worried that I'm holding out on you? I'll let you know as soon as I do. The lab is still working on coming up with a match. It would help if we had any clues as to what drug might be involved."

"I've just learned something. Congressman Glover's mother was living with him and his wife until recently. And then she died."

Tony's tone was puzzled. "Are you saying you think he killed his mother?"

"What I'm saying is that she had cancer. And she was on pain patches."

"Pain patches? That has to have been fentanyl." There was a long pause as Tony considered it. "Someone could scrape the fentanyl off the patches, dissolve it in rubbing alcohol, and then aerosolize it. It's possible."

Allison and Nicole exchanged a look.

"We'll check it out and see if it's a match, but that's going to take several days. But right now, I have to tell you I kind of like the idea."

249

Just showing that the drug was fentanyl wouldn't be enough to prove that Glover had done it. They needed more evidence. They had to work fast and hope that Glover wasn't one step ahead of them. Allison hurriedly drafted an affidavit for Nicole to swear off on. When it was done, they would take it to a judge to get search warrants for Glover's car, offices, and homes, both in Portland and in DC.

"What are you doing?" Allison asked Nicole as she put the finishing touches on the affidavit.

Nicole had been absolutely silent, tapping away on her laptop.

"I had a hunch, so I googled *Glover* and *smoke grenades*. Look at this." She handed over her computer to Allison. "It's a press release put out by Glover's office two years ago."

Congress Passes Funding for Oregon Defense Project

Congressman Quentin Glover has secured $2 million to replenish training and operational stocks of the M18 Grenade produced at Oregon's Umatilla Arsenal. The M18 Grenade is a small handheld grenade, approximately the size of a soup can, that emits a dense colored smoke and is used by all military services for signaling, marking, or screening operations. The M18 Smoke Grenade has been in high demand as a result of the wars in

250

Afghanistan and Iraq. Congressman Glover was honored for his support at an event in Umatilla.

Allison looked up at Nicole. Quentin Glover had just become their prime suspect.

CHAPTER 33
Channel 4 TV

The cameraman counted down with his fingers, and then Cassidy was on. Brad was sitting next to her, but this was her segment, and the camera focused only on her.

Even covering the gas leak downtown had been easier than this. But Allison had called to offer encouragement—and give a tantalizing hint about Glover—and even Nicole had sent a quick e-mail wishing her luck.

Cassidy took a deep breath. "These days, everywhere you look there are heart decorations and candy-filled displays. Valentine's Day is rapidly approaching. On the big day, many of us expect affection, romance, roses, chocolates, dinner out—or at least a card. But for others, the day only brings anxiety, fear, and violence. One in three women will experience domestic violence in her lifetime." She paused to give her words added weight. "I know, because I was one of these women."

Cassidy lifted her chin and looked directly into the camera. "Why am I coming forward now? To help others who are in the same horrible place I was. These victims need validation. They need to know they aren't alone. While I was dating my ex-boyfriend, I felt so isolated. I was in the public eye, but I felt cut off from everyone. Over time, my self-esteem was completely destroyed." She was thankful that her makeup hid the purple shadows under her eyes. Last night she had needed two and a half pills before she finally slept.

"My ex-boyfriend manipulated me and got under my skin. He took every grain of confidence I had. He called me names. He belittled me. And eventually he began to hit me. He also isolated me from my family and friends. The emotional manipulation took longer to get over than the bruises."

Cassidy took a deep breath. "I have decided to speak out to help any of our viewers who are being hurt and who will hear this broadcast. You need to know that you don't have to live in pain and isolation. You are not alone. I have stood in your shoes, I have walked the paths you are walking, and I managed to come out on the other side. I've reclaimed my life, and you can too."

With every word, Cassidy felt lighter. It had been a big, scary step to charge Rick with assault. But now she was the one who had the power. She was taking the skills she used every day at work—researching and telling a compelling story—and turning them into weapons against the man who had first proclaimed his love for her, then terrorized her. She imagined him sitting at home, watching her, grinding his teeth in impotent anger. And even if he wasn't watching, she was sure word would get back to him. All of his friends had known he was dating Channel 4's Cassidy Shaw. Rick had liked to show her off.

"Domestic violence can include sexual assault and physical violence. But it often starts small, with emotional abuse. Does your partner tell you that you are stupid, ugly, and unlovable? Does he insist that you no longer have contact with your friends and family? That is abuse. And the frightening thing about domestic violence is that it escalates. The abuser may destroy items you love. He—or even she—may threaten or actually harm your pets. May take control of your money. And the abuser may eventually attack you. The sad fact is that in America, a woman is at much greater risk of dying at the hands of a loved one than a stranger's.

"But we can break the cycle of domestic violence that is destroying our families, devastating our communities, and adding to an already overcrowded prison population. It begins with making a personal commitment to get involved if you suspect someone you know is affected. Yes, it is difficult. You might feel that it's not your business or that you don't know how to help. But if you don't reach out, it's possible that no one will.

"You can help by listening, without judging. When a person is being abused, she feels responsible, ashamed, and inadequate. She is afraid she'll be judged. I know I was." Cassidy nodded thoughtfully as she spoke. "But again, you can help by telling the victim that the abuse is not her fault. And that there is no excuse for violence—not alcohol or drugs, not being under financial pressure or being depressed, and certainly not any behavior of the victim's.

"Tell her she is not alone. Let her know that domestic violence tends to get worse and become more frequent with time, and that it rarely goes away on its own. And give your friend the number for the National Domestic Violence Hotline: 1-800-799-SAFE.

"Domestic violence is a brutal crime that can be prevented if we join hands. Hands are for holding, not hitting. Remember that this year on Valentine's Day."

After Cassidy walked out of the studio, staffers broke into spontaneous applause. People clapped her on the back, thanked her for her courage, and smiled at her.

She went into the bathroom. In the stall, she sat on the toilet and rested her head against the cool metal wall for a few blessed minutes. It was over.

She had done it. She had come forward and shared the secret that had paralyzed her for weeks.

Back in her office, Cassidy opened her work e-mail. The station had long made a practice of listing e-mail addresses for all of the on-air talent. Viewers responded by sending an amazing number of tips, photos, and videos. It took her e-mail a few seconds to open up, and when it finally did, Cassidy blinked. More than one hundred messages filled her in-box.

The first one heartened her. "You are so brave for coming forward and giving voice to the voiceless. Thank you for inspiring others."

Feeling much lighter, she clicked on the next e-mail.

"You're a fat whore" was all it said. And signed, strangely enough, Your fan.

The next few e-mails Cassidy opened continued to alternately delight and horrify her. But even though the vast majority were good comments, they did not hold as much weight as the bad, at least as far as Cassidy was concerned. People remarked on how she looked, acted, dressed, and even her age, calling her old and washed-up. It was as if, by opening up her own life to viewers, she had shown that she was just like them, and had only been pretending to be someone who deserved to be on camera. Who deserved to tell others the news.

Cassidy had thought she would be helping

others. But now she wondered—had she only hurt herself?

She had thought that her viewers would love her more for knowing that she had faced adversity and ultimately triumphed. Instead, many of them mocked her for it.

Had they ever loved her at all?

CHAPTER 34
Chapel Pub
Sunday, February 12

Nic sat with her back to the wall. She liked it that way. Something solid and impenetrable against her shoulder blades. And facing the door. She always wanted to see what was coming.

She was wearing jeans and a long-sleeved red shirt. Long-sleeved because her left arm was a wreck—bruised, cut, scraped—from all the elbow work she had been learning from her Thai boxing trainer. Out of old habit, Nic rested her hand over her glass of beer when she wasn't drinking it. Chapel Pub was nothing like the bars she had gone to when she was fresh out of college. Those had been dimly lit, with dance music thumping in the background. This place had white walls, dark rafters, and worn Oriental carpets, with plenty of babies and retired folks. If there was music, she couldn't hear it.

On a TV in the corner, she caught a glimpse of

Cassidy with an inset of Congressman Glover over her left shoulder. The lab had taken away boxes and boxes from his offices, homes, and cars, and was now painstakingly processing the evidence, looking for paper and fiber matches. Among the evidence were a number of fentanyl pain patches. But no smoke grenades.

Nic was so nervous she felt like she might explode. Or possibly implode. Or just shatter. But she had promised that she would be here.

The main door opened, and Leif walked through. His eyes found hers in an instant. He smiled, and warmth spread through Nic.

"Hey." He sat down and poured a glass from the pitcher she had ordered. "I see you thought ahead. I'll get the next one."

"This is my limit," she said. "And that's kind of why I need to talk to you. There are things you need to know about me. Before anything happens." She wanted to add "between us," but now it seemed too presumptuous. Her hands were slick, and she wiped them on the thighs of her jeans, glad they were hidden by the table. She sighed. "Look, I don't tell people this, okay? I don't tell *anyone*. And I would never tell someone at the Bureau."

Leif laid his hands flat on the table and leaned forward. "I'm not talking to you as a special agent, Nicole. I'm talking to you as a friend. This is for my ears only."

She looked into his light-colored eyes and thought of another pair of eyes, green ones, and her stomach twisted. Wanting to trust Leif, not knowing if she could or should. "The only person who knows everything is my mama." She dropped her gaze again. "And even she doesn't know everything."

Leif nodded. He didn't raise his beer to his lips, and his eyes never left her face.

"It was the summer after I graduated from college. I was still deciding what I wanted to do. I was thinking about going to law school, or getting an MBA. Maybe even going to medical school. I probably could have done anything. I know that sounds vain, but I'm good at school. But nothing really called to me. And it's not like employers were beating down doors to hire an English major. In the meantime, I was working as a waitress and living at home, saving money while I figured out what I wanted to do. One night I served these two guys just before closing. One was black and one was white. They were funny, smart, nice. At least they seemed that way." She could feel her upper lip curling as she spoke. "They invited me to have a drink with them at the bar next door after I got off work. I said yes." She swallowed. "That's how stupid I was."

"Nic," Leif protested softly.

She continued as if he hadn't spoken. "I remember having one drink. I remember ordering a second drink. After that, I don't really know what happened. Somehow I must have gotten home and made it into my bed. I woke up the next morning wearing all my clothes, but my panties were on inside out. I should have realized what that meant, but at the time I thought it was just one more weird thing I had managed while I was drunk, like getting home and not remembering it. Like getting bruises on my wrist but not remembering what happened.

"The next day I had a terrible headache, but I just assumed it was a hangover. But that night, the nightmares started. I woke up screaming, sweating. And it was the same thing the next night. And the next. Sometimes I cried. Sometimes Mama woke me up because I had woken her and Daddy up. The only thing about the dreams that I remembered was that I felt like I was trapped. Like something was on top of me. Crushing me."

Leif was completely still. His face could have been carved from stone. His eyes looked directly into hers.

"I thought it was the stress of trying to decide what to do with my life. My period was late, but I hadn't had sex in over a year. Finally I bought a test, even though I knew it couldn't be true. I just didn't want to believe I was that kind of girl. Some drunk slut."

Wincing, Leif shook his head, but Nic was caught up in her memories.

The grocery store had been full of pregnant women. Some lumbered, while others sported cute little bumps. One woman, belly jutting alarmingly ahead of her, sauntered along on four-inch heels Nic could never have worn, pregnant or not. She bought the cheapest pregnancy test, so generic it didn't even have a name.

At home, she made sure the bathroom door was locked before she peed on the white stick. A moment later, she watched the first pink line form. According to the instructions, that meant the test was working. When the second line began to appear, at first Nic told herself that she was imagining it. It wasn't that dark. It must be a false positive. She couldn't be pregnant. Not really.

Nic looked at the instructions again. Any line, no matter how faint, meant it was positive.

She called the advice nurse. "Is it possible it's a false positive?"

"Bless your heart," the nurse said.

Something inside Nic died.

Then the nurse added, "May I ask you something? Are you married?"

Instead of answering, Nic had hung up.

Now she told Leif, "I was going to have an abortion. I felt like garbage. Like a whore. I felt like everyone could tell, just by looking at me, what I had done."

Leif looked at her, bit his lip, looked away. Was he ashamed of her, embarrassed by her?

"Then my mama found me throwing up in the bathroom and figured out what was going on. You have to understand, my family is religious."

"And you're not?" Leif asked gently.

She thought of how she had begged God to make it not so, to take it away so that she could go back to her old life. "Not anymore, no. I don't want any part of a God that would let things like what happened, happen. If that's a problem for you"—her eyes flashed up to his—"then it's good you know it now."

"I'm listening," he said softly. "I'm not going anywhere."

"So my mama quoted some psalm to me, about how God knits babies together in their mothers' wombs. I tried to tell her it was just a blob of tissue. See, at that point, we both thought the same thing. That I had gotten drunk and made a mistake. We didn't know the rest. My mama and my daddy and my pastor—they all said people would help with the baby, that I could go back to school later, that God had given me this baby for a reason. And I listened to them. And then—and then the other shoe dropped when I was five months along and it was too late to do anything."

"What was the other shoe?"

"These two guys—Roy Kirk and Donny Miller—were arrested after a housekeeper found a videotape, still in the player, of them having sex with a passed-out woman. Roy had stacks of tapes like that, but only two of them had Miller too. When I saw their photos in the paper, I came forward. I wanted to see my tape." She took a deep, shaky breath. "But there wasn't one."

He put his hand over his eyes and asked, "What did they use, do you think?"

"At the trial, they said GHB."

Leif sucked air through his teeth and dropped his hand to the table. Colorless and odorless, GHB, or gamma-hydroxybutyrate, had a slightly salty taste that was easily disguised. A few drops could render a person close to unconscious for four hours or more, leaving them with little or no memory of events. And GHB exited the body within twelve hours, so victims were often tested too late. Five months after the fact, any proof would have been long gone.

Leif's low voice was edged with bitterness. "Yeah, why bother to use a gun or a knife when you can slip something into the drink of the girl of your choice? Not only will she not fight back; she won't even remember being attacked."

"You say that, but inside, even when everyone else started calling it a rape, I knew it was my fault. I had flirted and laughed with them. I had gone to the bar with them when they suggested it."

He groaned. "Nic, no."

"And now I was going to have a baby whose father was a monster. In an odd way, I felt sorry for it. For the baby. No one cared about it. I was its mother, and I didn't want it. I told Mama I was going to give it up for adoption. I couldn't raise it."

She remembered Berenice's reaction.

"Nicole, no," Mama had protested, dropping the wooden spoon she had been stirring a pot of soup with. "Have you prayed about it?"

Nic had straightened up. Anger shot through her, from the top of her head to the tips of her fingers. She felt more alive than she had since the night it had happened.

"Prayed about it? What kind of God would let two animals rape me in the first place? They drugged me and they used me like a piece of Kleenex. I don't care what God thinks. He didn't protect me. It's up to me to make decisions now."

"Oh, Nicole, don't say that!" Mama put her hand to her chest. Her eyes were bright with tears. "Look, when our people were slaves, many, many children were conceived in rape or from forced breeding. But those mothers still loved those children."

"Mama, I'm not a slave. And I can't do it. If I keep it, what kind of life will I give it? What will I tell people who want to know who the father is?"

"You just hold your head up high and say you are the mother *and* the father."

"And when the child asks me who the father is?

What then? A child can't live with that burden. A child can't live knowing that their father is the devil."

Mama reached up and put her hand on Nic's shoulder. "You just keep it simple. You just say that their father made a mistake and hurt you. But that you love them, no matter what."

Nic twisted until her mama's hand fell away. "I can't. It's not this child's fault, but it needs to be where it will be wanted and loved."

"And that's why you should keep the baby," Berenice had said. "*You're* the mother."

Now Leif said, "But you did keep her."

Nic sighed. "When my daughter was born, I was afraid if I held her it would make things worse, since I was giving her up. But then my mother held her, and the baby cried. The nurse held her, and she just squalled. Then finally the nurse brought the baby to me. She had just come on her shift, and I don't think anyone had told her I was giving the baby up. I reached out"—she demonstrated, holding up her empty arms—"and touched Makayla lightly on the forehead. She stopped crying right away and looked—I don't know—interested. She seemed to know me and be secure with me. And suddenly I was filled with love for this beautiful, innocent little creature. And maybe it wasn't fair to the parents who were going to adopt her, and maybe it wasn't fair to my daughter, but I decided to keep her. And she is the light of my life. She's one of two good things that came out of that horrible day."

"So what happened to those two guys?" Leif asked, looking grim.

"Kirk and Miller? Kirk got twenty-five years. Miller got thirteen." She had wanted to kick their teeth down their throats for ruining the lives of so many women. Instead, the resolution had hardened in her that no one would ever take advantage of her again.

"Did you testify?" The pain in Leif's eyes somehow made it easier for her to go on.

"In the end, they decided my case wasn't strong enough without video evidence. They had those other women on tape, and they testified. Before that, they had done a DNA test while I was still pregnant and determined paternity. It showed it was Miller's baby. But of course, he's not really Makayla's father. Not in the real sense of the word."

"Does she know?"

Nic shrugged and made a sound that was something like a laugh. "Actually, she's never asked me. I keep rehearsing what I'm going to say when she does. Sometimes I wonder if she knows I don't want her to."

Leif's expression softened. "What's your daughter like?"

"She's smart. Straight A's. Spunky. A little sassy. She's tall. Last summer, I had a couple of people

265

from modeling agencies ask me to give them a call."

"Did you do it?"

"No way. I don't want her to end up with a job where sooner or later people tell you that you're not thin enough, not pretty enough." Her stomach clenched. "She got the height from Miller. He's tall, like you."

Leif winced. "Does he know that she's his child?"

"He might. Even though my case was considered non-prosecutable, my name and the information about the pregnancy were in the pretrial discovery that Miller's attorney got. But he's never tried to contact me."

Leif's eye's narrowed. "You said he got thirteen years. How old is your daughter?"

"Ten. The thing is, Miller got paroled two weeks ago and put on electronic monitoring. They didn't even notify me until yesterday."

"Wait—he's here?"

"In Medford. It's where his mom lives." Medford was five hours to the south.

"Do you think he'll try to come up here?" Leif's hands tightened into fists.

"I don't think so. He's wearing a GPS monitor. Even if he wants to get revenge, I'm not one of the women who put him in prison."

"You said two good things came out of what happened." Leif touched the back of her hand with

266

the tip of his finger, and Nic felt it all the way down to her bones. And she didn't shatter. Instead, it felt like something inside her began to knit together. "What was the other?"

"During the course of the investigation, I was interviewed by a special agent, because Roy had raped girls in three states. That agent made a big impression on me. And when Makayla was two, I applied to join the Bureau. But I never talk about her father. To anyone. People have no right to know. And if someone asks, I just give them this look I have, and they don't ask again."

"You know what we call that look?" Leif's voice broke with relieved laughter. "The death stare."

CHAPTER 35
Channel 4 TV
Monday, February 13

Quentin Glover called a press conference at 12:15 to, quote, provide an update on the situation, end quote," Eric said at Channel 4's morning staff meeting.

"He's going to resign," Brad said with certainty. "That search warrant must have turned up something."

When Cassidy saw how adoringly Jenna regarded him, it was hard to keep from gagging.

"It's possible," Eric agreed. "Cassidy, I'm sending you and Andy over to cover it. We'll run it live on the noon news. Glover was already looking at jail time for his financial shenanigans, but there are rumors this is connected to Jim Fate's murder."

Cassidy felt a grim satisfaction. She had never liked Glover. Cassidy hated politics. Show her a politician, and as far as she was concerned, show her a liar. And now, it seemed, quite likely a murderer as well. If so, she couldn't wait to cover his trial and sentencing. It wouldn't bring Jim back, of course, but it might restore some balance to the universe.

An idea nagged at her, but when she tried to pin it down, it flew away. Something about Jim. Something she had seen recently that didn't seem quite right. But what was it?

The press conference was packed, but Cassidy judiciously used her elbows and high heels to maneuver her way to the front. Glover looked bad, sweaty and pale, his eyes wide as he faced two dozen microphones.

Looking at him, Cassidy felt zero sympathy. Let him suffer. Whatever anguish he was experiencing was nothing compared to what he had put Jim through.

"Some of you are probably here today expecting to see me slink away in defeat. But I won't."

Glover shook his head so hard that Cassidy saw a drop of sweat fly off his face.

"I want to repeat that I am innocent of these

accusations. I will not resign from the post that Oregonians have entrusted me with. I have been granted fifty-two years of exciting challenges and stimulating experiences and, most of all, the finest wife and children any man could ever desire. Now my life has changed because of a politically driven vendetta. That hack, Jim Fate, would not let up despite the lack of evidence. He did his best to destroy me and my family."

There was absolute silence in the room.

"Well, I'm happy to say that Jim's no longer here to badger me." Glover smiled, but it was more of a grimace. "But when those flapping gums of his were finally closed for good, the FBI, in its incompetence and its continued drive to persecute me, fixated on punishing me. So Jim continues to taunt me even from beyond the grave. I've come to realize that there is nothing I can do to escape these lies and slanders. Even though the man who set them into motion has been stopped, they still continue to spread, like the cancer that they are." A red stain spread up Glover's cheeks.

"Some people have been calling and e-mailing and telling me that they believe me. They know I'm innocent, that I never took a single dollar and that I certainly did not take Jim Fate's life. These people want to help. But in this nation, the world's greatest democracy, there is nothing they can do to prevent me from being prosecuted for crimes they know I did not commit. Jim Fate set into motion a juggernaut of political persecution and smears that have not only brought me pain, but have also hurt my family, friends, and colleagues! I had to watch my mother spend her last few weeks in agony because she couldn't believe the things Jim was saying about me." His words were coming faster, so fast he was almost spitting.

"Jim brought his own death on himself by the hate and lies he spewed. But while I understood the reasons behind it, I did not cause it. I have done nothing wrong. I ask those who believe in me to continue to extend friendship and prayer to my family, to work untiringly for the creation of a true justice system here in the United States, and to press on with the efforts to vindicate me, so that my family is not tainted by this injustice that has been perpetrated on me."

From the podium, with its Medusa head of microphones, he took three manila envelopes, two slender, one bulky. He looked off to one side. "John, could you take these, please?" One of Glover's staffers, appearing confused, stepped forward to take the two thin envelopes. And then Glover picked up the third and ripped it open. The crowd gasped.

It was a gun.

His face now oddly peaceful as he picked it up, Glover said calmly, "Please leave the room if this will offend you."

Around Cassidy, everyone pressed back.

John yelled, "Quentin, don't do this!" Others called out, "This isn't right, Quentin!" and "Quentin, listen to me!"

Glover held up one hand, signaling them to stop, while the other pointed the gun at the ceiling. "Don't try to take it, or someone will get hurt," he warned.

Cassidy felt like she was watching herself. It was as though the intervening weeks had never happened, and she was back in the home of the murdered Senate page, Katie Converse, with her eyes fixed on a gun. She couldn't move, couldn't even draw a breath.

Twisting his hand so that the gun was upside-down, Glover slipped the barrel into his mouth. People gasped and cried out.

Before anyone could move, he pulled the trigger and fell back against the wall. He slid down the wall until he was in a sitting position, his legs splayed in front of him. Blood poured from his nose and the exit wound at the top of his head.

All around Cassidy, people were screaming and swearing and crying out in shock. A few ran toward Glover as if to render first aid, but it was clear he was dead.

Come on! Half his head is gone, Cassidy thought, not moving. And then she had a terrible thought. Hadn't Eric said that Channel 4 would broadcast this live?

CHAPTER 36
Pastini Pastaria
Wednesday, February 15

Allison met Nicole outside Pastini's. "Have you seen Cassidy yet?" Allison asked.

Nicole was just shaking her head when Cassidy pulled her car up next to them. She got out, nearly getting run over in the process, seemingly oblivious to the honks and squealing brakes. On the sidewalk, she gave them each a hug. Underneath Allison's palms, her body seemed to hum. Cassidy had been through so much lately. Standing a few feet from a killer as he shot himself could not have helped her already stressed mental state.

"Cassidy, you can't park here," Nicole pointed out. "It's a fifteen-minute zone." The three of them squeezed closer to the car to let a mom with a double stroller pass by.

"I'll move it in a second," Cassidy said as she opened the passenger door and pushed the seat forward to reach into the back of the car. "Nicole, I just want to give you your birthday present before I forget. I know it's not for ten days, but with everyone's schedules being so busy . . ."

Allison felt a twinge of guilt. She had been so preoccupied with catching Jim Fate's killer that she hadn't given any thought to Nicole's upcoming birthday. The two of them watched as

Cassidy began to paw through the detritus that covered her front passenger seat: granola bar wrappers, a pair of Nikes, a tube of mascara, an umbrella, a crumpled McDonald's bag, and a couple of *People* magazines.

"It was just here," she complained, leaning in farther.

Cassidy had always aspired to be bone thin and worked hard to maintain a weight that Allison privately thought too low and Cassidy publicly felt was never low enough. But now it looked like she had given up the fight. Her narrow skirt was far too tight.

Allison turned to see if Nicole was registering the same thing. But instead of looking at Cassidy, Nicole was transfixed by something else inside the car. Allison followed her gaze. In between the seats was a cup holder that held, not a coffee cup, but a small dish of change. With something slightly larger resting on top.

"Here it is," Cassidy declared, unearthing a pink package about the size of a deck of cards. As she was straightening up, Nicole was leaning into the car.

"Hey!" Cassidy said in surprise as Nicole stood up again. All of them looked at the silver earring, shaped like a Chinese character, that now rested on Nicole's outstretched palm.

"What is this?" To Allison's ear, Nicole's voice was ominously casual.

Cassidy shrugged. "Half a pair of earrings. I don't know where I lost the other one. They're handmade, so I don't want to just toss it. I figure the minute I do, I'll find the missing one at the bottom of my purse or something."

"I've seen one just like this recently."

"Do you remember where? Because I would love to be able to wear them again."

"The one I saw is in an evidence bag," Nicole said without inflection. "Leif found it under Jim Fate's bed."

Cassidy's mouth made a small, round *O*.

"Tell me what you were doing there," Nicole demanded. "And in his bedroom."

"It's not what you think." Cassidy lowered her voice, and the three of them made a tight little knot on the sidewalk, no longer noticing the passersby.

"Oh no, Cassidy," Allison said, her heart sinking. "What do you mean that it's not what we think?"

"Jim and I have known each other for a long time. He wanted me to quit Channel 4 and take over Victoria Hanawa's job."

"What?" said Allison. Part of her couldn't believe it. Part of her realized it fit everything they had learned so far.

"So we made a recording at his condo like we were doing a show together. I went back there the morning he died so I could take it off his computer before anyone else found it." She looked from Nicole to Allison, seeking understanding. "I had already turned Jim down, but Channel 4 would have fired me if they had ever found out about it. I could have lost my job for nothing!"

"And you didn't think this information was worth telling us?" Nicole's eyes were blazing. "We've been searching for the woman the neighbor told us about, the mysterious blonde who left his apartment—and it was you, wasn't it? You lied to us, Cassidy. You said you were just friends with Jim. And you never told us that he wanted you to take over Victoria Hanawa's job."

"We *were* just friends. Basically. Jim wanted to be something more, but I didn't, which is where the earring must have come off. And I didn't tell you that I had been there because I didn't want you to think of me as a suspect."

"You withheld evidence, Cassidy! The fact that he offered you Victoria's job would have pointed toward Victoria being the killer."

Cassidy scuffed her toe on the sidewalk, looking like a five-year-old caught in a lie. "But I was worried about my job. I didn't realize that telling you about Jim and me would have pointed the finger at Victoria. But it worked out okay. You solved it."

Allison sighed. "Look, Cassidy, we can't keep secrets from one another. Not about important things."

She hung her head, her blonde hair falling on either side of her face like two wings. "I know. I'm sorry. I just didn't think it through."

Despite the apology, there was still a jangly feeling among them as they went inside. Nicole unwrapped her present—a bracelet made of polished tiger's-eye stones—and unfroze a little bit as she thanked Cassidy. When the waitress came, Allison ordered the ziti vegetariano, Nicole the linguini with chicken piccata, and Cassidy the ziti con molta carne.

After the waitress left, Cassidy asked, "Were you surprised when it turned out to be Glover?"

Allison said, "Surprised is maybe not the right word. And in some ways Glover's death makes things easier. Despite everything he's done, Glover still has some fans in this state. It would have been hard to find an impartial jury. And hard to convict him based on circumstantial evidence. But the fact remains that he hated Jim for good reasons, and his mother was on the same type of drug that killed Fate, and he had access to smoke grenades. The lab tests still aren't finished on Fate's blood, but I guess now it will be moot. The task force has already been disbanded. Now it's just Nicole and me tying up the loose ends."

"What was in the other two envelopes?" Cassidy asked. "The ones Glover handed to his aide?"

"One was his organ donor card. The other was a

suicide note." Allison had read it so often that she had it memorized.

The media and the FBI have accused me of so many things. In their bureaucratic world, there are no shades of gray, only black and white. In their false view, gifts from old friends became bribes. Cancers that needed to be cut out before they spread became fine, upstanding citizens, mourned by thousands. Personal matters were dragged out into the public square.

I think about my life and feel I've done most of the right things. I told the truth as I saw it. I paid what I was asked to pay. So why do I end up like this, with a target on my back? I can't go on. No matter what the outcome, people will look and point. I can't take that. I've only done what had to be done.

I'm sorry for what I've put my family through. You will be better off without me. I never meant to hurt you. My burden is so great that I can't go on with it any further.

Please, please, please, I ask the rest of you, please leave my children in peace.

"Do you think he was crazy?" Cassidy asked.

Nicole's mouth twisted. "Maybe crazy like a fox. Since Glover died in office before he was convicted of anything, his wife gets full survivor benefits from his pension. It turns out they don't have a suicide clause."

Their food came. Allison was tired of thinking

about Jim Fate, thinking about whether things really added up. She said, "I haven't had a chance to tell you yet, Cassidy, but I watched your piece on domestic violence. Good for you for coming forward. I mean, I volunteer at Safe Harbor, but that only helps one woman at a time. You offered hope to hundreds, maybe thousands of women."

Cassidy looked away. "I don't know if it was worth it. If I really got through. I should have thought about it more."

After a pause, Nicole said in a low voice, "Look, Cassidy, there was something I've been keeping to myself that I recently told one person. Just one. But it made me feel like it wasn't such a burden. Such a secret. Sometimes when you keep things to yourself, they feel heavier than they really are."

A spark finally lit up Cassidy's turquoise eyes. "So what was the secret?"

Allison was also intrigued. She guessed it had something to do with Leif.

"I promise I'll tell you guys sometime." Nicole looked past them. "Just not today."

Cassidy slumped back in her chair. "I keep thinking it would have been better if I had kept my mouth shut. People are accusing me of lying, imagining it. According to them, I'm crazy, jealous, vindictive, and a whore. And that's just the stuff I can say in public. I had to disable Google Alerts on my name, because all it was giving me were links to bloggers who call me fat or old or insane."

Allison bit her lip. "Aren't you hearing from other people, people who are glad that you came forward?"

With a shrug, Cassidy said, "Yeah. I mean, there are victims out there who say they're grateful that I spoke out. But in some ways I just feel like I made myself a target." She pressed her manicured fingers against her lips and was silent for a few seconds. "I've been thinking lately that I've been looking at things wrong. It's not like everyone out in viewer land loves me. It's not even like they know me. Not really. I mean, look at Jim. He didn't have any close friends, not really. His friends were like imaginary friends—all those people who tuned in to him every day. But that's not really a friendship. Not like what we have." She looked around the table, a smile trembling on her lips.

"So how are you dealing with all this?" Trying to forestall an automatic answer, Allison put her hand on Cassidy's wrist. "It seems like you've been right in the middle of every bad thing that's happened lately, from being friends with Jim Fate to being with Glover when he killed himself."

Cassidy blinked, and a tear ran from each eye.

"To be honest, I'm terrible. I've been having trouble sleeping for months. It started with Rick and then what happened at Katie Converse's house. Work has been awful. And everything has just snowballed since Jim died. He was the one who suggested I try taking Somulex so I could sleep better. Now I think I might be, well . . ." Her voice dropped to a near whisper: ". . . addicted."

Nicole leaned forward. "What do you mean?"

"I'm taking more than I should."

"But it's a prescription drug," Allison pointed out. "You should be able to only take so much."

Cassidy took a ragged breath. "But I take more than one doctor would prescribe. I'm actually going to three doctors now. None of them know about each other. I know it's stupid, but it's the only way I can get any sleep. But I've been doing some weird things. Like last night, I must have been sleepwalking. I woke up in the parking garage wearing just my pj's, and I was trying to open my car door with a fork! Thank goodness I was able to get back into my condo without anyone seeing me—but that was only because I had left the door wide-open. And the night that Jim died, I basically passed out in the bathtub after taking a couple of Somulex and then drinking wine."

"Oh, Cassidy," Allison said. "You need help now."

Cassidy's eyes flicked from one friend's face to the other's. "I can't—I'm too busy. There's too much going on."

"You're always going to be too busy," Nicole said matter-of-factly.

Allison squeezed Cassidy's wrist. "This is your life we're talking about, Cass. Look at you. You're shaking. You're not yourself anymore."

With a trembling hand, Cassidy raised her napkin to dab at her wet eyes. "I'm a professional. I tell myself I keep a distance between myself and what's going on. That it's not real. That's how I got through reporting from downtown when everyone thought it was terrorists. I just told myself that I had a job to do. That it didn't have anything to do with *me*." She poked herself in the chest. "But when I'm home alone at night, it all comes flooding back."

"You need to go to Narcotics Anonymous, girl," Nicole said. "They helped my brother turn his life around."

"She's right," Allison said. The only way Cassidy could conquer this was to turn it over to God, even if NA called Him "a higher power."

Nicole added, "When I get back to the office, I'll find out what meetings are near you and send you an e-mail."

Cassidy's back had gone rigid. "I'm not some junkie sticking a needle in my arm. I'm using a drug that was legally *prescribed* for me."

Nicole was unfazed. "NA is for anyone who has problems with drugs, street or legal. And anyone who is going to three doctors who don't know about each other certainly meets that definition."

"But there'd probably be people there who recognize me." Cassidy shook her head. "What if it
gets back to the station?"

"But in NA—," Nicole started to say, when
Allison's phone rang.

It was her office. She excused herself and took
the phone outside. Once there, she realized that
Cassidy had never reparked her car.

"Allison, I've got someone on the phone who says
he has to talk to you. But he won't tell me why."

"Who is it?"

"Chris Sorenson."

"Put him through . . . Chris?"

"Allison, I wanted to talk to you because I didn't
think anyone else would believe me."

"Believe you about what?"

"I've been watching the tapes of Glover's last
press conference."

Allison winced. "I wish they wouldn't keep
rebroadcasting it, even if they do cut away at the
end. It's ghoulish."

"The thing is," Chris said, "that's not his voice.
That's not Quentin Glover's voice at the press
conference."

"What? What do you mean?"

"Remember how I said Glover had called in
three or four times to threaten Jim? Whoever
called is not the same person who spoke at the
press conference."

"How can you be so sure?"

"Because I know voices." Chris's tone was matter-of-fact. "My whole job revolves around that."

Allison remembered his saying that he could recognize previously banned callers even if they called in on another person's phone.

"There's no doubt that was Glover who killed himself," she pointed out. "A hundred people were at that press conference, mostly reporters who'd been covering Glover for years. So that means whoever called you must have just pretended to be him."

"It was more than someone just pretending," Chris said. "The caller ID said it *was* Quentin Glover. It had his phone number, his name, everything. But I swear to you, it wasn't him."

Back in the restaurant, Allison found Cassidy calm, her tears wiped away. Nicole gave Allison a small nod that let her know that things were going in the right direction. And in front of them was a single plate filled with the restaurant's chocolate tartufo, a whipped cream–topped chocolate cake with a chocolate truffle center.

Nicole ceremoniously handed out the three forks. After first warning Cassidy that she couldn't run with this—at least not yet—Allison told them what Chris had said.

"The weird thing is that I believe him. But if it wasn't Glover who called the show, how could it say his name on the caller ID?"

"I think I know what happened," Nicole said slowly. "They used a spoof card."

"I can't remember what those are," Cassidy said.

"You can buy them on the Internet. They sell them for 'entertainment purposes only.'" Sarcasm colored Nicole's voice. "Right. Then you dial a toll-free number and key in the number you want to call and the caller ID number to display on the phone. On the other end, they see not only the fake phone number on the caller ID but even the name associated with that number."

"Isn't that illegal?" Cassidy asked.

"It's a gray area. Sometimes they're used for bad reasons. On the other hand, a social worker can use a spoof card to call an abused woman and spoof a safe number. That way the husband doesn't see a suspicious number on the caller ID."

Cassidy said, "But why would someone use a spoof card to make people think Glover was threatening Jim Fate?"

"To make us think Glover was the killer. I would bet the same person knew Glover helped get funding to make smoke grenades, and that gave them the idea to kill Fate with one." Nicole was speaking faster and faster as she began to connect the dots. "Karl tells me we haven't been able to match the grenade that killed Fate to any of the ones made here in Oregon. And so far, none of the carpet fibers from Glover's house, offices, or cars have matched the one in the package. We've got nothing that ties Glover to Fate except the fact that Fate kept riding him, and that Glover returned the favor by hating Jim's guts. And that he killed himself before we could ask too many questions."

"What if someone went to a lot of trouble to make sure all the clues pointed in Congressman Glover's direction?" Allison's words tumbled over each other. "What if they set him up—and then he snapped?"

CHAPTER 37
Mark O. Hatfield United States Courthouse

As soon as she got back to the office, Allison went to Dan and laid it all out for him. But as she spoke, she realized how insubstantial it was. All she had was one person's word that it wasn't Glover who had called the radio station to threaten Jim Fate. And even if that were true, there was still Glover's ready access to fentanyl pain patches, his connection to smoke grenades, his note that both denied and hinted at wrong-doing, and his last, desperate act of suicide as the net closed around him. Dan finally agreed to give the investigation more time, but he was clearly skeptical.

It was two in the afternoon before Allison finally went to the bathroom. And she saw blood. She stared at it stupidly, almost too tired to switch gears. How could there be blood?

On the phone, the nurse told Allison that she didn't need to worry unless the bleeding continued or she started to cramp. For the next hour Allison went through the motions of work, but her mind was on her belly. Was something wrong? Maybe. Did she feel crampy? Maybe. She went to the bathroom every few minutes. The bleeding wasn't slowing down. But it wasn't that much either. She tried to pray, but all she could manage was to touch the cross she wore around her neck, the one her father had given her, and think the word *Please*.

Finally she gave up and called the doctor's office again. They arranged for her to come in after work.

Then she called Marshall. "Can you meet me at Dr. Dubruski's at five?"

"Why?" His voice sharpened. "What's wrong? Is there something wrong with the baby?"

"It's probably nothing. I'm probably just imagining things." *Dear God, let it be true.* "I'm having a little bit of spotting, that's all. I just want to go in to be safe."

"I'll be there in five minutes. I'm taking you home so you can lie down."

"What? No, Marshall, I have too much to do. And besides, the nurse said if I was going to"— she hesitated, then made herself say the word—

"miscarry, that this early there wasn't anything they could do to stop it."

"This isn't up for discussion, Allison. I'll be there in five."

In a strange way, it was a relief to be told what to do, even if it might be more symbolic than anything else. She marked herself out for the day and took the elevator down to meet Marshall. If he showed up at work in the middle of the day, there would be too many questions.

At home, he insisted she lie down and then sat beside her, stroking her hair. But his very touch distracted her. She was listening. Listening to her body. Before, there had been a little hum of connection between her and the baby. Now it was gone. Or was it gone? Maybe she was just imagining it. Everything was probably fine.

Finally she asked, "Can you just hold me?" They lay together in the darkened room, his knees pressing into the backs of hers, each of them with a hand on her belly. Marshall whispered prayers into the nape of her neck until it was time for them to go.

In the doctor's office, the receptionist told them to wait. Allison turned obediently toward one of the flowered couches, but Marshall said to the receptionist, "Look, something might be wrong. Isn't there any way you can get us back there now?"

"Oh." The young woman nodded as she looked

from Marshall to Allison. "Of course. I'll see what they can do." It was only a few minutes before they were called back, a minor miracle.

The nurse weighed Allison—up one pound—and took her blood pressure—normal. They had to wait a few minutes in the exam room. Allison sat on the edge of the exam table. Marshall put his hand on her shoulder.

Dr. Dubruski finally came into the exam room. "How are you today?" She turned her head to look at them as she washed her hands in the sink.

"I've had some spotting." Tears slipped down Allison's face before she could will them away.

The doctor dried her hands and then handed Allison a tissue.

"I'm sorry," Allison said, trying to stop crying. Marshall put his arm around her.

"No, I'll bet you've been holding this in all afternoon, haven't you?" Dr. Dubruski wasn't much older than Allison and Marshall, but her words had the calming cadence of a mother's. "Let's check right now. Once we've heard a heartbeat, it's very unusual for spotting to mean anything serious."

She squirted jelly on Allison's belly. But no matter where the doctor pressed with the Doppler, nothing but an agonizing silence filled the room. Allison turned to look at Marshall. His eyes were narrowed in concentration as he listened for the sound that never came.

Dr. Dubruski finally lifted the Doppler. "We should really look with the ultrasound. With you only barely being at twelve weeks, sometimes the baby can just be in the wrong position for us to hear it on the Doppler. I'm sorry. I should have thought of that."

Marshall helped Allison pull on a gown, and they walked down the hall to the ultrasound room. There the doctor began to move the ultrasound sensor over Allison's belly. Allison watched Dr. Dubruski's kind face as she leaned toward the screen. She looked serious, but not worried. That's what Allison kept telling herself. That the doctor simply looked intent.

Dr. Dubruski peered closer at the screen, then pulled back a little. At the same time she moved the sensor around, picked it up, put it down, pushed it from one side to the other, tried a new angle, started again.

"I know this must be uncomfortable," she said at one point. "I'm sorry."

And there all along on the screen was the baby-shaped gray blob inside the black space of Allison's uterus, quiet and still.

"I'm not seeing what I want to see," Dr. Dubruski said. "But I am not sure . . ."

Minutes passed. Marshall moved to Allison's side and took her hand, his forehead creased with worry. She willed herself to be quiet. She was not going to jump to conclusions. She was not going to panic.

She was not going to be the one to say it first.

Finally, the doctor stopped looking. "Let me take some measurements," she said. "Yes, I think . . ." she said, and looked down. "This is measuring at about eleven weeks. And I can't find a heartbeat." Dr. Dubruski looked at them. "I'm so sorry."

Even though she was flat on her back, Allison felt as if she were falling. The table couldn't keep her from tumbling into the abyss.

CHAPTER 38
Hedges Residence

Moving like a sleepwalker, Nic shuffled up her front steps, past the overgrown camellia. Pink-tipped buds were already showing. She needed to trim it back, but just thinking about it made her feel even more exhausted. She was so tired. So tired. The string of eighteen-hour days was catching up with her. And now, with Chris Sorenson claiming that it hadn't been Congressman Glover's voice on the phone, it felt like she couldn't even put the Jim Fate case to bed. Plus, there was the little matter of Cassidy's Somulex addiction. Sometimes Cassidy got on her nerves, but seeing her so vulnerable had touched something inside Nic.

Letting herself inside the house, she locked the door behind her. With the alarm beeping, she hurried to the back of the house and entered the code on the control panel next to the back door. She left the alarm off, because Makayla would be home soon. In her bedroom, Nic took off her jacket and unbuckled her holster. She put her gun in the safe on her closet shelf, and then set her keys, hand-cuffs, and badge on the bureau.

She looked longingly at the double bed that no man had ever slept in. She should probably eat before she went to bed, but it seemed like too much trouble. And Mama would have fed Makayla before bringing her home.

She was taking off her jacket when she heard the front door open and her daughter cry out. Just one word, but it held a bottomless well of terror and fear.

"Mama!"

Nic ran out into the hall, her stockinged feet slipping on the oak floor. In the living room, a tall white guy was holding her daughter's shoulder in one hand. In his other hand he held a gun. Nic identified it as a SIG Sauer. And, though she hadn't seen him in nearly ten years, she identified the guy holding it as Donny Miller.

"She's tall like me," he observed.

The words flew out of Nic's mouth before she could weigh their wisdom. "She is nothing at all like you." Her blood ran hot in her veins. She wanted to take each finger that was touching her daughter and snap it off like a stick.

"Mama, he shoved the door open as I was locking it," Makayla said, as if she would get in trouble.

Miller pushed Makayla toward Nic. Nic's rage turned to ice. Her daughter ran to her and wrapped both arms around Nic's waist, pressing her head against her chest. Shaking so hard it was a wonder they both didn't fall over.

"Makayla, did he hurt you?" Panic gripped her as she felt Makayla tremble. But then she saw the smallest of head shakes.

A smile flitted across Miller's face. "So that's her name? Makayla Miller? That's pretty."

Makayla lifted her head a fraction. Now only her eyes moved, darting back and forth between Nic and Miller. Her green eyes. Just like Miller's.

Her mind moving at warp speed, Nic took stock. Her gun was locked in the gun safe. Her handcuffs and cell phone were on the bureau. There was a landline phone in the kitchen and another in her bedroom. The kitchen, with its lovely knives, was so far away. And even farther was the alarm panel, with one button labeled with a little blue shield that would immediately summon the police. If Miller hadn't cut the line. If he had, then neither the landline phones nor the alarm panel would work.

The only weapon left to Nic was her own body. If she could get close to him, she could attack him with her fists and elbows, knees and shins. But if she wasn't fast enough, or if she made a mistake, then there was Miller's gun. The gun that might hurt her daughter.

The chance seemed too big to take.

"I just wanted to see her," Miller said. "I'm her father, aren't I? Just like it said in those papers my lawyer got. And you've kept her from me all these years."

Nic remembered that voice now. Flat, almost affectless.

"No, you're not." Nic spit out the words. "You're nothing. You're nobody." She looked down at her daughter, still clutching her waist. She was learning the news that Nic had always dreaded giving her, but now even that was eclipsed by something more terrible.

"Go, Makayla. Go now." She pried her daughter's arms away from her. "Run out the front door to Mrs. Henderson's. And don't look back."

"Don't." Miller's voice was eerily calm.

"Run!" Nic urged, giving her daughter's shoulder a little push, trying to turn her toward the door. "He won't shoot you." She knew it in her bones.

"That's right, honey." He lifted the gun and pointed it at Nic's head. "I won't shoot you. I'll shoot your mother. The woman who doesn't want to admit that I'm your daddy."

Makayla froze.

"Don't listen to him, sweetie." Nic didn't allow any fear into her voice. "Go to Mrs. Henderson's."

"Makayla," Miller said, "don't pay attention to her. I'm your daddy. Your daddy!" He attempted a smile. "And if you do exactly what I say, no one will get hurt. Because I don't want to hurt anyone. I really don't. But if you don't do what I say, then I will be forced to shoot your mom. You don't want me to do that, do you?"

Makayla said nothing, her eyes darting from Miller to the door and then back to her mother. He continued to stare at her until she finally shook her head.

"Good. Now I want you to get your mom's cell phone and your cell phone and bring them to me. Do it right now. And don't be tempted to call anyone." He gestured toward Nic with the gun. "Or else."

Makayla took one quick look at Nic and then scurried to her mother's bedroom. He must have cut the phone line, Nic thought. Otherwise he wouldn't risk letting her out of his sight. She wondered if Makayla might still chance trying to call when she was in the bedroom, out of sight. And what Miller would do if he caught her. She didn't pray anymore, didn't believe in God, but she sent up a silent plea. Just one word. *Please.*

The Donny Miller who had raped her had been

a coward who needed a drug and the urgings of a buddy to commit his crimes. But ten years in prison was guaranteed to change someone. And not in a good way.

The second Makayla left the room, Miller was at Nic's side in two quick strides. He put one arm loosely around her shoulders and with the other pressed the gun against her temple. She could feel every hair on her skin. Could feel where the bullet would enter her temporal lobe. Could imagine Tony Sardella looking down at her body on the autopsy table as he switched on the circular saw.

Nic did not move.

Makayla came back in with Nic's phone and then took her own cell from her back pocket. She held them out toward Miller. Her eyes were so big they seemed to fill up her face.

"That's my good girl." He offered her another dead smile, which made everything seem worse. "Now, turn them off and take out the batteries."

Makayla did as he ordered, her hands trembling. After he instructed her to drop the phones on the floor, he crushed them with his heavy boots, the barrel of the gun digging into the thin skin of Nic's temple as he stomped.

"Now bring me something I can tie your mom up with. Scarves, belts, something like that. I need a lot."

As soon as Makayla scurried out of the room for

the second time, Nic tried to look at Miller, but all she could see was the black barrel of the gun. "If you touch a hair on her head, I'll make you beg to die."

"What do you think I am? She's my daughter. Mine. Whether you admit it or not. But don't worry. I'll be merciful to you, as long as you don't do anything stupid. You are the mother of my child, after all."

She realized that whatever Miller knew, he did not know what she did for a living now. He might still think she was a waitress. He probably didn't know that she wouldn't hesitate to kill him. And that she could, if only she didn't have a gun pressed against her head.

"What are you going to do to us?" she said in an even voice.

"I just want to make up for lost time, that's all. Don't worry. I won't hurt her. I would never hurt her." He didn't say anything about his plans for Nic.

Makayla came out of Nic's bedroom. A bundle of scarves and belts filled her arms. She dropped them at Miller's feet. Automatically, he started to lean over to pick them up.

And then Nic saw what else was in her daughter's hands. Nic's Glock. Makayla must have seen Nic key in the combination to the gun safe enough times that she had memorized the numbers.

Her daughter raised the gun, holding it out in front of her with two shaking hands.

Nic threw herself sideways, not to protect Miller, but to knock him off balance so that he couldn't shoot Makayla.

Time slowed down. Makayla's index finger curled on the trigger and pulled it back.

Boom! A bullet tore into the ceiling. Nic's concentration was so fierce that she barely registered the sound. White plaster sifted down on them.

Makayla stumbled backward, still holding the gun. Nic's vision narrowed. All she could see was Miller's gun, which he was now raising to point at Makayla.

Nic spun toward him, her raised elbow slashing through the air. It connected with Miller's left eyebrow, and suddenly blood was sheeting down his face. Swinging her right leg back, Nic arched her back and snapped her leg out from the hip, delivering a high round kick to his wrist.

The gun flew away. She heard it slide along the hardwood floor, but she knew they weren't safe. Not yet.

Nic grabbed Miller's shoulders and delivered a knee strike to his solar plexus. A deep part of her thrilled at the sound of the grunt as all the air left his lungs. She moved her hands to the back of his neck and pulled his head onto her knee, skipping in place as she drove first her left knee and then her right into his face, unloading them against his nose and cheeks. She heard the soft and splintery sound of bones cracking.

And then Miller fell to his knees, wailing and spitting blood, and Makayla slipped Nic's gun into her hand.

CHAPTER 39
Bridgetown Medical Specialists

We have some choices," Dr. Dubruski told Allison and Marshall. Her narrow face looked drawn, the skin stretched tight over her cheekbones. But she never looked away from them; she let them see that their pain was hers as well. "We could do a D & C. There's a slight risk associated with that. Or you can wait and let your body miscarry on its own. But some people find that too painful."

As she would in a courtroom, Allison sought clarification. "Physically, you mean?" She had become all mind, no heart. She could calculate, communicate, prevaricate.

The doctor shook her head. "It's not a comfortable process, no, but I meant more emotionally. The waiting can get to some people. It can take up to two weeks."

Marshall looked at her, and Allison realized this was one decision that only she could make. "I think I would rather wait for it to happen." Part of her just wasn't ready to admit that it was really true. She hoped that if she had to wait for it, she would also come to accept it.

"Okay. But remember you can discuss it at home. If you change your mind and decide you want a D & C, just call me."

When Dr. Dubruski hugged her, Allison's arms stayed limp by her sides. When the doctor pulled back, her eyes were wet, but Allison couldn't cry. Wouldn't. Not anymore.

All she could do now was wait.

Marshall insisted that she not try to work, so Allison told the office she was sick, without getting into specifics. He stayed home from the advertising agency the first day, but then she made him go back. It was bad enough having one of them slowly going crazy. When he left for work, she tried to pray, but her thoughts could not find a fix on anything.

The time dragged on. The only thing that distracted her was talking to Cassidy and Nicole. Cassidy reported that her doctor was doling out a reduced amount of Somulex, one night at a time, and that she had already attended four NA meetings. She also was growing desperate from lack of rest, and Allison tried to assure her that eventually she would sleep through the night.

But it was Nicole who had the most exciting story, even though she didn't say much about it. She and Makayla had fought off an armed intruder, although ultimately only he had been hurt. Closing ranks and pulling a few strings, the FBI had managed to put a damper on the news. Allison sensed there was more to it than Nicole was telling, but she was too focused on her impending loss to try to get more information.

On the second day, when the shock had lessened a little, Allison wanted to read in more detail about what would happen. But none of her pregnancy books had more than a paragraph or two. It made sense, she supposed. After all, these were pregnancy books, and a miscarriage ended a pregnancy. *Nothing to see here. Please move along.*

"I guess it *is* possible to be a little bit pregnant," she told Marshall that evening.

"What?" He looked up from the minestrone soup he had made her, clearly lost in his own thoughts. He was the person she needed the most, but how could they comfort each other when they both were in agony?

"I always used to think that being a little bit pregnant was the stupidest idea," she said patiently. "You were either pregnant or you weren't. But that's exactly what I am. I'm in limbo."

On the third day, in her restless search for more information, Allison found the *Fit Pregnancy* magazine Marshall had picked up for her at the newsstand a few weeks earlier. On the cover, a woman in a yellow bikini, her dark hair flowing past her shoulders, rested her hand on her baby bump, smiling proudly at the camera. Allison had never even had much of a baby bump. She had kept her pregnancy a secret, and now she would suffer in secret. The stupid girl on the cover looked ten years younger than Allison. She could have a dozen more babies, easy.

But what about Allison? She might not ever have a baby. "Why, God?" she cried out. "Why? It's not fair!"

She whirled and threw the magazine across the room. It slapped against the wall and then fell to the floor. She picked it up and began to rip it apart, page by page. Pictures of bellies ripe with promise and adorable babies and pregnant women doing yoga and running barefoot along the beach.

Twenty minutes later, that's where Marshall found her when he came home at lunchtime to check on her. On her hands and knees, weeping amid strewn scraps of paper.

That evening the bleeding started. Heavier than she expected. Marshall sat with her as she lay on the bed, biting her lip. The TV was on, but neither of them paid any attention to it for more than a few minutes, even when Cassidy came on and began talking about the Jim Fate case, pointing out that there were still loose ends. All Allison's thoughts were concentrated on the work of her body.

An hour into it, she suddenly felt panicky,

breathless, and nauseated. Marshall ran out of the room and came back with a blue and white ceramic bowl, and before Allison could tell him not to be ridiculous, of course she was not going to vomit in the same bowl she mixed cookie dough in, she was throwing up into it.

The worst part was over by morning. She even managed to sleep a little.

When she woke up around ten, she felt as if she'd been emptied of everything. Of blood, of tears, of pain.

Of life.

Pastor Schmitz visited that afternoon. "We don't know why we suffer," he told Allison and Marshall gently. "Even Jesus said, 'Father, take this cup from Me.' Suffering, and being with others who are suffering, is part of what it means to be human."

Allison nodded, but the word *suffering* seemed inadequate to describe the aching void inside her.

That evening Marshall brought her a bowl of potato and leek soup he had spent all afternoon simmering. She managed to swallow one spoonful, two, but then her throat closed, and she set the tray aside. He took it without comment and was back twenty minutes later. "There's someone here to see you," he said.

It was not even 6 p.m., but completely dark outside. How Allison longed for spring! She shook her head. "Marshall, I don't feel up to seeing anyone." Her physical strength was coming back, but her emotions were numb.

"I think you might make an exception." Before she could protest again, he opened the door a little wider. "Go on," he urged someone. "It's okay. Um, *está bien.*" Then a tiny figure slipped through.

Estella. Something in Allison cracked open at the sight of her grin.

A young Hispanic woman who shared the same plump cheeks and dark eyes as Estella stood in the doorway, smiling shyly. *"Gracias,"* she said. "Thank you for helping my daughter."

Estella toddled over to Allison. One soft hand patted her cheek. *"Hola,"* she said in a high, piping voice.

Looking at Estella's perfection, Allison felt the tears come again. But this time, they left her feeling cleansed.

The next day, Allison boxed up the few baby things she had allowed herself to buy. A tan, soft, plush rattle shaped like Paddington Bear. A pair of Robeez booties made of red corduroy. She had bought a couple of maternity suits, modeling them with the pregnancy-shaped pillow the shop offered, and those, too, went into the box. Pushing away the memory of how she had grinned with delight and amazement at the dressing room mirror, Allison carried the box down to the basement. It was surprisingly light.

She spent the afternoon paging through her Bible, finally finding comfort in the book of Lamentations:

"I have been deprived of peace; I have forgotten what prosperity is. So I say, 'My splendor is gone and all that I had hoped from the LORD.'
I remember my affliction and my wandering, the bitterness and the gall.
I well remember them, and my soul is downcast within me.
Yet this I call to mind and therefore I have hope:
Because of the LORD's great love we are not consumed, for his compassions never fail."

As the afternoon drew to a close, she started when the doorbell rang. Allison opened the door to find Cassidy and Nicole on her front step. They hugged her, a little awkwardly, and then Cassidy ran back to the car and returned with a basket of food from Elephants Delicatessen. There was a still-warm roasted chicken, green grapes, Italian cheese, salami, almonds, olives, and a fresh-baked baguette. And, of course, a huge chocolate brownie.

"We figured if you couldn't come out to dinner,

dinner should come to you," Cassidy said, grinning.

Tears sprang to Allison's eyes. It seemed like anything and everything could make her cry. But it was better than being numb. "Oh, you guys, this is so thoughtful."

"I can't take any credit," Nicole said. "It was all Cass's idea."

Allison didn't let her expression change, but she thought it was the first time she had heard Nicole call Cassidy by her nickname. She sent up a quick prayer of thanks. Things were shifting among the three women. Cassidy was facing her problems, Nicole seemed to be opening up a sliver, and Allison had allowed her friends to see that she, too, was vulnerable. Even gathering in her home was a new step.

When Marshall came home twenty minutes later, there were hugs all around. Then he said, "I'm going to catch up on some work in my office." He put a little bit of everything from the basket—except for the brownie, which he knew was off-limits—on a plate.

Allison shot him a grateful smile. She waited until the door to his office was closed before she said to Cassidy, "I'm not the only one who's been going through things. How's it going getting off the Somulex?"

Cassidy bit her lip. "It's been hard. First I had to tell my primary doctor that I had been going to two other doctors. He called that 'drug-seeking behavior,' which made me kind of angry until I realized he was right. Anyway, he's slowly tapering me off. I won't lie to you. I miss the way I used to sleep back when I first took one pill and it would just knock me out for the night. Now when I try to sleep, my skin itches and my heart feels like it's going to come out of my chest.

"But the alternative? I'm sure that would have been worse. So thank you, guys. This is going to sound all sappy and everything, but lately I've been realizing I can always count on you." She turned to Nicole. "Nicole even took me to my first couple of meetings."

A rare smile lit up Nicole's face, but she still shrugged. "You would have done the same for me."

"How about you, Allison?" Cassidy asked. "How are you doing? Really?"

"Physically, I'm back to normal." Allison realized she was resting her hand on her now-flat belly. "Emotionally—well, first I was sad, then numb, then scared. I've also been angry, and depressed, and through it all I've been exhausted. Now I'm back to sad. But I've been praying a lot, and I feel like God is really walking beside me."

"How can you say that?" Nicole asked. For once it sounded like a question, not an accusation. "You had this horrible, horrible thing happen to you. How can it have anything to do with God? If He really loved you, wouldn't He have stopped this from happening?"

It was a question Allison had asked herself, and she tried to answer as honestly as possible. "You know what, Nic? I don't really have an answer. But I'm coming to terms with that. Life is full of mystery. Not everything folds up neatly into boxes. But I believe that God sometimes allows something to happen that in His wisdom and power He could prevent. I will probably never know why. Maybe I'm not capable of knowing why. The peace I'm beginning to find isn't something I can explain in words. It comes from knowing that God is good, and from looking for the good that can come from this."

She watched Nicole as she spoke. Allison knew her friend wouldn't argue with her, not when she was so raw, but she was unprepared for the tiny flicker of vulnerability in Nicole's eyes. It was like she was really hearing Allison's words.

Cassidy said simply, "I'm so glad to hear that."

Allison added, "All I can do is get through each day the best I can. But I need something to focus on. That's why I'm going back to the office tomorrow."

Cassidy looked shocked. "You're not going back to work?"

"What am I supposed to do? Sit around at home and think about what happened? I feel like God is telling me to move forward. I'm tired of talking about me and thinking about me. I'd much rather think about my cases. Especially Jim Fate."

"You're not the only one who can't stop thinking about Jim Fate," Nicole said. "And I've got news for you. Right before I came here tonight, I got the lab results on his blood."

"And?"

"It was fentanyl after all."

Allison's mouth opened in surprise. "Fentanyl! Then Glover *must* have done it." Despite his claims, Chris must not be as good at telling voices apart as he had thought.

Nicole's nose wrinkled. "One odd thing was that the dosage was amazingly high. The lab people are still trying to figure out how Glover was able to concentrate it like he did."

"So what does fentanyl do to you when you inhale it?" Cassidy asked.

"They say it would have caused an almost immediate opioid-induced apnea," Nicole said. "Basically, he would have wanted to breathe, but his lungs wouldn't have cooperated."

Cassidy winced. "That sounds painful."

"Everyone says it only took a couple of minutes for him to die," Allison said. She didn't point out how long a couple of minutes could be. She had once won a conviction on a murder case by simply asking the jury to think about the strangling victim while she timed two minutes on her watch.

Two minutes had proved to be an eternity.

CHAPTER 40
Channel 4 TV
Monday, February 20

Allison Pierce is here to see you," the receptionist told Cassidy.

"Great. Could you send her down?" Cassidy wanted to get a little bit more work done before she took off. She didn't have any stories on tonight's news. Her entire day had been spent working on the half-hour special about Jim Fate—"Death of a Talk Show Host"—that was scheduled to air at the end of the month.

The special would have a beginning, a middle, and an end. But something about Jim Fate's death still felt like unfinished business.

"Hey," Allison said. "Are you ready to hit Nordstrom Rack?"

The plan was to do a little window-shopping and then grab a bite to eat, with Nicole joining them if she could. Cassidy guessed that Allison just wanted to check up on her and see if she was doing okay. But the joke was on Allison—Cassidy wanted to do the exact same thing to her.

"Give me a minute, would you?"

"What are you working on?" Allison leaned down to look over her shoulder. One side of Cassidy's computer showed the transcript of an interview she had conducted with a nationally known talk show host right after Jim's funeral. On the other was the script she was writing. As Allison watched, Cassidy copied two sentences of the interview and pasted them into the script.

"That special on Jim. It's going to cover his life and times, as well as his death. I certainly have plenty of footage for the part of the story where Glover committed suicide rather than face the consequences of his crimes." She swiveled in her chair to look up at Allison. "The thing is, the more I think about Glover killing himself, the less clear-cut it seems. What if—and I know they've already put this case to bed—but what if Glover killed himself just because he was worn down and desperate, knowing he was probably going to jail for taking kickbacks?"

Allison straightened up and bit the edge of her thumbnail. "I've been thinking about it too, Cassidy. All the evidence we have is circumstantial. Glover hated Jim Fate, and he had access to both fentanyl and smoke grenades. But if hating Jim Fate was a crime . . ."

Cassidy finished the thought: ". . . then there are a lot of people out there who are guilty."

"And the fentanyl and even the smoke grenades aren't so unique that only Glover could have gotten his hands on them. And he never came out and admitted to killing Jim."

"I guess there's no way we'll ever know for sure." Cassidy sighed. "I'm almost done. Let me just check this B-roll footage of Jim at one of the governor's press conferences. I'm thinking I could use it to illustrate how good he was at getting people's goats." In a new window on her computer, she clicked on the file that held five-year-old footage.

The clip began to play. Allison leaned over Cassidy's shoulder again.

At the same instant, they both sucked in their breath. There it was. The missing piece. The thing that had been nagging at Cassidy for days.

Only it wasn't a thing.

It was a person.

Allison tapped a short fingernail on the screen. "Isn't that . . . ?"

Cassidy turned the knob to shuttle back the footage. The cameraman had panned the audience of activists. And there in the middle was a familiar face. One she had seen recently in person. Only in this footage, the woman wore her hair in two swinging braids and was dressed in black Carhartt overalls. At Jim's funeral, her hair had been in a sleek twist, and she had worn a tailored black suit.

Willow Klonsky. Jim Fate's intern.

Somewhere in the intervening years, Willow had gone over to the other side, gone corporate, forgotten her roots as an activist.

"Wait," Allison said. "What group is this again?"

"Some kind of environmental group. But narrow.

I'm trying to remember. They focused on . . ." Cassidy thought a moment. "On food. Stuff like keeping antibiotics out of animal feed, more frequent factory inspections, banning that additive they give milk cows now."

Allison peered at the frozen photo of Willow. "Looks like she parted company with the group. I can't really see one of those activists going to work for someone like Jim Fate."

"She couldn't have been much out of high school in this photo. Maybe not even." Cassidy felt the final puzzle piece fall into place. "So Willow grows up, forgets about her youthful ideals when she realizes that otherwise she'll never be able to keep herself in iPods and Nikes, decides to go corporate, and starts working for a guy who opposes all kinds of governmental regulations. But what if one of these people"—she pointed at the blurry figures in the background—"saw what she did as a betrayal?"

"Jim Fate was a big name," Allison said slowly. "The kind of guy who always had an army of people to do his grunt work for him—clean his house, pick up his dry cleaning, get him coffee. The kind of guy who would have someone else open his mail. But he always insisted on doing it, because he sometimes got personal items in the mail."

Cassidy almost got sidetracked, wondering what those items had been. She dragged her tired mind back to the question at hand. "So maybe the package was never meant for Jim at all? What if they addressed it to him, knowing that it would throw the cops off the scent, but they expected all along that Willow would open it?" She started to pick up the phone. "We need to talk to her."

Allison put one hand on top of the receiver. "No. Law enforcement needs to handle this. I'm going to go talk to Nicole, see what she knows about this group. Do you remember their name?"

"It was something like SAFE or SANE. Some four-letter acronym that started with *S*."

"Okay. But I'm serious, Cass. Do not call Willow. If her group did target her, we don't need her alerting them."

"I promise. But you have to let me have first dibs on the story. If I didn't have this footage, you would never have seen this."

Allison nodded, already grabbing up her purse. As soon as Cassidy saw her turn the corner, she grabbed her keys and hurried the other way, toward the parking garage. She had promised not to call, but she hadn't said a thing about not talking to Willow in person. This was her scoop. This was the story that might put her back on top.

And Cassidy ignored the little twinge she felt that maybe, just maybe, this wasn't the right thing to do.

CHAPTER 41
KNWS Radio

It was five thirty by the time Cassidy got to KNWS, and the parking lot was beginning to empty out. The receptionist was putting on her coat as she told Cassidy where to find Willow's space. The cubicles Cassidy passed along the way were mostly empty.

Willow's cubicle looked like it had been assembled out of rejects. The once cream-colored head-high walls were stained, and the desk chair she sat in, typing away on her computer, was orange and lacked arms.

"Willow?" Cassidy said.

"Yes?" The girl turned around and stood up.

"Hi. Cassidy Shaw from Channel 4. I just need to ask you a few questions. I'm working on a memorial piece about Jim."

"Now?" Willow's brows pulled together. "It's the end of the day."

"Would you mind? It wouldn't take long. And I'm on deadline." She gave Willow her best smile, one that had disarmed an uncounted number of people.

"I really don't know that I have that much to say about Jim. I mean, I was just his gofer."

Cassidy lowered her voice. "Look, Willow, I found out about your past."

314

The girl's face froze. "What do you mean?"

"You were an environmental activist, but then you left that life behind and went to work for Jim. And your old comrades didn't like that, did they? You betrayed their beliefs. They knew you were his gofer, so they figured you opened his mail too. They sent the package to Jim, but you were the target."

Willow laughed, a single short burst of sound. She sounded both surprised and amused. She shook her head and said, "Really—that's what you think happened?"

"If it's not, then tell me what did happen. I was looking at some old footage, Willow. And there you were, at the governor's press conference about food safety. You gave all that up, but they weren't ready to give you up, were they?"

Willow stood totally still for a long moment. Cassidy could tell she was balanced on the edge, trying to decide whether to tell a truth or a lie. Cassidy had been in that same position so many times herself. Finally Willow got her purse from a drawer.

"Come with me," she said. "There's something I want to show you."

Cassidy followed Willow down a corridor. Fumbling in her purse with one hand, Willow opened a door with the other. Inside was a long room filled with banks of equipment, watched over by a silver-haired man wearing headphones.

A glass window separated the control room from a radio studio, this one empty.

The man pulled back one of his headphones, looking confused. "Willow, what are you doing?"

"You need to leave, Greg. Now. Leave or die."

Leave or die? What? And then Cassidy saw what Willow had just taken out of her purse—a small, black gun. She had seen far too many guns recently. Far too many guns, far too much blood, and far too many dead people.

Greg stared at Willow, uncomprehending. "But I can't leave. I'm running the board."

Cassidy felt like she was about to burst out of her skin. She had seen what guns could do, and she didn't want to see it again. "I think she means it, Greg," she said. At least that's what Cassidy meant to say, but it came out as more of a shriek. "Get out now. Get out!"

Greg yanked the headphones off, set them down, and left in a hurry. Her eyes never leaving Cassidy, Willow went to the door and turned the lock. Then she opened a drawer, scrabbled through it with her free hand, and tossed Cassidy a roll of silver duct tape. "Sit down in that chair and tape your ankles together. And do a good job."

Cassidy's eyes darted around the room, looking for something she could use as a weapon. Nothing. Then she remembered her purse, which was still slung over her shoulder. She could stab

Willow with a pen or a metal nail file, or squirt hair spray in her eyes.

But there were problems with these ideas. One was that a gun was a far more efficient and effective weapon. The second was the near impossibility of actually locating any given item in the bottomless depths of her tote. Her only hope was that Allison was sure to be right behind her.

"So you did it," Cassidy said as she leaned over and taped her ankles together, trying not to do it too tightly. "Not your old friends."

"What? No." She shook her head. "SAFE is all about lobbying. Or, if they really feel like pushing the envelope, demonstrations. They're not willing to put their lives on the line. When I saw that they were just going to stick to their petitions and their protests, I decided someone needed to really fight back. The big food companies have deep pockets. They can get stories swept under the rug, pay people to go away and forget about what happened. But I can never forget. Never. Which is why Jim Fate had to die."

Whatever this was about, Cassidy realized, it was personal. "What is it you can't forget?" she said softly.

"I had a little sister, Sunshine. We called her Sunny. She died when she was six." Willow's mouth trembled and then firmed into a thin line. But the gun never wavered. It was pointed right at Cassidy's chest.

317

"What happened to her?"

"She ate peanut butter crackers. Something millions of little kids do every day. But the peanut butter was contaminated. She started throwing up. The next day she had bloody diarrhea, and my parents took her to the emergency room. She ended up in pediatric intensive care. In agony. They kept giving her painkillers, but they didn't help at all. She just lay there and whimpered. My parents were talking to the doctors when Sunny started crying and saying she knew she was going to die. And I was saying of course she wasn't going to, she was going to be okay, the doctors would help her." Willow's eyes shone with tears. "I was so scared, but of course I had to say those things. And at the time, I believed them. I still trusted the system to work.

"An hour later, she had a massive heart attack. All the doctors and nurses were there, trying to get her back, shocking her poor little body, but it was too late. They said there were no signs of brain activity. I was only sixteen years old, but I knew what that meant. They let us hold her, and then they unplugged the machines."

"Oh no," Cassidy breathed.

But Willow wasn't done. "A year to the day after my sister died, my mom killed herself. She was the one who bought those crackers for Sunny."

"I am so, so sorry," Cassidy said, meaning it. If she could just get the gun out of Willow's hand

and some sense into her head, this would make great TV.

"Sorry doesn't bring them back, does it?" Willow shook her head as if to clear the memory. "Now, tear off some more long pieces of duct tape so I can tape your wrists together."

As Cassidy did so, she said, "But it was contaminated peanut butter that killed your sister, not Jim. Why go after him? He's not a food manufacturer."

"Jim Fate had millions of listeners who hung on his every word. And he was always telling them that we didn't need more regulations." Behind Cassidy's back, Willow wrapped the tape tightly around her wrists. "That we could count on the laws that were already on the books. What a joke! Every day, manufacturers decide to gamble. One positive salmonella test can mean dumping thousands of dollars' worth of product. When the alternative is to ship it out, make money, and cross your fingers that with luck, A, no one will get sick, and B, if they do, they will blame something or someone else, not you."

"But why didn't you reason with him?" Cassidy thought of Jim. He had a soft side, even if many people didn't get to see it. "He would have cared about your sister. He would have listened to you."

Willow's laugh was real. "How can you seriously ask me that? You knew him. You couldn't *reason* with Jim. Jim Fate didn't listen to anyone but himself. It would be like trying to argue with Hitler. Would you try to get Hitler to see that what he was doing was wrong? Or would you shoot him down like a dog?"

Hitler! Anger heightened Cassidy's senses. She could hear the rasp of Willow's breathing. The edges of everything she saw were sharper. So were her words, spilling out before she could think twice about their wisdom. "You've obviously got a gun—why didn't you *shoot* him? But no, you didn't even have the courage to look Jim in the eyes when you killed him."

Willow waved the gun at her. "Don't tempt me, okay? And I did see him that day. I was watching through the window when he opened the envelope. It only took a few minutes for him to die—it took three days for Sunny. Three days! I did him a favor, killing him the way I did."

Cassidy felt her attention widen past the round eye of the gun, past Willow's sad and crazy explanation. "So what's going to happen now?" More important, what was going to happen to her?

"I figured I'd get caught eventually. Step number one was stopping Jim Fate from standing in the way of real reform that will clean up our food supply. But there's always been a step number two."

"And that is?"

"I now have access to millions of listeners. I'll be able to get my message out, and you can be

320

sure it will be broadcast again and again when they cover this story, and be reprinted in magazines and newspapers. And now that you're here, I can use you to get it on TV as well."

Before Cassidy could protest, Willow slapped a final piece of tape over her mouth. Even though her nose was clear, Cassidy immediately felt like she was suffocating.

"First I need to buy us some time," Willow said, and Cassidy hoped it was a good sign that she'd said *us*.

Willow took the white pages of the phone book down from a shelf. Opening it at random, she stabbed a page with her finger, and then looked up at Cassidy and said, "Now watch me be . . . hmm." Willow looked back down, squinted at a name. "Myra Crutchfield."

Picking up the phone, she began to key in a string of numbers, pausing to grin up at Cassidy. "I have a card that lets me be anybody. Anybody at all, as long as I know their phone number. It can even alter my voice so that I sound like a man. Or if I wanted, I could call your old boyfriend right now and tell him that I want him back, and he would see your number on the caller ID and think it was really you. But right now, it's going to be 911 that's going to believe that Myra Crutchfield is watching a world of hurt."

So Chris had been right, Cassidy thought—the voice on the phone hadn't belonged to

Congressman Glover. Instead Willow had framed him so effectively that he had been pushed into suicide.

Willow finished dialing the long string of numbers and then put the phone to her ear. "Yes," she said in an old lady's quavery voice, "this is Mrs. Crutchfield on Southwest Thirtieth. My neighbor's house is on fire. I tried to go over there with a garden hose, but it's too hot. Flames are shooting out of the roof. And I can hear little kids screaming. Oh no! One of them is trying to crawl out a second-story window!"

Without saying anything more, Willow hung up. Cassidy imagined the firefighters and police being dispatched to the neighborhood, hearts pumping, only to find—nothing. And Mrs. Crutchfield denying that she had been doing anything but watching TV or making dinner.

But Willow wasn't finished. She selected another page in the phone book, and again her finger stabbed down, choosing a name. "Here's one in Southeast Portland. Got to keep them busy."

After dialing another long string of numbers, Willow whispered, "Help me! I'm hiding in the basement. There are four men here, and they are beating up my housemate and demanding money. And I think they shot my sister. I heard a gun go off, and I saw a lot of blood. We don't have any idea who they are, and we don't have any money, but they don't believe us." She let out a gasp. "Oh no, someone's coming down the stairs!"

Willow disconnected the phone. Her eyes were alight with a strange glee.

"Let's mix things up a little," Willow said. "How about if I be Victoria, or at least Victoria's cell phone?" This time when 911 answered, she said, "I'm at the Lloyd Center Mall, and there's some guy, he's on the upper balcony, and he just leaned over and started shooting. There are bodies everywhere! He's by the Jamba Juice."

She hung up and grinned at Cassidy, her eyes shining. "There. That should keep everyone busy for a while. I was always good at acting. How do you think I've been able to stand working with Jim, anyway?" She ripped the duct tape away from Cassidy's face. It was more painful than any visit to the aesthetician.

Cassidy couldn't wipe her mouth on her sleeve, so instead she spit the taste of glue into her lap. "The cops and firefighters will figure out you're lying."

"Sure, sooner or later. But in the short run, they have to take it seriously. It's just one way of throwing a wrench in the works." Her grin widened. "And now you're going to help me throw another one. Tonight we are going to take back KNWS and give it to the people. Tonight we're going to start waking up America."

"What do you mean?" Cassidy wasn't sure she wanted to know.

"I'm going to broadcast some cold, hard truths about the food supply. And you are going to help me." Then Willow explained to Cassidy what she had to do.

At night, KNWS normally broadcast shows that were national feeds. But not this night. Tonight it would be the Willow Klonsky show. And if Willow had her way, it would be broadcast on more than one venue.

After dialing the number Cassidy gave her for Channel 4's station manager, Willow pressed the button for the speakerphone.

Cassidy tried to put as much urgency as she could into her voice. "Jerry, it's Cassidy. You need to listen to me. I have been taken hostage."

"What?" In the single syllable, she could hear his confusion and disbelief.

"I'm down here at KNWS. I came to interview Jim Fate's intern, Willow Klonsky. Jerry, it turns out she's the real killer."

"Not Glover?"

"No. She killed Fate and then tried to make everyone think Glover did it. And now we're in the control room of KNWS, and she is going to broadcast a manifesto about food safety."

"Food safety?" His tone was dubious.

"And, Jerry, she says she will kill me unless you broadcast it live on Channel 4 as well."

"A manifesto?" Jerry finally seemed to be following. Unfortunately, he was heading in another direction. "Cassidy, are you drunk? You haven't been yourself lately."

Willow shot her a smirk.

"No, I am not drunk, Jerry. I'm being held hostage." Cassidy only hoped that as soon as they were off the phone, he would call 911. But would they even believe Jerry now that they had been sent on three wild goose chases? "And Willow will kill me unless Channel 4 simulcasts the same message."

"Are you serious? With just the audio? No visuals at all, except maybe a big photo of you on the screen? Nobody is going to watch that."

"Jerry, this is my *life* you're talking about."

"Could we run it on a tape delay this evening? After prime time?"

Cassidy couldn't believe her ears. Had it come to this? That Jerry was willing to dicker for her life?

"Look," Willow said leaning into the speaker, "if you want Cassidy Shaw to live, you will put her on, unedited. Now. And I have a TV in here, so I can see whether you do it or not. Her blood will be on your hands if you don't obey."

There was a long pause, long enough for Cassidy to imagine that Jerry was going to turn Willow down.

Finally he said, "Okay, okay, but it's going to take at least twenty minutes."

"I'll give you fifteen. And if I don't see it then, you'll hear me execute your reporter. Live. On the radio." Willow stabbed the button to disconnect the call.

CHAPTER 42
KNWS Radio

After learning that the board operator at KNWS had called 911, reporting a gun-toting hostage-taker, Allison drove as fast as she could to the radio station. She was torn between burning anger that Cassidy had gone behind her back and cold fear that her friend had now gotten herself in trouble so deep she would never get out. The car radio was tuned to KNWS, but so far it was only playing a national feed. For a second, the radio went silent, and in the quiet Allison could hear her heart beating in her ears. Then she heard a familiar voice.

"Hello. My name is Cassidy Shaw. You might know me from Channel 4 news, but I'm here tonight at the KNWS studio, where I am being held hostage." Cassidy enunciated each word carefully.

So it was true, then. The police had already told Allison about the spate of false 911 calls. She had been hoping that this was just one more.

Cassidy continued, her voice slow and even. "I've been asked to introduce this important message about our nation's food supply. I have been told that I will be shot if I do not comply. You may think that this is some kind of joke, but I can assure you, it is not." Her voice dropped. "This is real."

Unexpectedly, Allison found herself smiling. Even with a gun trained on her, Cassidy was still a professional, still using her tone, choice of words, and well-placed pauses to command attention.

Then another woman's voice broke in, angry and strident. "Wake up, America! When you sit down to eat, when you give your children a hamburger or milk and cookies, how do you know it's safe? How do you know there isn't salmonella in your spinach, campylobacter in your peas, *Listeria* in your cheese, *Shigella* in your bean dip, *E. coli* in your hamburger?

"Well, you know what? You don't know. Every forkful you put in your mouth is a gamble. Every day our food supply can and does kill someone. Our food is being contaminated by rats and cow manure, mold and dead birds, bacteria you can't see, taste, or smell, but that can still kill you. It's not just a matter of turning your stomach. It's a matter of life and death.

"And you know who is the most likely to die? Our most vulnerable. Your baby, your grandmother, your friend who is fighting cancer. And maybe when they die you'll think it was the flu, or old age, or some kind of bug—but it was completely preventable. Thousands are dying each year who don't need to.

"Now weigh that against the fate of a single man. A man who called people like me 'Chicken Littles.' Who mocked us as the food police and supporters of the nanny state, and falsely claimed that it was too expensive to really keep our food safe. You know what? Tell that to my dead sister. Tell her that it cost too much to keep bacteria out of her peanut butter. Tell the kids whose kidneys fail that safe food is too much of a hassle. Tell your grandmother that it's too much of a burden to make sure her salad isn't teeming with pathogens.

"Because that's what Jim Fate did. He mocked those of us who cared. Millions of people listened to his lies. And as a result, Jim Fate had the blood of innocents on his hands.

"We must demand that the federal government take on the responsibility of policing our food. That inspections are frequent, and the consequences dire. When a company weighs whether to keep contaminated food off your table, they need to know that they might go out of business if they don't."

Despite Cassidy being held at gunpoint, despite Jim Fate's murder, Allison found Willow's words striking a chord with her. The girl's approach was dead wrong—but were her ideas?

Up ahead she saw the flashing lights of emergency vehicles. It was like a nighttime replay of the day Jim Fate had died, minus the panicked crowd on the street.

It was a nightmare.

Thank goodness you're here," Nicole told Allison on the sidewalk outside KNWS. Leif nodded, and the three of them huddled close. They were surrounded by uniformed cops, guys in suits holding cell phones to their ears, and men in black commando outfits complete with helmets, bullet-proof vests, and submachine guns. "We called Willow, and she actually answered. But she'll only speak to you."

"Me?" Allison echoed in surprise. "Why me?"

"She says she liked you from when you interviewed her." Nicole's smile was rueful. "I reminded her that I was there, too, but I guess you're the one Willow liked. So you're going to have to be our negotiator."

It was suddenly hard for Allison to draw a breath. "But I don't have any training."

"I'll be right here so I can guide you," Leif said. "I'll be able to listen in on an earpiece. There's no other way to get Cassidy out, not if we don't persuade Willow. She's holding her in the station's control room." He pointed to the building's entrance. "There are cameras on the front and back doors so that whoever works at night can buzz people in. Unfortunately, they feed into the control room. We can't risk spooking her. We're working on breaching the windows, but again, we can't make any noise."

"Is there a window into the control room?" Allison asked. "Could you use a sniper?"

Leif shook his head. "No exterior windows. The only good shot would be if we could get someone inside, get them into the main studio, and have them shoot through the glass that separates it from the control room. That's if we could get them inside. Even then the board operator says the glass is four panes thick."

"What about using tear gas or some other kind of gas?" It would be an ironic twist.

Nicole answered, "The second Willow realized there was something in the air, we believe she would shoot Cassidy."

Leif held up a cell phone. "In a minute, I'll dial this for you. Your goal is to connect with her, just the way you must have done in the interview. We need you to slow things down and take out some of the tension. We don't need Willow to panic."

Allison felt like the panicky one. Her knees were trembling. "I can't do this!"

Nicole put an arm around her shoulders. "Look, Allison, it's just like choosing a jury. You need to build a rapport with her. Don't ask questions that can be answered with just a yes or a no. Get Willow talking. She must be tired of living a lie day after day. So give her the chance

330

to vent. Repeat what she tells you so that she knows that you get it. But most of all, just keep her talking."

Leif said, "We need to take the pressure off her. Speak slowly. Give her a chance to think this through. Ask her if she's hungry, and if she is, ask her exactly what type of food she would like. Keep her focused on the details. That will help stretch things out and give us time to come up with a plan."

Allison touched the cross under her blouse. *Dear God,* she prayed, *help me not to make any mistakes. Protect Cassidy and even Willow. Don't let anyone get hurt.*

Leif dialed the phone and handed it to her.

"Yeah."

If Allison hadn't known it was Willow, she didn't think she would have recognized her voice.

"This is Allison Pierce. How are you doing, Willow?"

"How do you think I'm doing?"

Allison decided not to reinforce Willow's panic by suggesting that she was panicked. Instead she said, "It's dinnertime. You must be hungry." She pitched her voice softer and lower than Willow's, subtly sending a signal of calm. "Would you like us to get you some pizza or something?"

"Right, and have the deliveryman jump me? No thanks."

So much for sending a signal of calm. "What

would you like, then? You name it, and I'll see if I can get it."

Leif nodded and gave her a thumbs-up.

"What's the point?" Willow asked. "I killed Jim Fate. And now I'm a kidnapper. I'll be in jail until I'm old. I might as well be dead."

"Willow, it won't help anything if you die," Allison said quickly, worried that Willow was on verge of making decisions that couldn't be taken back. "It won't help your cause."

Except that maybe it actually could, she couldn't help thinking. The media paid more attention to dead bodies than it did to standoffs that ended peacefully.

"Just tell me what you want, and we'll figure out a way to get it to you."

Willow's voice strengthened. "Then bring me a car. With no tracking devices. And no one follows me. I'll take Cassidy with me. Once I'm sure no one is following, I'll let her go."

Or tumble her out of the car with a bullet in her head, Allison thought.

"Focus on the details," Leif whispered in her other ear. "Buy us some time."

"What kind of car do you want? Four doors? Two? A hybrid?"

"I want your car."

"What?" Allison sputtered.

Even Leif was struck silent.

"I want your car. The one you came here in.

Drive it over the sidewalk and up to the front door so that it's in full view of the camera. Back it up so that I can leave right away. Leave the keys in the ignition. And do it in the next three minutes, or I'll know you are messing with me. And I want everyone back thirty feet with their weapons holstered, or lying on the ground with their hands empty. If I see a single gun pointed at me, I'll shoot the hostage."

The phone went dead.

"What should I do?" Allison begged. "What should I do?"

"It's a very, very bad sign that she is referring to Cassidy as 'the hostage,'" Nicole said, her voice grim. "She's depersonalizing her. I think you're going to have to do what she said. And you had better hurry."

A minute later, Allison backed her Volvo onto the sidewalk until it nearly touched the front door. Then she got out and joined the wide ring that waited for the door to open and the two women to come out.

The front door finally edged open. Willow had her left arm looped around Cassidy's neck, and her right hand held the gun pressed under her chin. The two of them were as close as conjoined twins, only with one dark and one fair head. Cassidy's eyes were wide, her mouth opened as if she wanted to scream, but she didn't make a sound.

One step. Two. Willow went to the passenger side door, opened it, and nudged Cassidy in with the barrel of her gun.

A grenade spun across the pavement and landed right at Willow's feet. A second later there was a huge flash of blinding light and a thunderous *BANG!* The concussive force of the blast sent Allison stumbling backward.

Her ears were ringing, but Allison thought she heard the sounds of a gun firing and a woman screaming. But she was still blind from the flash.

CHAPTER 43
Papa Haydn
Thursday, February 23

Three days later, Allison sat in the semidarkness of Papa Haydn, listening to the clink of silverware on china. The menu featured halibut cheeks, bison au jus, and pasta with wild boar, but the restaurant's real draw was the huge dessert case.

"Here you go," the waitress said, setting down a plate. "One serving of our chocolate torte, and forks for everyone." Four glorious layers of chocolate buttermilk cake separated by espresso ganache and glazed with milk chocolate ganache lay in front of them.

"I shouldn't," Nicole said, picking up her fork.

"Maybe just a couple of bites," Allison said, cutting off a sliver.

"Delicious," Cassidy mumbled through an already full mouth.

As she looked at her two friends, Allison could feel her heart expand in her chest. They had come so close to losing Cassidy. "I still don't understand, Nicole, why you didn't tell me you were going to use that, that . . ."

"Stun grenade," Nicole said. "Otherwise known as a flashbang, for obvious reasons. The flash blinds you. The bang and the percussive wave mess with your ears and your balance. It buys you a little bit of time. In this case, just enough to disarm Willow and grab Cassidy."

"And I thank you for that." Cassidy lifted her glass of wine. "Although when Willow's gun went off, I was sure I was dead. Thank God she didn't hit anyone. But if you had let her drive me away, I would have been dead for sure."

Nicole said, "And the reason we didn't tell you, Allison, is that it's standard operating procedure not to tell the negotiator if a rescue attempt is being planned. Willow was listening to you, watching you get out of your car. We couldn't risk you giving things away through your words, your tone of voice, or even your body language."

"But where did Willow get the fentanyl to kill Jim?" Cassidy asked.

"It wasn't fentanyl," Allison explained. "She had a friend who worked for a large animal vet, and he stole this drug called Carfentanil for her."

Nicole said, "Carfentanil is an analog of fentanyl, which is why the lab thought it had turned up in Jim Fate's blood, only somehow concentrated. It's an animal tranquilizer that's a hundred times stronger than fentanyl. It was used in the Moscow theater hostage crisis, the one where hundreds of people died when the Russian military pumped in gas."

"Maybe it was really fast then," Cassidy said. "I sure hope so." She looked at each of them. "There's something else I have to tell you guys. One of the last things Jim ever told me was that when you're on the radio, you should pretend you're talking to your best friend. He said you should imagine that they are right there in the studio with you. Well, when Willow forced me to help with her so-called manifesto, all I could think of was you two. All the time I was talking, I was thinking of you."

A rare smile pulled at the corners of Nicole's lips. "How are you doing, anyway? Are you sleeping worse now because of this? Are you keeping away from the Somulex?"

"Last night I slept for over six hours. Without drugs. It sounds crazy after everything that's happened, but it's true."

"I'm so glad." Allison leaned forward and patted Cassidy's shoulder. "Good for you. How are you doing it?"

"It's like they say in NA: one day at a time. It's

336

totally boring, but I've been going to bed at the same time every night. Even on the weekend. I'm committed to going to yoga three times a week and NA meetings five times a week."

Nicole took a deep breath. "Since it's true confession time, I have one for you guys. That man who broke into my house didn't just pick us out randomly. About ten years ago, someone slipped something into my drink . . ." Her words came slower and slower. "And I was . . . was raped."

Cassidy and Allison froze.

Allison did the math. "So Makayla?" she said after a long moment.

Nicole nodded.

Cassidy put down her fork. "Does she know?"

"She didn't. Now she knows a little. But she knows the important thing. That I'm her mother and that I love her."

"What happened to the guy?" Cassidy asked.

"He was on parole, but now he's back in jail. He was supposed to be on electronic monitoring, but you can just cut those bracelets off with scissors. I guess it makes sense—you wouldn't want someone to get caught on a piece of machinery or something. It does send an automatic alarm when it's cut, so they knew he was loose. They notified the victims—but they didn't think to notify me, since I wasn't one of the people who had testified against him. Not very many people knew that I was carrying his baby, but he did."

Allison shivered. "How did he find you?"

"He was slick. He called my little brother and pretended to be from a delivery service with a package for me. He said someone had spilled coffee on it and smeared the address. My brother thought he was doing me a favor by helping this guy. One good thing is that Miller's willing to plead guilty. I don't want Makayla to go through a trial. At least she didn't really shoot him." Nicole pressed her lips together, and her eyes got wide.

If Allison hadn't known her better, she would have said that Nicole was fighting off tears. But Nic never cried.

"We found all these stuffed animals and dolls in his car. Actually things that were more suited for a younger girl. I think he really had some fantasy about being her father."

"Everyone dreams about being a parent," Cassidy said with what Allison thought might just be a wistful smile. She looked at Allison. "Has the doctor said whether you and Marshall can have another baby?"

Nicole lightly slapped her arm. "Girl—it is too *soon* to ask her that. Just let her be."

"No, it's okay," Allison said. "She said we could start trying again in a few months. But part of me gets worried about going back to that place when we were trying to get pregnant and couldn't, month after month. Everything that's happened recently has brought Marshall and me closer. Even

338

my finding that little girl on the day that Jim Fate died. Yesterday, I brought a few things over to Estella's family. They're barely scraping by."

"Doesn't it bother you that they're illegal?" Cassidy asked.

"It would bother me more if I knew they were hungry and cold, especially a little child who didn't have any say in where she was born. Jesus said, 'I was hungry, and you fed me.' He didn't say, 'I was illegal, and you deported me.'"

"Good point," Nicole said, surprising Allison. Usually any God-talk was met with a skeptical silence.

"If Jim were here, I'd bet he could come up with a half-dozen arguments against what you just said," Cassidy said. "But he's not." She sighed. "You know, I miss him more than I would have ever guessed."

"To Jim," Allison said, raising her glass of wine.

"To Jim," the other two women echoed, leaning forward to clink their glasses together.

"And to the Triple Threat Club," Nicole said.

"Long may it reign!" Cassidy said.

And the three friends drank their wine and smiled at each other.

A NOTE FROM LIS WIEHL

A funny thing happened when I asked key radio personalities to read and endorse *Hand of Fate*.

They eagerly agreed. But with their endorsements came a similar theme of "Come on, you can tell me. I'm really the inspiration behind Jim Fate, right?"

Seemed only fair to share some of these letters— all written in fun —with our readers. Hope you'll enjoy them as much as I did.

So who was Jim Fate really modeled after? Hmmmm . . . now that's a mystery probably best left unsolved!

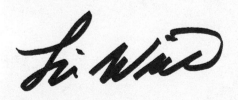

FOX NEWS channel
A UNIT OF FOX TELEVISION

Bill O'Reilly
Anchor

12/18/09

Wiehl,

Nice work on the book! But could you not have tried a little harder to disguise me?

I'll forgive you this time.

Bill O'Reilly

Lis Wiehl
Fox News Channel
New York, NY

Lis . . .

   Your book series is fantastic! That Jim
Fate sure seems like a great guy . . . West
coast digs and that great 2nd Amendment
baseball cap on the wall of his office. I'm
really flattered that you'd base a character
on me . . . even if he does end up dead. At
least he beat the new Obama estate tax
rules, right?

   Can't wait to see who you kill next!

                    Best Wishes

                    Lars

The Mark Levin Show

Lis,

So Jim Fate is "The Great One," huh?
That's very funny. Thanks for basing him
on me. Best of luck with the series. We
need to talk about this on my show so
you can explain yourself!

Mark R. Levin

NewsTalkRadio
77 WABC
The 50,000 Watt Beacon of Freedom

Hi Lis:

I was sitting in my radio studio today when the police arrived to question me about the death of Jim Fate. I cooperated fully and have an airtight alibi, of course, but none of us in the talk radio business is above suspicion. Sure, he was controversial, but he was also a true champion of the First Amendment. His killer wanted to silence him—and the rest of us who believe in free speech. Thank goodness the Triple Threat Club is on the case.

Monica

—Monica Crowley
   Host of the nationally syndicated "The Monica
      Crowley Show"
   Political Analyst, Fox News Channel
   Panelist, "The McLaughlin Group"

READING GROUP GUIDE
(Warning! This guide contains spoilers.)

1. Are there certain functions, such as ensuring the safety of our food supply, that require more government regulation to keep us safe? Or are we in danger of becoming a nanny state, as Jim charges?

2. Jim Fate chooses to stay in his studio, rather than risk his co-workers' lives. Do you think you could have done that if you were in his shoes? Or do you think that one never knows how one will react until the moment happens?

3. Have you ever been in in a situation where people were panicking? Rudyard Kipling wrote, "If you can keep your head when all about you/Are losing theirs . . . you'll be a Man, my son!" How hard was it to keep your head?

4. It's been nine years since the 9/11 terrorist attacks. Do you think people have grown more complacent thinking that it won't happen again?

5. Do you have a strong friendship with a small group of people the way Cassidy, Allison and

Nicole do? Or do you think that kind of close friendship is too hard to maintain in today's hectic world, with the pull of work, school, and family?

6. Cassidy becomes addicted to a sleeping aid, called Somulex in the book. Do you think our society has become too reliant on drugs to help with common problems like sleep-lessness or anxiety? Have we made it too easy for people to get drugs?

7. In *Hand of Fate*, the city of Portland is on the brink of a huge disaster. Have you made any family preparations in case of a disaster? What are two or three things you could do to be prepared in case you had to shelter in your home for several days? Have you made plans for what to do in case you are not with your family when a disaster hits?

8. Many children are born in America to parents who entered the country illegally. Obviously these babies have no say in where they are born. Does automatically conferring citizen-ship make our country stronger or weaker? Is America a melting pot, a salad bowl, or something else entirely? What about children who are brought to this country as toddlers or small children? They may have no familiarity

with their "home" country, but still face deportation.

9. Like Allison, many Americans do not speak a second language. Only one in four Americans can speak a second language well enough to carry on a conversation. English has become the default second language in most parts of the world. Do you think it hurts Americans if they can't speak another language? Many high schools require two years of a language as a graduation requirement. Do you think that's a good idea?

10. Does listening to talk radio make you anxious or energized? Has the country become too polarized, with arguments verging on the extreme on both sides?

11. As an African American woman in the FBI, Nicole often feels like she's a double minority. Has there ever been a time when you felt out of place? Why? What did you do about it? Have you ever seen someone feeling out of place in a group? What did you do to make them feel welcome?

12. Do you think that the twenty-four hour news cycle has been detrimental, focusing on fleeting, unimportant stories? Or does it bring

to light problems that were previously ignored, or help solve crimes, such as in the case of the kidnapped Elizabeth Smart?

13. Some think that political campaigns have moved too far away from the issues to focus on exterior, unimportant things like unflattering photographs of candidates looking crazy or overweight. What do you think? If a campaign focused only on truthfully reporting the issues, could it succeed?

14. Jim gets hate mail every day, mostly via e-mail. Do you think e-mail has made people less civil? Or is it that words can sound harsher when delivered in an e-mail? Have you ever had a misunderstanding due to an e-mail being taken in a different way than it was meant?

15. Cassidy goes on air to talk about her experiences with domestic violence. Do you think people are still reluctant to speak openly about domestic violence? Have you tried to help someone who was in a violent relationship? Was your help welcome?

16. Allison has to deal with the loss of a pregnancy. Have you ever had to deal with a loss that seemed unbearable? What was it and how did you deal with it?

ACKNOWLEDGMENTS

Someone said "it takes a village." Well, that's true for this novel: O'Reilly . . . thank you again . . . from Wiehl (we're on a last-name basis after doing a national radio show together for seven years). And Roger Ailes, the fearless leader of the FOX News Channel, thank you for taking a chance on hiring a certain "Legal Analyst." Dianne Brandi for always being in my corner. And my still "favorite" brother Christopher; his lovely wife Sarah; and son Christian. Mom and Dad; son Jacob; daughter Dani; and husband Mickey a/k/a Michael Stone.

Thanks to all my friends who wrote letters and blurbs (especially those of you in radio and TV with a sense of humor). Thanks for being willing to play along. Pamela Cooney, law clerk; Ryan Eanes, LisWiehlbooks.com Web site creator extraordinaire; John Blasi, the smarts and vision behind Billoreilly.com; Garr King, U.S. District Court judge; Jeff McLennan, F-ABMDI, senior medicolegal investigator for Clackamas County; Bob Stewart, retired FBI agent (along with many FBI agents and other sources who wish to remain anonymous); and Matt Trom, call screener.

Our book agents, Wendy Schmalz of the Wendy Schmalz Agency, and Todd Shuster and Lane

Zachary of Zachary, Shuster, Harmsworth Literary and Entertainment Agency, have worked tirelessly along with the wonderful folks at Thomas Nelson, who saw the potential and drama in this series: Allen Arnold, Senior Vice President and Publisher of Fiction (and even with that long title a really nice guy); Ami McConnell, Senior Acquisitions Editor (with the patience of a saint); and Editor L.B. Norton (with the amazing ability to catch all errors and revise with a smile). And the exuberance of Belinda Bass, Natalie Hanemann, Daisy Hutton, Corinne Kalasky, and Becky Monds of Thomas Nelson continues to inspire. The Thomas Nelson sales team has the stamina and creativity of a true dream team: Doug Miller, Rick Spruill, Heather McCulloch, Kathy Carabajal, and Kathleen Dietz just to name a few. Last but definitely not least, Jennifer Deshler's fantastic marketing team, including the dynamic Katie Bond and Ashley Schneider with the ever-spunky intern Micah Walker. All of the mistakes are ours. All the credit is theirs. Thank you!

Center Point Publishing
600 Brooks Road ● PO Box 1
Thorndike ME 04986-0001 USA

(207) 568-3717

US & Canada:
1 800 929-9108
www.centerpointlargeprint.com

X